# Surrender to Sultry

# MACY BECKETT

Copyright © 2013 by Macy Beckett
Cover and internal design © 2013 by Sourcebooks, Inc.
Cover design by Dawn Adams

Sourcebooks and the colophon are registered trademarks of
Sourcebooks, Inc.

All rights reserved. No part of this book may be reproduced in any form
or by any electronic or mechanical means including information storage
and retrieval systems—except in the case of brief quotations embodied
in critical articles or reviews—without permission in writing from its
publisher, Sourcebooks, Inc.

The characters and events portrayed in this book are fictitious or are
used fictitiously. Any similarity to real persons, living or dead, is
purely coincidental and not intended by the author.

Published by Sourcebooks Casablanca, an imprint of Sourcebooks, Inc.
P.O. Box 4410, Naperville, Illinois 60567-4410
(630) 961-3900
Fax: (630) 961-2168
www.sourcebooks.com

Printed and bound in the United States of America.
VP 10 9 8 7 6 5 4 3 2 1

*Many thanks to Deputy D. Cooper of the Clermont County Sheriff's Department for the enlightening ride-along. I hope the other deputies have stopped using ballpoint pens on your touch-screen computer.*

# Chapter 1

"WELL, IF IT AIN'T CRAZY COLT!"

Sheriff Colton Bea pushed to standing and slammed his cruiser door hard enough to rock the front end. Tipping back his Stetson, he glared down his nose at the floppy-eared, gray heifer tethered to a cedar tree an arm's length away. A crisp November breeze stirred the loose hair at the base of Colt's neck, cooling his temper by a few degrees, but doing nothing to disperse the pungent stink of manure. Under any other circumstances, the sight of a prize Brahman wouldn't faze him—not in Sultry Springs, where cattle outnumbered cowboys two to one—but there were a couple problems on this particular morning.

For starters, a clearly intoxicated Tommy Robbins was hell-bent on riding the humpbacked heifer, barefoot, bare-assed, clad in nothing but a pair of leather chaps and a Texas Rangers ball cap. Even more concerning, the location for this impromptu rodeo was the Sack-n-Pay parking lot, right off Main Street.

Colton shook his head. It was too early for this shit.

"Been drinkin', Tommy?" Colt asked out of habit, though the shifting focus in Tommy's red-rimmed gaze said he was "stilldrunk," that three-hour window the morning after a bender when a guy could still blow twice the legal limit. It was a condition Colt had known mighty well back in his younger days.

"Gimme a leg up, will ya?"

Tommy tried hitching an ankle over the Brahman, but the old girl wasn't having it. With a snort of protest, she clopped aside, leaving Tommy hopping on one foot to close the distance while his wedding tackle dangled for all to see.

"Nope," Colt answered.

The heifer took to munching a patch of grass that had pushed through a crack in the asphalt while Tommy freed his leg and stumbled back a few paces. "Man," he whined, "I remember when you used to be fun."

If *fun* meant reckless, arrogant, and stupid, then yeah, Colt couldn't deny he'd been a whole boatload of fun. At least until a couple of years ago, when the consequences had caught up with him. Now he had neither the time nor the inclination for jackassery.

Squeezing the microphone clipped to his shoulder, Colt radioed, "Sheriff to base. See if you can get—" he scanned the cow's rump until he spotted a faded *JD* brand "—Jackson Dean to come down to the Sack-n-Pay to fetch a stray heifer." The Dean ranch was three miles outside of town, and Colt wondered how the hell a barefoot inebriate had managed to tow the thing so far.

An outbreak of chortles from behind the Dumpster gave him his answer. He should've known Tommy hadn't managed this alone.

"Out," he ordered. "Now!"

Then, like a parade of dunces, half his old defensive line bumbled into view, five equally pathetic schmucks who'd peaked in high school and now spent their free time getting hammered and rehashing the glory days. If brains were dynamite, Tommy Robbins couldn't blow his nose, and he was the smartest of the bunch. Colt couldn't believe he used to run with these fools. It especially stuck in his craw that he'd let them ruin the best thing that had ever happened to him.

*No one held a gun to your head*, he criticized inwardly. And that's what cut the deepest. He'd made his own choices, and on stagnant nights when insomnia forced him to lie awake and replay past mistakes, he knew like gospel that he had nobody to blame but himself. Still, he hated running into his old crew — they reminded him of what a moron he'd been.

Plus, they were a bona fide pain in his ass.

But Colt decided to look on the bright side. Once he locked up these yahoos, he wouldn't have to see their ugly mugs for at least two days. "Sheriff to base," he repeated into his mic, letting a smile lift the corners of his mouth. "Tell Horace to bring the van for six drunk-and-disorderlies."

———

One hour and two cups of coffee later, Colt stood facing a pile of invoices, Post-it notes, and "urgent" phone messages from the mayor — a step up from dealing with drunkards and cow shit, but not by much.

An all-too-familiar set of tingles along his lower back warned him he'd better take a seat before the spasms set in. Only nine o'clock and already his muscles were tighter than a gnat's bunghole. By lunchtime, his spine would be on fire, and he'd wish he hadn't shredded his painkiller prescriptions. But he'd seen firsthand how addictive Oxy was, and when it stopped taking the edge off, folks moved on to harder substances, like heroin.

No, thanks. Despite his surgeon's advice, Colton would make do with ibuprofen and his trusty heating pad. A little suffering never killed anyone, even if his staff did complain that he was a cranky bastard.

Before he had a chance to sit down, two soft knocks sounded from the office door frame, and his secretary, Darla, stepped inside with a bulky black garment draped over one arm.

"Got your new vest," she announced, lifting it for show like one of those babes on *The Price Is Right*.

Colt groaned. "I hate Kevlar. Makes me all sweaty."

One corner of Darla's ruby-red lips slid into a grin. She'd wanted to get him sweaty for years, and she'd made no secret about it. As far back as Colt could remember, girls had followed him around like bears to honey. Something about his Cherokee complexion and blue, Scots-Irish eyes had made panties disappear. He'd never complained before, but once in a while the attention complicated matters, like with Darla. Everyone knew you didn't dip your pen in company ink.

"Better than dead," she chided. "You know the rule—either put it on or sign the waiver."

"Yes, ma'am."

Without further protest, he unbuckled his utility belt, then got to work on the buttons of his short-sleeved shirt. Once he shrugged it off, Darla's eyes locked on his chest, tracing the pink keloid scar that puckered the planes of his upper torso and stood in sharp contrast against his russet skin. From there, her gaze moved down past his abdomen and lingered on the bulge beneath his fly. He knew that look.

"I can take it from here," he said firmly.

"Sure, boss." She ran her tongue along her upper teeth, big brown eyes flicking to his and back down to his crotch just as quickly. "Let me know if you change your mind." Then she took the hint and backed out, closing the door behind her.

Colt let out a breath and strapped on his leaden vest. There was a time when he'd never have refused a pair of hot, willing lips and an eager tongue. Girls like Darla— with their bleached hair, stilettos, and big jugs—had turned his head and stiffened his junk every time. He'd gorged himself on cheap sex like a hog at the trough, and pickings had never been slim.

But not anymore.

Easy women made him twitch. No lie. When temptation presented itself, his body and brain conspired against him, issuing painful reminders of Barbara Lee, who'd run him down in her Ford Taurus after a one-night-stand gone wrong. These days, he behaved like a monk, which didn't help his mood any, but at least it'd kept him alive. And truth be told, he didn't really miss the empty encounters, the endless rotation of nameless, faceless women.

Still, it had been an *awfully* long time. The worst part of his newfound celibacy was that it robbed him of the gift of distraction, forcing him to face demons he'd failed to exorcise over the years. One demon in particular, who was really more of an angel…

"Shit." Colton shook his head hard enough to dislodge his Stetson. He needed to get out of here and blow off some steam. After buttoning up his shirt and refastening his belt, he decided to let the messages wait. The mayor wasn't going anywhere.

He grabbed his keys and sunglasses and ambled past the front desk, calling to Darla, "I'm going on patrol." With a wave, he ignored her reminders of meetings and obligations, continuing out the door into the parking lot.

Already he felt fifty pounds lighter, despite the heavy vest tugging his shoulders. This was where he belonged—out among the people, not shackled to a desk. He slid on his Ray Bans and pulled his long black hair into a ponytail while making his way to the cruiser.

Gripping the car's door frame, he gingerly lowered to the leather seat and then started up his mobile laptop, which took a few tries because Darla had changed the damned password again. Once he'd finally logged in, he pulled onto Main Street and began scanning the area for signs of trouble.

It was a typical Monday, as yawning workers mourned the death of the weekend and shuffled slowly along the sidewalks, lattes in hand. Most waved when he drove by, with only a few exceptions, like Rachel Landry, who shot him the bird. Not very ladylike, especially for a former homecoming queen, but he just smiled and touched the brim of his hat in a sarcastic greeting. She'd hated him since high school, and he couldn't resist needling her.

Through his open window, Colton noticed a couple of business entrances that needed a little reinforcement, their wood doors marred by old break-in attempts. He also noticed that Warren Swain was still driving with expired tags, despite the warning Colt had given him last month. If the irritating SOB thought he'd get another reprieve just because he hunted quail with the mayor, he was dead wrong. Colton slowed his cruiser and reached to flip on the overhead flashing lights when an out-of-state license plate turned his attention to a gleaming, pearly Cadillac Escalade.

Didn't see many of those in Sultry Springs.

"Minnesota," Colt murmured to himself. Someone was a long way from home.

He followed the Escalade away from downtown, trailing two car-lengths behind as he tapped the plate number into his computer. The registrant's name popped up, along with the guy's photo—a middle-aged Latino with a crew cut and a salt-and-pepper beard. Colt leaned forward in his seat and squinted at the driver's slender neck and her white-blond hair. "You sure don't look like Benito Alvarez to me, honey."

Half the time when the driver's description didn't match the registrant, it meant someone was operating on a suspended license. But that wasn't enough to pull her over. He needed just cause.

Which she promptly gave him by making a right turn without signaling.

"Gotcha." Grinning to himself, he turned on his flashing lights and radioed to base, "Bea. Traffic stop, intersection of Main and Route Fifty."

Minnesota pulled onto the shoulder—again, without signaling—and cut the ignition. Through the SUV's expansive side-view mirror, Colt spotted her slim, ivory fingers gripping the steering wheel hard enough to make the leather bleed.

Oh, yeah. This chick had something to hide.

He carefully hoisted himself to standing and approached the Escalade, pushing his Ray Bans higher up the length of his nose. Out of habit, he sniffed the air for

the smoky-sweet scent of pot, but noted only the lingering odor of exhaust. A quick glance through the tinted
side windows revealed a discarded pretzel bag and an
empty bottle of Snapple, nothing out of the ordinary.

Hands on his hips, he glanced at the driver and
drawled, "License and registr—" then froze in place
with his lips still pursed in *R* formation. He quit breathing, and his heart may have skipped a few beats. It was
hard to tell because all the blood left his head in a rush.

"Hello, Colton." Still facing forward, she handed
the documents out the open window, not the least bit
surprised to see him.

Was he dreaming? This wouldn't be the first time his
subconscious had summoned her, but she was usually
naked during those fantasies. He tore off his sunglasses
and blinked once. Twice. Three times before he was able
to process what his eyes had already told him: Leah was
back. After ten excruciating years, she'd finally come
home. Still unable to believe it, he snatched her license
and ran one trembling finger over the text.

*McMahon, Leah Nicole, HT: 5-02 EYES: BLU*

It was Texas-issued, dated yesterday with her father's
address listed as her residence.

"God damn," he whispered. It really *was* her. Colton
reached out a hand to steady himself but missed the mark
and stumbled a few steps, knocking his shin against the
running board. The pain didn't even register.

Once he recovered his balance, he barked, "Step out
of the car," louder than he'd intended. There was no
reason for the command other than his need to see her—
all of her. "Please," he added in a softer tone.

He moved to grasp the handle for her but drew back.

She probably didn't want his help, not after all the things he'd done. The tight set of her mouth confirmed it. He took two steps back, giving her space to swing open the door and climb down.

One tiny ballet flat whispered against the asphalt, then the other. She pivoted to shut the car door before clasping both hands behind her back and peering up at him beneath long, blond lashes. The little color that existed in her fair skin had drained away, her pulse thumping visibly at the base of her throat as she gnawed on her bottom lip. She'd gazed at him exactly like this the first time he'd kissed her, so nervous she'd trembled in his arms.

Christ, she hadn't changed at all.

Her hair fell in gossamer waves that reached her slim waist and shimmered in the early-morning sunlight. That was the first thing he'd noticed about her all those years ago, her hair. She'd reminded him of a Christmas angel, so radiant she'd stolen his breath. Though, naturally, he'd played it off in an attempt to look cool in front of his idiot friends.

But, oh, how he'd burned for her.

His eyes followed the outside swell of her breasts, the feminine curve of her hips, visible beneath a simple black dress that stopped just above the knee. Her legs looked every bit as smooth as he remembered, like she'd been carved from a block of flawless white marble. When he was seventeen, he'd gazed in wonder at the contrast of those ivory limbs wrapped around his waist. Together they were light and dark, snow and fire, saint and sinner. He might've been a hell-raiser back then, but making love with Leah was pure heaven.

By the time his gaze returned to her soft blue eyes, it occurred to Colt that if he stared at her any harder, he'd sear a hole through her forehead.

So, what now?

He'd had a decade to chew on what he'd done to Leah, to obsess over what he'd say if he ever got a second chance with her. How many nights had he lain awake imagining this very moment? At least a hundred. And now he couldn't manage to choke out a single apology. All he knew was this: he couldn't let her get away again.

Should he arrest her? No, that'd probably do more harm than good, and besides, he didn't have legal cause. Shit. He had to do something—she was waiting. On impulse, he opened his mouth and forced out five words.

"Get back in your car."

—◦◦◦—

Thank goodness Daddy had prepared her for this, because if Leah had rolled into town and come face-to-face with "Crazy Colt" Bea wearing a cop uniform, she would've assumed he was on his way to a bachelorette party. As the entertainment.

But this was no flimsy tear-off costume. Twin patches embroidered on his short sleeves proclaimed him *Sultry County Sheriff*, displaying three words she'd never before associated with Colton: *integrity, courage, valor*.

He wore a thick black belt low on his hips, laden with pistol, taser, handcuffs, mace, plus half a dozen other testost-o-gadgets she couldn't identify. A gold star winked at her from above Colt's fickle heart, and she couldn't help noticing that a bulletproof vest strained the brass buttons lining his chest. Its bulk concealed the hard, sinful contours she knew lay beneath—not that she cared about Colt's chest. Or any of his other manly parts, for that matter, like the rounded biceps in her direct line of vision that seemed to have grown in direct proportion with the rest of him. No, she didn't give a fig for those.

Maybe she should just get back in the car like he'd asked.

"Okay." She opened the door and scaled the massive Escalade, trying to sound like someone who hadn't shoved a fake ID beneath the front seat moments earlier. "Is there a problem?"

Instead of replying, he turned on his booted heel and stalked slowly back to his cruiser.

That didn't seem like a good sign.

Ten minutes later, she began to worry.

In an effort to steady her quickening pulse, she unclenched the steering wheel and drew a deep, slow breath. Why was Colton detaining her so long? Did he know what she'd done? Had he sensed it?

No, of course not, no need to act paranoid. It's just that she'd always been a terrible liar, and when she'd stepped onto the street and faced him, it had taken all her willpower not to break down and confess everything.

*God, give me strength.*

So much for getting through the next month without crossing Colt's path. She hadn't even made it a full twenty-four hours. From now on, she'd have to do a better job of avoiding him, maybe call the county office and learn his schedule, then plan her trips into town when he was off work. She should swing by the library, too, and stock up on books to keep her occupied at home. The only other safe haven in the county was Daddy's church. Colton would never set foot in there—too much risk of spontaneous combustion.

She glanced at him in her rear-view mirror, wondering what was taking so long. He kept opening and closing his trunk, but retrieved nothing new. With her documents in one hand and the other resting on the butt of his pistol, he paced a slow circuit in the middle of the road, not even bothering to glance over his shoulder for oncoming traffic.

With a loud curse, he opened his car door and slid behind the wheel with the exaggerated care of someone in a great deal of pain. Misery was part of Leah's job, and she recognized the grimace distorting Colt's stunning face, his one visible fist clenched so tightly he could squeeze water from a stone.

Daddy had told her about the accident a couple of years ago. No, not accident—attack. Some psycho stalker had run over Colton with her car.

It was clear he needed physical therapy, but that was none of her business. The therapists at Sultry Memorial were every bit as skilled as she was—even more so, since they were accredited. The last thing she needed to do was to get anywhere near Colt's body.

To err was human, to forgive, divine, but to fall for the same shtick twice was just plain stupid. She'd forgiven Colton—had to for her sanity—but that didn't mean she wanted to be friends. Besides, if he had any intentions toward her, she'd bet dollars to doughnuts they weren't friendly in nature. Once a selfish prick, always a selfish prick, pardon her language.

Leah checked her watch. The drug store would open

soon, and she needed to pick up her daddy's Lovenox injections so she could regulate his blood coagulation level. Nothing wrecked a brand-new mechanical heart valve faster than a clot. And with Daddy so frail, she didn't like leaving him alone more than a few minutes at a time.

"Hey," she called out the window. "Is this going to take much longer?"

Colton flinched as if he'd forgotten she was there. Then their pseudo-reunion got a whole lot weirder. Without another word, he tugged his car door shut, started his engine, and pulled a u-turn, flinging tiny bits of gravel in his wake as he tore back into town...taking her license and Benny's registration with him.

"Wait!" Leah waved one arm to hail him down, but he made a left on Main Street and sped out of sight. For the next few minutes, she stared at the intersection and waited for him to return.

He never did.

Well, nuts. What was she supposed to do now? Did he expect her to follow? Or keep waiting there? She checked her watch again and then punched the Cadillac's fancy ignition button. To heck with it. She was heading to the drug store. What was he going to do, arrest her? She hadn't done anything wrong.

At least not anything Colton knew of.

# Chapter 2

COLT FLIPPED ON THE SIREN AS HE BARRELED FROM Route Fifty to the courthouse, cursing every dawdling bastard that stood in his way. At the intersection of Main and Third, he had to resist the urge to ram the tailgate of Jim Jenkin's idling Chevy pickup. Damn it, this was an emergency! Colt needed to reach the one man in Sultry Springs who would know why Leah was in town—or any other gossip, for that matter—his grandpa, the county judge.

After the longest sixty seconds of his life, Colt skidded to a halt in front of the three-story justice building, straddling two parking spaces and not giving a rat's mangy ass about the quizzical looks he'd drawn from the nearby clerks. If it weren't for Colt's injuries, he would've bounded up the limestone steps like an Olympic hurdler, but as it was, he gripped the handrail and made his way inside the courthouse at geezer pace.

The rubber soles of his work boots squeaked against the waxed floor, a slow creak-pause-creak-pause that continued to remind him he wasn't as light on his feet as he used to be. As if he could forget.

His family kept saying he was lucky to be alive, but Colt would gladly trade a couple decades of mortality to have his old body back. He wanted to run again, or even manage a brisk walk. Maybe toss the pigskin every once in a while. Hell, he'd love to go cruising on his Harley for more than an hour without having to stop and massage his lower back like an invalid.

Once he'd navigated the labyrinth of halls leading to the judge's chambers, he stopped at the clerk's desk just outside his granddaddy's office door.

"Mornin', Ty," Colt said, handing over Benito Alvarez's registration. "Run a quick check on this guy, will you?"

"Sure thing," Ty said. "Listen, a bunch of us are meeting up tonight at Shooters for dollar—"

"—draft night," Colton finished, cutting off the invitation. He made a mental note to set up a DUI checkpoint on his side of the county line, then turned and continued on his way. "No, thanks." He strode forward, knocked twice beneath Granddaddy's brass nameplate, and let himself in without pausing for a reply.

He should've waited.

Because what he saw on the other side of that door would stay with him forever, kind of like the roll of prepackaged cookie dough he ate last week. He kept forgetting that his granddaddy wasn't an old bachelor anymore—he'd married the widow Foster nearly two years ago.

At over six feet tall and built like a linebacker, the bride had resembled a geriatric drag queen standing next to her groom, who'd reminded Colt of a short, potbellied Albert Einstein in a bolero tie. Colton had always hoped their union was in name only, because the two of them would make an especially gruesome beast with two backs. But judging by the gusto with which they sucked face on the leather sofa, their relationship was the real deal. Someone would lose a denture if they kept carrying on like this.

Before clearing his throat, Colt raised his gaze to an assortment of fly-fishing lures mounted on the wall above the sofa. "Sorry to interrupt, but I need a minute."

Pru drew a sharp breath, clapping one man-hand over her breast. Or rather where her breast used to be before it'd migrated south. When she turned to face him, two spots of color appeared high on her withered cheeks. It made Colt smile. He'd never seen a granny blush before.

"Well, I reckon we gave you an eyeful," she said, tucking a stray lock of hair into her bun.

Granddaddy leaned in for one last peck on the lips. "Boy got what he deserved, sneakin' up on us like that." He lowered his bushy eyebrows and demanded, "What's got your boxers in a bunch so early?"

Colt closed the door behind him, awkwardness forgotten as he recalled why he was here. "You'll never guess who I just pulled over, driving an Escalade of all things."

"Oh." Pru pointed a bony finger at him. "Little Leah McMahon."

"Yeah. How'd you—" Colt mentally smacked himself. Of course Pru would know. She probably spent more time inside the Holy Baptism by Hellfire Church than the preacher did. Colt's step-granny threaded the Bible Belt through her knickers and wore it on the tightest notch.

"When'd she come back?" he asked.

"Yesterday," Pru told him.

A whole day in town and the news hadn't reached him? Around here, a man couldn't sneeze at the breakfast table without rumors of his death circulating by lunch. "She's been gone a long time," he added.

"'Bout seven years, I think."

"Ten," Colt corrected.

"Mmm-hmm." Pru made a disapproving noise from the back of her throat. "Broke her daddy's heart runnin' off like that. No warnin', neither. And not one letter in all those years. For all he knew, she was lyin' in a ditch somewhere. Or worse—shackin' up."

"She here to visit, or for good?"

"Guess you could call it a visit." Using the armrest as leverage, Pru heaved herself to standing. She shuffled to the mahogany desk and retrieved her handbag. "Her daddy had open-heart surgery last week. You probably heard."

Colt hadn't, but he nodded anyway.

"Well, it turns out Leah's one-a-them nurses who stays on with people while they're—"

"A home health aide?" he interrupted.

"Mmm-hmm, and she's gonna live with her daddy till he's back on his feet, then head up North."

That explained a few things, like why nobody had been able to find Leah in the national databases after she'd run away. Some occupations, like construction or in-home health care, were conducive to staying hidden. When cash changed hands under the table, there were no taxes to file. No public records. And if Leah had let her certification lapse and lived with her clients, she'd never have an official address to report. But what that didn't explain was why she'd gone to such extremes to lay low, or why she'd stayed away so long without a word.

Still deep in thought, Colt scratched a patch of stubble he'd missed while shaving. "If she didn't stay in touch, how'd she know about the preacher's surgery?"

Granddaddy piped up from his place on the couch. "She said the Lord called her home."

"A miracle," Pru added with a smile, turning her gaze skyward.

"Uh-huh." Colt's bullshit detector started beeping. Someone had tipped off Leah, and he wanted to know who. Over the years, he'd shaken down every single one of her uptight friends to find her, but they'd all claimed ignorance. The mole was probably Rachel Landry. She'd shave her head, grow a beard, and bat for the other team before lifting a finger to help him. "The Lord works in mysterious ways," he said.

"Amen." While nodding in agreement, Pru eyed him approvingly. "Why don't you join us at Sunday's service?"

Because he'd rather wax his balls, that's why. "I'm busy." Then he flagrantly changed the subject back to Leah. "So how long until the pastor's back on his feet?"

Like a redneck pirate, Granddaddy narrowed one beady eye. "Why do you care?"

Colt faked a casual shrug. "Leah's—" *the one who got away.* "An old friend."

"Mmm-hmm." Granddaddy gave him a look that said his own bullshit detector was blaring. "Didn't you two date for a while?"

"I guess," Colt muttered. "If you wanna call it that."

For reasons he couldn't quite identify, it felt wrong to admit that someone so flawless had belonged to him, like it might sully her by association. In truth, Leah had been his girl for the best one month, six days, and seventeen hours of Colt's miserable existence. Until he'd stabbed her in the back like the immature coward he was back then. But she got the last laugh.

For the past decade, the sight of every long-haired blonde had made Colt's breath catch, only to send his heart plummeting to the ground when he realized it wasn't her. At Christmastime, every blond-haired angel tree-topper taunted him with reminders of what he'd lost, until he began to dread the whole damned season.

"So, what'd she say?"

"Hmm?" Colt asked, still distracted.

"Leah." Granddaddy made a *come on* motion with one hand. "Why'd she disappear like that?"

That's what Colt wanted to know. He'd always thought Leah's daddy was too strict. Maybe the preacher had taken the old saying *Spare the rod and spoil the child* literally. But if that was the case, it didn't make sense for her to run away, then suddenly show up and nurse him back to health before leaving again. When Colt had pulled her over, he'd sensed she was in trouble, or at least hiding something. Maybe if he'd had the capacity to utter more than *step out of the car* and *get back in your car*, he'd have found out what.

"Didn't ask," he said.

He fished Leah's driver's license from his shirt pocket and locked his gaze on her image as if to confirm he hadn't hallucinated the whole encounter. Her pink lips were curved into a smile that didn't quite reach her eyes. Was it his imagination, or did he detect a hint of sadness in those baby blues? It made him wonder what kind of life she'd made for herself in Minnesota, assuming that's where she lived. Suddenly, it occurred to Colt that she might have a family. He hadn't noticed a ring on her finger, and her last name was still McMahon, but that didn't mean anything. She could very well be married. A sickening chill uncurled in the pit of his stomach. Wouldn't that be the ultimate punishment for his past transgressions—to find her after all these years only to discover she belonged to another man?

"Six weeks, tops," Pru said, pulling him back to present company.

"What's that?" he asked.

"You asked how long till Pastor Mac's on his feet. Shouldn't take much more'n a month."

"Oh." That was less time than he'd expected. Colt swallowed hard, pushing down something that tasted an awful lot like fear. He knew it would tip his hand, but he couldn't resist asking, "Did her daddy mention if she's got a husband?"

Pru and Granddaddy shared a long, knowing look— the kind folks exchanged when they were about to spring bad news on some poor, unsuspecting sap. Colt's gut twisted while he braced himself for the worst.

"He didn't say anything."

Colt released the breath he'd been holding. Pru's answer wasn't a no, but it wasn't a yes either. His relief didn't escape Granddaddy's detection. Those haywire brows knitted together while the man studied him from the other side of the room.

"Careful, son," his grandpa said. "A person changes a lot in ten years. I dunno where Leah's been, but I'll wager she's not the same girl you remember."

Well, no shit. Of course she wasn't the same girl, just like Colt wasn't the same wild and reckless juvenile de- linquent who'd stolen as many hearts as cars. But while time might've drained a bit of the youthful innocence from Leah's features, some things never changed—like a person's core, the essence of who they were. No matter where she'd traveled or what she'd done, Leah would always have the purest heart on earth. Colt knew it instinctively. What he didn't know was why she'd bother with the likes of him. He didn't deserve a second chance, but if she was single, he was sure as hell going to take it.

"You got nothin' to worry about," he told his grandfather. "Like I said, she's just a friend."

"Mmm-hmm." The old guy wasn't fooled. "Suit yourself."

Colt grinned, nodding a good-bye as he backed toward the door. "Always do."

---

"Careful, now," Leah said. "Nice and slow."

Supporting Daddy's elbow, she helped him lower onto the same corduroy recliner where he'd once rocked her as an infant. In response to the burden, the chair's wooden frame groaned and crackled, sagging beneath Daddy's considerable weight until she worried he'd drop to the living room floor like Goldilocks. Except Daddy had no locks. He'd lost his hair and doubled his body mass since she'd been away, which explained the heart attack.

"I'm going to find you a wife," she threatened. "Someone who'll make you eat grilled salmon instead of quarter-pounders and walk you like a dog after dinner."

Daddy's laugh sounded more like a symphony of wheezes. "I wouldn't want to marry the kind of woman who'd have me. I'm not exactly a catch, Pumpkin." His smiling eyes found Mama's portrait, mounted above the television where it'd hung for the last twenty-seven years. "Besides, I already have a wife waiting for me."

Leah glanced at the portrait of the woman who'd delivered her into the world. She had her mother's fair coloring and blue eyes, and Daddy'd always claimed she had the same gentle spirit too. But Leah wouldn't know. Thanks to preeclampsia, she'd lost her mama before they'd even met. Anyway, Leah's spirit didn't feel gentle these days. Just broken.

"Well," she said, trying to brighten her voice, "you're going to meet her way too soon if you don't start taking care of yourself. And I don't think she'd want you to leave me yet."

Daddy's gaze softened, staring through Mama instead of at her. He fell silent for a few beats before giving a nearly imperceptible shake of his head and whispering, "No, she wouldn't want that." Covering Leah's hand with his own, he turned to her with a smile back in place. "She loved you so much," then added with a wink, "almost as much as I do."

Leah dropped a kiss on his bald head. "Love you too, Daddy. It's good to be home."

"Amen to that. Talkin' to you on that video phone doesn't compare to having you here."

"Oh, that reminds me." She lowered her voice as if someone might overhear. "We have to be careful."

The hardest part of maintaining their ruse was pretending that they hadn't emailed twice a week for the last ten years before discovering Skype. Or that Daddy's "missionary trips" weren't really visits to Minnesota. That instead, she'd run away from her rigid Baptist daddy because she'd hated their life together. Nothing could be farther from the truth.

"I saw June at the drug store," she said, "and I almost called her by her married name." Leah wasn't supposed to know that her childhood friend had married Luke Gallagher, or that they'd finally gotten pregnant after a year of trying. She hated lying to the whole town like this. It was just a matter of time before she slipped up.

"Have you called Rachel yet?" Daddy asked.

A heavy sigh puffed Leah's cheeks, and she sank onto her haunches, resting her chin on Daddy's knee. "No. I'm waiting for the right time."

"The right time, huh?"

He didn't need to say more; they both knew what he was thinking. There *was* no right time to apologize to the BFF she'd abandoned without so much as a good-bye, especially when that best friend was bound to ask questions. Which meant more lies.

"First we need to get our stories straight," she said. "I'm sure people are already talking. Won't take them long to compare notes."

"I say we keep it simple." Shrugging one shoulder, Daddy suggested, "I'll tell folks that word got back to me about what you and Colton had done, we had a nasty blow-out—said some things we regret—and you left."

"Sounds good," Leah said a few octaves too high.

She couldn't believe it, but the mere mention of "what she and Colton had done" brought a flush to her cheeks. Without warning, she felt the ghost of his hot breath stirring against her throat, the graze of his teeth scraping her shoulder. Seductive whispers caressed her ear, bringing chills to the surface of her skin. *I'll stop whenever you want, Angel, just say the word.* She remembered vividly that while she'd wanted to say the word, she hadn't asked Colt to stop. He'd bewitched her with those wicked fingers and his dedicated tongue, and the only command that had left her lips was *more*.

A heavy warmth settled low in her belly at the flashback, reminding her of how long it had been since she'd enjoyed a man's touch. But that wasn't something she wanted to contemplate with her daddy in the room. She cleared her throat and hoped he couldn't see her blushing.

"Colton pulled me over," she said. "About an hour ago."

Daddy gripped the faded corduroy armrests. "Everything go okay?"

"Mmm-hmm. He didn't say much. I think he was surprised to see me."

"I'll bet," he said, letting go a relieved chuckle. "I'm not surprised he nabbed you. That Caddy's about as inconspicuous as a porcupine in a balloon shop. He write you a ticket?"

"No, but he drove off with my license and Benny's papers."

"Huh." Clearly, it didn't make sense to him either. "That boy always was an odd duck."

More like something that *rhymed* with duck.

"Hey," she said, turning the subject away from ducks and scoundrels, "I was thinking of buying June's old car to use while I'm in town." June had been hanging flyers when Leah'd run into her at the drugstore. The old purple hatchback for sale wouldn't win any beauty contests, but the price was right.

"What about the Escalade?"

Leah was grateful to her boss for the loaner, especially considering she didn't have a credit card and thus couldn't rent a car, but it was too nerve-wracking driving something that cost more than a double-wide.

"I'm scared I'll ding it," she said. "Besides, now that I've got a real license, I can title June's car under your address." For the first time in her twenty-seven years, she would own a vehicle. The idea made her smile. Better late than never.

"Whatever you want, Pumpkin. Sure was nice of Benny, though."

"Yeah," she agreed. "He's been real good to me." *Like a second father*. She kept that last bit to herself, not wanting to hurt Daddy's feelings. "The least I can do is keep his pride and joy nice and shiny."

Daddy made a noise of agreement, but his averted gaze and slackened smile warned her a change was coming in their innocent small talk. And sweet Lord, he didn't disappoint.

"I bet his real pride and joy is that boy of his. A doctor, right?"

Leah's stomach dropped. She didn't want to talk about Ari.

"Have you, uh…" Daddy began awkwardly, then paused to swallow. "Have you two worked things out? Last we talked, you thought he might change his mind about—"

"No." Leah lifted her chin and pushed to standing. There was nothing to work out. Ari wanted something she couldn't give, so he'd broken their engagement. It was as simple—and as painful—as that. She hooked a thumb toward the kitchen. "I'd better get started on breakfast. It's already late."

"Sorry, hon. His loss." Daddy caught her hand before

she could get away. He gave a playful tug, trying to lighten her now sour mood. "If you're cookin', I'll have a bacon, egg, and cheese biscuit."

Leah laughed without humor. "Well, that's not what you're gonna get." Not on her watch, anyway. "You'll have oatmeal."

"Aw, come on, Pumpk—"

She silenced him with a flash of her palm. "There's what we want, and there's what's good for us. The two are almost never the same." Boy, had she learned that lesson the hard way. "It won't be so bad. I'll add some cinnamon and vanilla."

"And chocolate chips?"

"Nope."

"Syrup?"

"Unh-uh."

"Brown sugar?"

"No deal."

"Need I remind you that I'm the head of this house?" Daddy asked.

"You know what they say, Daddy." Leah strode into the kitchen, calling over her shoulder, "You're the head, but I'm the neck. I'll turn you whichever way I want."

But despite her tough words, Leah pulled a tub of raw honey from the pantry when she gathered her ingredients. In her heart, she understood how it felt to choke down life's bitter lumps, and she couldn't deny her daddy a little sweetness.

She grabbed a pot and stood before the old stove, its electric burners scrubbed to a dull black and revealing gleaming silver bowls beneath. Daddy's kitchen was cleaner than she'd expected. *Too* clean. No traces of

dried tomato sauce or smudges of grease existed anywhere except the inside of a white microwave oven that
stood in odd contrast to the original harvest gold ap-
pliances. That's how she knew Daddy didn't cook for
himself. A well-used kitchen was never this spotless.
If she had to guess, she'd say he subsisted on Hungry-
Man dinners and takeout. To test her theory, Leah took
three steps toward the fridge and tugged open the freezer
door. A waft of cool air greeted her, along with two
dozen boxes of Salisbury Surprise, Mexican Fiesta, and
Pub Favorites.

Mmm-hmm. Just as she thought.

Shaking her head, she returned to the stove, where
she combined two parts skim milk with one part rolled
oats. She added a teaspoon of cinnamon and vanilla, and
before long, the mixture had come to a rolling simmer.
Moist steam swirled up from the pot, smelling of bland,
watery grain, and eliciting a frown in response. Leah
would never admit it to Daddy, but she didn't like oatmeal either. In fact, she detested it.

She hated everything about oatmeal—the dull flavor,
mushy texture, the way it lingered in her stomach like
mashed lead. What she *really* craved was an ooey-gooey
chocolate éclair with an extra-thick layer of fudge icing.
Richman's grocery made them fresh, right down the
street, and she still remembered the culinary ecstasy of
sinking her teeth into one. Her toes almost curled when
she imagined the way that sweet custard would burst
across her tongue when she'd take a big, sinful bite.

Oh, heavens. Was she drooling? Sadly, yes.

She wiped a hand across her lips and returned her attention to the oats before they stuck to the bottom of the

pot. Like she'd told Daddy, what she wanted and what she needed were two different things.

Or at least she'd always thought so. These days, she was beginning to wonder.

For the last ten years, she'd forgone happiness in the interest of doing what was right, hoping the Lord would reward her sacrifices. Even her relationship with Ari had started that way. They'd been friends at first, and she hadn't wanted anything more. But when the spark behind his eyes had told her he felt differently, she couldn't turn him down, not after his father had taken her in and given her a new life. Besides, Ari was a genuinely wonderful person, so she ignored the way his thin lips had never fit against her own, or that his embrace didn't set her insides on fire. She didn't need lust, just the love of a good man, and Ari had offered her that. Loving him back should have been safe…but look how that'd turned out.

Was God trying to tell her she wasn't forgiven? That even when she settled for less than her ideal, she still wasn't worthy of a family? Or was it just bad luck? She didn't know, but darn it, that chocolate éclair sounded mighty good right now. Her eyes darted toward the living room, where the theme song to *Monday Morning Ministry* played on the television. If she was quiet, she could sneak down to Richman's and be back before Daddy even knew she was gone. The oatmeal needed a few minutes to thicken anyway. Wasn't she entitled to a little splurge? Heck, maybe Daddy too. A few bites wouldn't hurt him.

*Yes!* she decided with a nod, turning off the stove with one hand and plucking her purse from the countertop with the other. A spoonful of sugar, and all that. Creeping on her tiptoes, she crossed the kitchen and slipped on her shoes, then fished her Escalade keys from the wall hook beside the back door. She'd just reached for the doorknob when three loud knocks sounded from the other side. She flinched back, clapping a hand over her heart and dropping her keys in the process.

"Who is it, Pumpkin?" Daddy called from the front room.

"Crumbs," Leah whispered to herself. So much for her sneaky donut run. "I don't know."

She pushed aside the curtain to identify their visitor and came face-to-face with a pair of turquoise eyes shaded by a tan Stetson. A flutter tickled Leah's chest, spreading to her stomach when Colton's full lips curved into a sexy, crooked grin and he tipped back his hat with one finger. She dropped the curtain, but the image of Colt's stunning face hovered in the air like a specter. He'd always been a gorgeous boy, but time had hardened his features—sharpening the angle of his jaw, strengthening his forehead, and drawing out his Cherokee heritage until he'd transformed from gorgeous into downright decadent. She hated that he still had the power to give her butterflies, but he did all the same.

She composed herself and opened the door.

"Hey," he drawled, slow and deep, leaning against the doorjamb with one booted foot crossed over the other. He folded his muscled arms as if he'd come here to shoot the breeze with an old friend.

But they weren't friends, and she made that clear with a tight nod.

He glanced over her shoulder into the kitchen. "Somethin' smells good."

"Mmm-hmm."

"Gonna invite me in?"

"Nope."

He patted his shirt pocket. "But I've got your registration."

"Good." She extended one hand, palm up. "Then give it here."

Whatever he wanted from this ridiculous visit, it must've occurred to him he wasn't going to get it, because his coy smile faded and he removed his hat, then raked a hand through his shoulder-length black hair.

"I, uh," he began, "don't have your license, though. Left it in my office." He gestured to the sheriff's cruiser parked on the curb. "Why don't you come with me, and we'll go get it real quick?"

Leah shook her head at the stone-cold, sneaky son of a motherless dog. She'd dip herself in honey and roll in a nest of fire ants before spending one minute alone with him. "I'm not going anywhere with you, Colton Bea."

"It'll only take a few—"

"Never mind," she interrupted. "Just keep it." She closed the door and locked the deadbolt with extra force, so he'd hear it and get the message.

To his credit, Colt didn't linger more than a few seconds. His heavy boots clopped slowly down the wooden steps, and soon she detected the sound of his car starting and motoring off into the distance.

"Who was it?" Daddy called again.

Leah kicked off her shoes, tossed her purse onto the counter, and padded to the stove, where she dished up two bowls of nice, safe oatmeal—a breakfast that, while bland, had never hurt anyone. She wasn't in the mood for éclairs anymore.

Joining Daddy in the living room, she shrugged and told him, "Nobody."

# Chapter 3

THE NEXT MORNING BROUGHT A FLURRY OF VISITORS, as nearly half of Daddy's congregation circulated through the living room to wish him well. Most of his guests came bearing gifts of tater-tot casseroles, fruit pies, creamed soups, and cookie bar mixes sealed in Mason jars. While Leah knew their hearts were in the right place, it was the occasional crossword puzzle and handheld video game she really appreciated. Those were the kinds of distractions Daddy needed—to keep his hands busy and his mind occupied so he didn't munch himself into another stay at Sultry Memorial.

To her relief, she and Daddy worked well as a team, fielding questions about her ten-year absence with a generic, "We had a falling out, but we're mighty grateful the Lord brought us together again." If anyone pushed for details, Leah told them she didn't want to dwell on the past, and that generally shut them up. And when Miss Pru asked if Leah was single, all talk of family rifts abruptly shifted to matchmaking. No less annoying, but at least it took the pressure off.

After lunch, June and Luke Gallagher stopped by to transfer the title to June's old car. A cold front had moved in, so Leah grabbed her cardigan before following the couple down the street, where they'd parked behind half a dozen of Daddy's friends.

Poor June had adopted that third trimester waddle,

pushing out her distended belly while supporting her lower back with both hands. Despite the chill, her face was dewy with perspiration, her ankles so swollen she'd been forced to wear flip-flops. But bless her heart, she didn't complain once. June's rounded cheeks exuded the radiance of a woman who'd finally earned everything she wanted out of life: a devoted husband who couldn't go thirty seconds without touching her and a healthy baby girl on the way.

It warmed Leah's heart to see them together. June and Luke had graduated a few years ahead of her, but she remembered the way June had always gazed at Luke...and the way he'd gazed back when he thought nobody was looking. Leah had hated to miss their wedding. She'd missed a lot of nuptials over the years...like Rachel's. *And the divorce that came shortly afterward*, she thought with a prickle of guilt.

"Well," Luke said, stopping in front of a purple spray-painted hatchback, "here's old Bruiser." He gave the hood a hearty smack. "Not much to look at, but he's tougher than a two-dollar steak. I don't think he'll die on you, but if he does, I'm sure whoever wins the pool will split the pot with you."

"People are betting on how long it runs?" Leah craned her neck and glanced at the mismatched hubcaps— one silver, one black—which drew her attention to a baseball-sized rusted hole near the gas tank.

"Yup." Luke's eyes darted to a sarcastic *wash me* message traced on the front fender. He erased it with the side of his fist. "Last I heard, it's up to five hundred."

"Oh, god." June bit her lip, covering her face in shame. "I feel awful asking anything for this heap." She splayed both hands in front of her and begged, "Just let me give it to you."

"No, no, no." Leah dug into her back pocket to retrieve her cash, then thrust the wad at June. "I can't."

"Pleeeeeeease?"

"No, really." Leah appreciated the offer, but she couldn't handle freebies. Instead of enjoying gifts, she always felt obliged to repay them with kindness, which probably explained why she'd said *yes* to a first date with Ari five years ago. "Thanks, but it'd make me feel—"

"Believe me," Luke said, gripping his hips, "I get it. Nobody likes taking charity, least of all me." He accepted her money, but counted out a couple hundred dollars and handed it back. "How's that? Now neither of us has to feel like shit."

"Language!" June chided with a light slap.

Leah laughed and shook Luke's hand. "It's a deal."

While the two of them pocketed their money, June cradled her swollen belly between both palms, stroking it and making gentle shushing noises as if Luke's curse had injured the child nestled within. A contrite Luke knelt at his wife's puffy feet and lifted her shirt so he could whisper apologies through her navel.

"Daddy's sorry, Sweet Pea," he crooned while June lovingly swept the hair from his forehead. "I'll go easy on the swears from now on. Promise."

At first, it was positively the most adorable thing Leah had ever seen. But then she began to feel a tug of envy in her stomach, a dropping sensation like she'd missed the last step at the bottom of the porch. Before she knew what she was doing, she'd pressed one hand to her own abdomen, directly over her hysterectomy scar.

Her chest knotted, pulling tighter as she watched Luke nuzzle his wife's belly. Leah would never share this moment with a man, never place his palm on her tummy to feel their baby's tender kicks. Never. And she wanted it so badly she ached.

June must have seen the longing in Leah's face and mistaken it for embarrassment, because she tugged her shirt down and backed away from her husband, leaving him on his knees making kissy noises into empty air.

"Sorry," June said. "It took a long time for us, and we're still kind of slap-happy."

"Don't apologize." Leah swallowed her self-pity and found a smile. June and Luke were good people, and they deserved this joy. "I think it's sweet."

Luke stood and dug through his pockets until he found the hatchback keys, then handed them over. "Sickeningly sweet, probably." He laid the title on the hood and fished for a pen. "I used to roll my eyes at couples like us."

"Me too," June said, offering Luke a Bic from her purse.

Leah shrugged. "I like seeing people happy. It gives me—" *hope*—"warm fuzzies." Nodding at June's baby bulge, she asked, "When're you due?"

"End of January."

*Holy bones, two and a half more months?* Leah fought to keep the shock from parting her lips. By June's size, she'd guessed the baby would arrive in a few weeks, tops. "Well, you look great." Every pregnant woman needed to hear that once in a while, even if it was a little white lie. Or a clanker of a lie.

"Aw, thanks." June laced her fingers together, resting them atop her belly while she studied Leah in silence for a moment. "Hey," she said, tipping her head in appraisal, "Grammy told me you're not married. Do you have anyone special back home? 'Cause if you're not—"

"*Junebug*," Luke warned. He glanced up from his paperwork to shoot her one of those scolding looks married couples gave each other.

"What?" June asked innocently.

"You know what."

They proceeded to communicate through a silent dance of raised brows, narrowed eyes, jerking heads, and slashing hand gestures. Clearly, they'd discussed this issue before arriving, and Leah wondered which eligible bachelor June had in mind for her. Not that it mattered, because she did have someone special back home. Just not the way June had meant it.

"I'm not here to date," Leah said. "But thanks for thinking of me."

"See?" Luke said to his wife while handing Leah the title. "She's not interested."

"He's *your* friend," June hissed. "I'm just trying to help."

"*Friend* is putting it loosely. Real loosely. It's not like we're—"

"Whatever," June cut him off and turned to Leah. "Just promise you'll keep something in mind." When Leah nodded, June left her with a cryptic, "People really can change."

"*Jooooonbug*," Luke warned again.

With a roll of her eyes, June relented. As she climbed into Luke's dusty, black F-250, she asked Leah, "You're coming to Trey's potluck, right?"

"Who's Trey?"

"My brother-in-law," Luke answered. "He and my

sister have been living in Dubai the past couple years, and we're throwing 'em a homecoming."

"Oh, Bobbi got hitched?" Leah asked, pretending not to know that Luke's little sister had married his best friend. "I think we were in the same preschool class."

"Yep." After closing his wife's door, Luke strode around to the other side and opened his own. "Friday night at the church fellowship hall. Six o'clock. Don't worry about bringing anything. We've got it covered." With a wave, he started the truck and drove away.

Once he'd disappeared from view, Leah took a minute to study her new ride.

"Well, Bruiser," she said, patting the side-view mirror, "you're no looker, but that's okay. I'll bet you're pretty on the inside, and that's what matters."

Pocketing her title, she strolled toward the driveway with a light breeze tossing her hair and the faint scent of burning leaves filling her nose. She pulled a deep breath into her lungs and savored it—the sweet, crisp smell of Texas in autumn. Lord, she'd missed that smell. Right now in Minnesota, the air was so frosty it would have stung the inside of her nose, and no sweater was thick enough to combat those brutal Northern winters. Her hands had been perpetually cold for the last decade, like she'd caught a chill in her soul.

As if in consolation, the November sun broke free of the clouds and caressed the apples of Leah's cheeks. She lifted her face to the heavens, and by the time she reached her front porch, she didn't want to go inside.

Tucking both hands into her sweater pockets, she stood on tiptoe to peer through the front windows. Daddy still had plenty of company, so she decided to linger a while. She took a seat on the bottom step and crossed her legs at the ankles, letting her dark jeans soak up the sun's warmth. With a contented sigh, she leaned back on her elbows and glanced at the yard.

The really overgrown yard.

For the first time since returning home, she noticed that crabgrass had choked out the lush fescue lawn she remembered—the one that'd felt like a carpet of cool satin beneath her feet. The flowerbeds were in even worse shape. Leah couldn't tell what kind of weed had replaced her cheery mums, but their tall, prickly stems and poofy white tips reminded her of cotton's evil stepsister. Her old dog, Samson, was buried there, and his grave seemed desecrated by the overgrowth.

When Leah studied her neighbors' modest-but-immaculate homes, then glanced over her shoulder at the flaking paint and loose shutters on the brick ranch behind her, it became apparent that Daddy had let more than just himself go.

Maybe she *should* find him a wife. Or three.

While she sat there wondering how to rehabilitate her father's heart *and* his home in one short month, more trouble rolled in, this time on a cherry-red 1978 Harley-Davidson.

Leah recognized the distinct sound of its high-performance engine long before it pulled into view, its low roar tearing at her eardrums, rumbling the air until she felt it in her teeth. She'd know that hog anywhere, and more important, the pig riding it. Colt had put her on the back of that bike a time or two, though it hadn't been fully restored then, more like a rude, crude tornado

of bolts. Still, at seventeen she'd thought it was sexy as
hell, pardon her language.

But she'd matured since then. Danger didn't get her
revved up anymore. She'd collect her license and registration, then send the good sheriff on his merry way.
She stood and took a defensive stance—feet planted
shoulder-width apart, arms folded—to steel herself
against another butterfly attack.

Colt parked beneath the shade of an old oak tree
across the street and cut the engine. With a booted heel,
he kicked the stand and leaned the bike gingerly to the
side before swinging one leg over the seat. He started to
remove his helmet, but something caught his eye, and
he paused to buff a smudge of dirt from the body with a
clean rag he'd pulled from his back pocket. Leah snickered to herself, half expecting Colt to ask the bike, *Your
place or mine, honey?*

He shrugged off his leather jacket and slung it over
the handlebars while Leah shifted her weight to one hip,
wishing he'd hurry up already. But then he reached up to
pull off his helmet, and the hem of his T-shirt rose a few
inches—just enough to reveal a sprinkling of inky-black
hair that covered his hard, flat abdomen and trailed off
beneath the waistband of his Levi's.

Oh, mercy.

A wave of desire slammed Leah with so much force,
she actually swayed on her feet. And just when she'd
regained her footing, Colt shook back his loose hair and
locked those aqua eyes on her, making her mouth go
dry. This was bad. Very bad. Not to mention pathetic.
He hadn't even touched her, and already her blood had
rushed to all the right places. She had to get rid of him.

"Got my license?" she shouted.

Instead of answering right away, he took his sweet time, waiting until he'd crossed the street and joined her at the foot of the porch steps to say, "Unh-uh." He swept a leisurely gaze over her body, heating her in every single spot it landed. "It's still in my office. If you want it, you're gonna have to come get it."

Not in this lifetime. "Then why're you here?"

"To talk."

"We've got nothing to talk about."

"Yeah, we do." He shoved both hands in his pockets, drawing her attention to parts of him she shouldn't want. She dropped her gaze to her shoes. "I need to apologize, Leah."

Her heart gave a tiny leap. It was the first time he'd spoken her name in that buttery drawl, and she wished it didn't sound so delicious on his lips.

"Don't worry about it," she said in a rush. "It's ancient history."

"Not for me." Something in his tone darkened, and she peeked up to find him staring into the grass. "Not at all."

Leah gnawed on her bottom lip. She didn't like the way he'd gone all somber, as if he really was sorry. She didn't want him to be sorry. His contrition pulled the already painful knot in her chest even tighter. In order to regain some power, or at least the illusion of it, she skirted around him and climbed the porch steps until she met his height, then turned and demanded, "Why are you really here?"

"To tell you I'm sorry for what I did. I want to explain wh—"

"Are you apologizing to all the women you've seduced?" If so, he'd better clear his schedule for the next six months.

"No." His gaze burned into hers, deadly serious and tugging that knot until her ribs threatened to crack. "There's only you."

The crisp autumn air turned to soup, thick and steamy and impossible to breathe. *There's only you, Angel.* That's what he used to say every time she'd laced her fingers behind his broad neck and asked if he loved her. But Colt did *not* love her, probably never had. He was toying with her now just as he'd done back then.

"I forgive you," she said. "So you can go now."

"Liar."

She pulled her sweater sleeves over her clammy hands and shrugged one shoulder. "If you don't believe me, that's your problem."

"I don't believe you, and we're not done talking."

"Oh, yeah?" She'd show him otherwise. Raising one brow, she backed slowly up the stairs. "'Cause I think we are."

"What're you afraid of, Leah?"

There it was again—her name dipped in the chocolate of his voice. "*Afraid?*" she scoffed. "Don't flatter yourself, CJ." Instantly, she realized what she'd done, and her cheeks went up in flames. She hoped he hadn't noticed that she'd called him by his old nickname, the one she'd only used when they were...*alone*.

His eyes brightened, and a sly smile curved his lips, teeth flashing white against his dark skin. He'd definitely noticed, darn it. "Okay, honey." Still grinning like a hyena, he hitched a thumb toward his Harley. "I'll leave you alone, for now. But sooner or later, we're gonna have that talk."

"What-*ever*." Oh, Lord. She sounded seventeen! "I've gotta check on Daddy." And before she could humiliate herself any further, she retreated into the house.

—⁓—

An hour later, she occupied herself with the task of tidying up after Daddy's guests. The wave of visitors had crested, and only one remained—the associate pastor, Brother Mike, who sat beside Daddy on the sofa as they discussed Sunday's sermon.

Leah shuttled half-full glasses of watered-down iced tea and Coca-Cola from the living room into the kitchen and loaded the dishwasher. When she'd finished wiping the rings off the coffee table, she laid out a pound of chicken breasts to thaw for supper, then brought Daddy his daily dose of Coumadin and baby aspirin.

She'd just sat down for a break when her iPad chimed from its resting place atop the corner curio. Reflexively, her eyes widened and met with Daddy's across the room. They both knew who was calling. She only Skyped with one other person, and she didn't want Brother Mike, or anyone else, to find out whom.

"Excuse me," she said to Mike as she jumped to her feet to grab the tablet. "I'll take this in the other room so I don't disturb y'all."

*Y'all?*

Three days in Texas and already her accent was prairie-dogging it. She ran down the hall into her bedroom and shut the door before swiping her index finger across the glossy screen. Bold white lettering announced

*Noah Ackerman calling.* She tapped the screen and waited for the three-second delay to pass before greeting her son.

"Hey, Bud."

A blur of colors filled the screen, and then Noah's image came into focus—sea-blue eyes smiling above russet cheeks, a mop of black hair brushing his shoulders. He flashed the classic gap-toothed grin of a nine-year-old. "Hi, Miss Leah."

She'd always been painfully aware that Noah favored his father, but having just seen Colt in the flesh, the resemblance seemed even more striking. Noah had inherited Leah's peaceful nature and Colt's...well, everything else. It seemed his DNA had unceremoniously elbowed hers aside, but considering the way he'd demanded center stage in life, why would his genes behave any differently? If she hadn't been conscious during delivery and seen Noah with her own eyes, she wouldn't have believed the child was hers.

*Not mine*, she scolded inwardly. *Not really.* No matter how open the adoption, Noah called another woman "Mom." That would never change.

She glanced at the bedside alarm clock. "It's only three," she said. "Why aren't you in school?"

"I'm sick."

She brought the iPad a little closer to scrutinize Noah's image. He didn't look sick. Didn't sound it, either. "What's wrong?"

"I had a tummy ache, but I'm okay now."

"Good. I'm glad you feel better."

Instead of responding with an account of his day, he fell silent and slouched. That wasn't like him. Usually he rattled on about Pokemons, Bakugans, and other assorted Japanese–ons she didn't understand.

"What's wrong?" she said.

He perked up as if he'd been waiting for her to ask. "Mom won't let me play Mario Kart. She says if I'm too sick to go to school, then I'm too sick for anything else."

Leah smiled. "My daddy used to say the same thing, but with TV instead of video games. He always made me stay in bed when I was sick."

"Don't you think that's a stupid rule?"

She took a moment to form a careful response. Diane was a good mother to Noah, and Leah didn't want to undermine her authority. "I think you need to respect your mama by doing what she says."

That wasn't what Noah wanted to hear. He'd always known Leah was his birth mother, but until the last six months, he hadn't matured enough to understand what that meant. Since then, he'd begun testing the boundaries, trying to play her in a game of "divide and conquer" against his parents every time they disciplined him. But Leah refused to surrender, no matter how good it might feel to give Noah what he wanted and be his hero for a change.

"Can you talk to her for me?" he begged.

"I'm not going against your mama, Bud."

Black brows formed a slash over his eyes as he jutted out his bottom lip. "Fine. I gotta go."

"Okay," she said with a casual shrug. It stung to know he'd only called for permission to play his video game, but she hid her disappointment. "Love you."

He grumbled something she couldn't make out before abruptly disconnecting.

Leah's heart sank. Like any child, Noah had his quirks, but he was usually a sweet boy. He'd never hung up on her before. Numbly, she powered off her iPad and set it on the nightstand, then curled up in bed to stare at the wall.

Since the day Leah discovered she was pregnant, she'd put Noah's needs ahead of her own, but it had been an excruciating journey. Nothing—absolutely nothing on earth—hurt worse than leaving the maternity ward with empty arms, breasts swollen with milk for an infant who belonged to someone else. During those early days, she didn't think she'd survive it. And just when she'd thought life couldn't kick her any harder, she'd hemorrhaged, and the doctors were forced to take her womb.

Still, she'd resisted the screaming maternal urge to reclaim Noah for herself. Jim and Diane loved her baby more than life, and she knew they'd give him the kind of stability she simply could not provide. At seventeen, Leah couldn't even remember to feed the dog, and Colt had just been arrested again. Placing Noah with the Ackermans was the most selfless thing she'd ever done.

And the most shameful.

She'd kept Noah's existence a secret from Colt, afraid he'd insist on letting their families raise the baby. Her child deserved better than being tossed between three grandparents. She'd wanted him to have one stable home with a mom and dad who loved each other. With rules and consistency and maybe even siblings. So, after talking it over with Daddy, she'd skipped town right before prom to live with Jim and Diane in Minnesota.

She'd lied—claiming not to know who'd fathered her

child—and had hidden like a thief to make sure Colt couldn't find out in time to overturn the adoption. She'd insisted on an open arrangement, and the Ackermans had agreed, understanding that a mother would always be a mother. She loved them for that. Over the years, she'd borne the pain in silence, settling for monthly visits with Noah and the occasional video conference call.

Logically, adoption was the right choice, but that didn't stop her from lying awake some nights, too guilty for dreams. What would Colt say if he knew she'd given away their son?

She didn't want to think about it.

"Pumpkin?" A knock on her bedroom door brought her back to the present. "Brother Mike's gone. Everything okay?"

"Yeah." She rolled out of bed, shook off her funk, and joined Daddy in the hall. "Noah's just having a bad day and taking it out on me."

Daddy gave her arm a consoling pat. "Congrats, hon. That means you're a real parent. He wouldn't push your buttons if he didn't feel safe around you."

"I know, but it stings all the same." She nodded toward the master bedroom. "Come on. Let's get you cleaned up, and then maybe you should take a rest."

After changing the bandages on his chest, she tucked him in like an overgrown child and lowered the shades. Before shutting his door, she asked, "Hey, is Rachel still living at home?"

"Far as I know. She took over the hardware store when her daddy passed, so you can try her there too."

Leah told him to holler if he needed anything, then headed to the kitchen, where she stared at the old rotary phone affixed to the wall. She couldn't put it off any longer—she had to call Rachel. Not only was it the right thing to do, but she needed a friend right now. Even a furious friend who'd demand answers Leah wasn't at liberty to give.

Taking a deep breath, she lifted the phone from its cradle and dialed the number she knew by heart.

"Hello," Rachel spat after the third ring. Her phone greeting had always sounded exactly like this—accusing, as if she'd been on the verge of curing cancer before you'd had the nerve to interrupt her.

"It's me," was all Leah said.

"Tinkerbell." The smile was thick in Rachel's voice. "It's about damn time."

# Chapter 4

"LISTEN UP, DIPSHITS," COLTON HOLLERED AT HIS deputies during Friday morning roll call. Instantly, half a dozen men bolted upright and quit their jabbering. "Stop using an open pen to tap the LCD panel in your cruisers. You're leavin' ballpoint ink on the touch screens."

That equipment was expensive as hell, and he'd kissed a lot of ass to get it covered in the budget. "Next guy I catch marking up his laptop is gonna spend two months detailing the whole squad." Pointing at his chief deputy, he added, "I'm lookin' at you, Horace."

"Yeah, yeah." Horace waved him off before scratching his potbelly with a Bic cap.

"And speaking of equipment," Colt said, "if y'all want new pistols next year, you'd better start writing tickets." After court fees, the sheriff's department only kept about twenty percent of the total fine, and Glocks weren't cheap. "Folks are haulin' ass on Route Fifty. It'll be like shooting fish in a barrel."

His lower back muscles clenched, and he sucked a mouthful of black coffee from his Styrofoam cup, letting the flavor of roasted beans distract him from the pain.

"Another thing," he muttered. "When you're serving warrants, see if you can get a snitch on whoever's stealing the AC units on Front Street." When the economy tanked, theft skyrocketed, and people were snatching anything that wasn't nailed down. Crazy fools had even stolen the brass valves out of the new auto-flushing toilets at Shooters. "The perp's probably selling the parts over in Hallover County."

Horace nodded a little too enthusiastically and checked his watch, no doubt eager for the free country platter Miss Stacy served him each morning at the diner. "We done?"

"Not yet." Colt cleared his throat and pretended to study the warrants tacked to his clipboard. "Y'all probably heard Leah McMahon's back in town."

"Mmm-hmm," came a few replies.

"She in trouble?" Horace asked.

"Unh-uh." Not yet, anyway. But last night Colt dreamt she'd been kidnapped by Troy Aikman. The quick-fingered bastard had thrown Leah over one shoulder, huffed into the end zone, and then spiked her onto the Astroturf. While the logical side of Colt's brain understood the absurdity of it, the echo of her screams still rang in his ears, and he hadn't been able to think straight all morning. What if the nightmare was an omen? Yeah, he knew that sounded crazy too, but he didn't care. He finally had Leah back in his life—more or less—and he wasn't taking any chances with her safety.

"I want you to keep a special watch on her," he said. "Make sure she's okay. Be there if she needs a hand."

Someone snickered from the other end of the table, and Colt fired a glare that would freeze the balls off a brass monkey. The laughter died real friggin' fast, but to make sure his men knew he wasn't dicking around, he threatened, "If she so much as stubs her toe while she's here, I'll have your asses." After a stern glance all around, he added, "We clear?"

"Yeah, Chief," they muttered.

He gave the boys a terse reminder about Saturday night's spaghetti supper at the firehouse before dismissing them for patrol duty and returning to his office. When he hobbled down the hallway and shoved open his door, his already lousy morning took a hard left into Shitville.

"Hey, jerkwad." Homecoming queen turned man-hater, Rachel Landry, occupied his chair, resting her fugly garden clogs on the corner of his desk. The eight-by-eight office seemed to shrink in her presence, probably because her bitterness took up all the room.

Colt glanced over his shoulder toward the reception desk and kneaded his lower back with one fist. "How'd you get in here?"

"Darla." She flashed a faux-sweet smile, shaking back her shiny chestnut hair. Rachel was girl-next-door pretty, but she sucked the fun out of the air like a possessed leech. "We were co-captains on the varsity cheer squad, remember?"

"Must've slipped my mind." He stalked behind her and jerked back the rolling chair, forcing her to hop to her feet. And because he knew it would put a burr in her britches, he said, "I arrested your idiot husband on Monday. He make bail?"

Rachel's eyes turned to slits, exactly as he'd hoped. "He's not my husband, and you damn well know it."

"I'm pretty sure you're still married in God's eyes." Colt didn't believe that one bit, but it was too much fun watching Rachel's mouth prune up like elephant ass.

"Go to hell, Colton."

"Sure thing." He lowered to his chair and groaned with relief. "I'll say hello to your mama while I'm there."

"My mama's still alive, moron."

"Exactly." He pointed one finger at her. "And living with you. If that's not some serious hell on earth, I don't know what is." Before she had a chance to strike back, he added, "Do us both a favor and take a hike, Landry."

"Believe me, I can't stand sharing oxygen with you either." To prove her point, she curled her upper lip and raked a glare over him from Stetson to Laredos. "I think your chair just gave me herpes. But I'm here for my girl, Tink. You want me gone?" She held out one hand and waggled her fingers. "Give me her license and papers."

*Tink.* He'd always hated that Leah's friends had nicknamed her after some dumb fairy, just because she was tiny and blond. Anyone with two brain cells to rub together knew she was an angel. "No dice. I can't release official documents to you—it's a privacy violation. Leah's a big girl. She can come and get 'em herself."

"Turns out I'm not the only one who hates sharing oxygen with you."

The words hurt as real as any buckshot, but he didn't let it show. He couldn't believe Leah despised him that much. Sure, she'd hung up on him the last three times he'd called, but her reaction during his visits—the way her ivory throat pulsed like she'd just sprinted the twenty-yard dash—said she liked sharing his airspace a little too much.

Instead of dwelling on that, he asked, "She mention why she ran away?"

Rachel lifted a shoulder as she moved to the opposite side of the desk. "Just the same bullshit excuse she's shoveling all over town. But if you ask me, it's your fault."

"Me?" Colt couldn't hide his reaction this time. He

drew back, feeling his brows skyrocket into his scalp. *His* fault? He'd nearly lost his mind when Leah disappeared, and nobody had worked harder to track her down. Nobody. Not even her own daddy. "I think some of Tommy's stupid rubbed off on you."

"Oh, please. Don't play innocent. You completely trashed her reputation."

Colton opened his mouth to defend himself, but bit back his retort. There was no point in denying he'd blackened Leah's name. He felt guilty just thinking about it. "True," he said. "Maybe that's part of the reason she left, but not why she stayed gone ten years without a word for her own daddy."

The shrew didn't have an answer for that. For several beats, Rachel sucked on her top teeth and stared him down, clearly searching for a way to blame it on him but coming up empty.

"Yeah, I guess not," she finally admitted.

"You think maybe he hit her?" Colt asked. "I've heard those hardcore preacher types can be—"

"No way," she interrupted. "Pastor Mac couldn't punch a clock, let alone his little girl. You didn't grow up around here—you never saw the way he doted on her."

Colt wasn't convinced. He didn't need a Texas birth certificate to see that things between Leah and her father didn't add up. "Well, something happened between them—something bigger than a fight about me. You don't turn your back on family for that long without a good reason."

With that, the ceasefire they'd wordlessly negotiated seemed to end as Rachel's tone shifted from mean to bitchtastic. "Whatever happened, it's none of your business. You did enough damage last time." She jabbed an index finger at him. "Leave her alone and call one of your floozies if you want a score. You've got a whole army of them."

Heat crept into Colton's face, building like steam inside a pressure cooker until he feared the top of his skull might blow through the ceiling. "I'm not that man anymore," he ground out between clenched teeth.

Rachel didn't know him—never really had—and it infuriated him to think she might drip that poison in Leah's ear, filling her mind with tales of Colt's drinking and whoring without bothering to mention he'd changed.

His fury must've shown, because Rachel quit tapping her nails on his desk and took a step back. "You know what they say about leopards and spots."

"Get out," he ordered in an eerie calm that alarmed even himself. "Before I find a reason to throw you in the tank with Tommy."

Rachel cocked her head to the side. He could practically see her wheels turning—calculating the risk of slipping in one more insult. She wanted the last word so badly her mouth twitched. But she must have thought better of it, because she turned with a huff, flinging her hair over one shoulder like a country diva as she charged into the hall.

Colt stared after her a minute to make sure she'd really left before turning his attention to the stack of citizens' complaints on his desk. But after mindlessly scanning the same page three times, he accepted the fact that Rachel had screwed with his focus, and he shoved the paperwork aside.

Damn it, his goal to win Leah's trust was hard

enough without her friends meddling in his business. Leah already knew about his crazy teenage years, but she had no idea how he'd self-destructed after she left. He'd hoped to keep it that way.

He'd done a thorough job of wrecking himself back then. Moonshine, honkytonks, titty bars—he'd used them all to forget Leah. Or to try. He never could put her sweet face out of his mind for long, so he'd doubled his efforts, hurtling through life with his pants around his ankles and a perpetual buzz fogging his brain.

It had never occurred to him before, but what if Leah couldn't forgive him for all the women he'd slept with? Because the idea of her making love to another man sent bile clawing a trail through his esophagus.

He needed to apologize to Leah before Rachel turned her against him for good. Of course, there was the minor complication of getting Leah to speak to him first.

He pulled her driver's license from his shirt pocket and gazed into those sad, blue eyes. "Stubborn girl," he told her. "Hide all you want, but I'm not gonna quit on you."

The direct method had failed, so maybe he needed to change strategies. To get sneaky. The more he thought about it, the more it made sense. He was mighty good at sneaky—an expert, if he did say so himself. While it seemed backward to trick Leah into forgiving him, he didn't have much time before her dad got better and she'd leave again. Already, he'd wasted a week in a misguided attempt to do the right thing.

So now that he'd resolved to trust his more wicked inclinations, how was he going to get Leah alone? She hardly left her daddy's house, and there was no way she'd invite him inside.

He bounced one booted heel against the floor, considering his options. He'd heard she planned on coming to Trey Lewis's homecoming potluck tonight. Maybe he should confront her there. Not the ideal situation, as half the town would turn out, including Leah's sisterhood of cockblockers, but Colt would have to make it work. The only question was how.

Thirty minutes and two broken pencils later, he'd just hatched the beginnings of a plan when his sister knocked on the door and peeped inside.

"Hey." Avery bit her bottom lip, apologizing with her eyes. "Sorry to bug you."

"Don't be." Smiling for the first time that day, Colt pushed back from his desk and waved her inside. "I hardly get to see you now that you've taken up with that accountant."

"Consultant," she corrected.

"Whatever." He didn't give a rip what her boyfriend did for a living. The guy didn't make Avery cry, and that's all that mattered. Colt and his sister weren't as close as most fraternal twins, but he still wanted to tear the nads off any bastard who screwed with her head. And since her "baby daddy" had split for Reno, there'd been a lot of candidates for Colt's neutering services.

"Come on in," he said. "I could use a distraction."

"Oh, yeah?" Her face brightened. "I'm glad you mentioned that, because," she tugged his niece into view, "I need a favor."

"Hi, Uncle Colt." Apropos of nothing, Emma stretched both arms above her head and told him, "This is how ballerinas dance." She demonstrated by rising to her tiptoes and staggering into his office like a drunken mule in high heels. Before he had a chance to open his mouth, she pinched a handful of her bedazzled jeans and said, "These are really tight, but they're fashionable. Don't you think they're fashionable?"

"Sure, honey," he told her, giving Avery a questioning look.

"Can she hang out here for a couple of hours?" Avery asked. "I have a doctor's appointment, and my sitter canceled."

Colt glanced at his niece, who'd begun whipping her head back and forth, smacking herself in the face with her own ponytail. Emma wasn't a bad kid, but Colt suspected she was powered by nukes instead of cornflakes.

"Why can't she go to school?" he asked Avery.

Emma hopped on one foot and interjected, "I'm in kindergarten!"

"Teacher work day," Avery explained.

"What about Granddaddy?"

"He's in court."

Without warning, Emma pitched forward into Colt's lap, knocking his rolling chair back a few inches and filling his space with the smell of peanut butter. "What's that?" she asked, making a grab for his pistol.

He pushed her little hand aside and told Avery, "Just take her with you. I see kids at the doctor all the time."

"I can't." Avery backed out of the room and hovered in the doorway, tensing as if to make a run for it. "It's the lady doctor." Then she felt the need to gross him out with details like, "I'm getting fitted for a new diaphragm. I'll be naked from the waist down, spread-eagled with my feet in stirrups, all my business wide open for everyone to—"

"Christ, Avery!" Colt held up one hand to block the image. He didn't want to think about his sister that way. He liked to pretend she didn't have girly parts or a sex life—that Emma was conceived immaculately. "Just go."

"Thanks. I owe you." She blew a kiss at her daughter and told Colt, "Don't give her any candy."

He scoffed, shaking his head. Of course he wouldn't give the kid any friggin' candy—it was nine o'clock in the morning. What kind of moron did Avery take him for?

"How about a doobie from the evidence room?" he asked. "Can I give her one of those?"

"Love you too, Colton," she sang in an unnaturally high-pitched voice, her child-friendly way of saying *Fuck you, and the Harley you rode in on*. "Be a good girl, Em," she added before rushing off to her appointment.

Emma didn't miss a beat. "Look, Uncle Colt." She thrust out her belly to display a sticker, pointing to a cartoon character dressed in a harem girl costume. "She's my favorite princess."

"Oh, yeah?" He scanned the cartoon's heavy-lidded bedroom eyes and the cleavage spilling from her off-the-shoulder halter top. Jeez, whatever happened to Strawberry Shortcake and Rainbow Brite? He shook his head. "She's not my favorite."

Emma's tiny pink lips parted with a pop. "She's not?"

"Unh-uh."

"Then which princess is your favorite?"

Colt scrambled for a name, coming up empty. "Uh," he made a wide circle with his hands and guessed, "the one with the poofy dress."

"Belle or Cinderella?"

"Cinderella." He recognized that one. Nodding at Emma's sticker, he said, "I don't like the way this girl is showing off her tummy and her—" *ginormous tits* "—uh, her bosoms."

"Oh." Emma nodded in understanding. "Her bubbies." She craned her neck to inspect said bubbies. "She's sexy. One day I'll have big bubbies too, then I'll be sexy."

Good God. As if kids these days didn't have enough to worry about. "You're only six, hon. I don't want you thinking about what's sexy."

"But my friend Shayla said boys like big bubbies. She has three brothers, and they told her so."

"Well, first of all, that's not true." In all the years since Leah left town, he'd never seen a pair of breasts that compared to her flawless, pink-tipped B-cups. But he wasn't about to share that tidbit with Emma. He thought for a moment, then warned, "And besides, you wanna stay away from boys. They're gross."

"Really?"

"Yep. They pick their noses and don't wash their hands." Then he hastily added, "Except for me."

A new voice from the doorway said, "You wash your hands after you pick your nose?"

Colt glanced up to find Leah watching them. A thrill ricocheted up and down the length of his body from groin to chest. "Every single time," he told her. "I have standards, you know."

"Hmm. I've heard mixed reports on that." She folded both arms beneath those magnificent bubbies, and Colt's mouth broke into a grin. No matter how exotic, that buxom cartoon character had nothing on Leah.

He let his eyes trace the gentle curves of her denim-clad thighs and a teasing swell of hips peeking out from beneath an oversized Vikings sweatshirt. Nothing screamed *sexy!* like a woman who loved football, even if she did pull for a shitty team like Minnesota. Leah didn't need to put all her goods on display to make Colt's heart thump. She was a natural beauty without even trying.

"Emma," Colt said when he'd finished ogling, "this is Miss McMahon. She and I were real good friends once."

Emma turned her wide, brown eyes on him and tipped her head. "But you're not friends anymore?"

He glanced at Leah and lifted his brows, a silent message that it was entirely up to her.

"Is she yours?" Leah asked, ignoring the question.

He shook his head. "My sister's. You never met Avery. She was still in Oklahoma when my folks sent me to live here. She moved to town about seven years ago, right before she had Emma."

"Nice to meet you," Leah said, crouching down to Emma's height. "I like your sparkly pants. Oh, and your sticker! She's my second favorite, right behind Ariel."

With that, Emma was sold. She skipped over to her new best friend and began twirling Leah's hair between her fingers. "I like Ariel, too, but I don't think Uncle Colt does."

"No?" Leah asked. She raised her gaze to his. "Why not?"

Colt shrugged. He didn't know Ariel from an areola.

"'Cause he don't like it when girls show off their belly and their bubbies."

Leah tipped back her blond head, laughing in a warm, high tinkle that settled in Colt's chest and radiated outward until his fingertips went tingly. She glanced at him with those crystal-blue eyes all lit up like the noonday sky, and for an instant, she was his angel again.

It felt like heaven, but it didn't last nearly long enough. The smile died on Leah's lips, her gaze dimming as she pushed to standing and took two steps toward his desk.

"Rachel said you wouldn't give her my license." She pressed her lips together and peered at him a moment before taking a sudden interest in his stapler. "I need it so I can get tags for my car."

"Oh, sure." He stiffened his spine in an effort to hide his disappointment. "Got that right here in my desk," which was a bald-faced lie. He kept her license in his shirt pocket, where he could pull it out during the day and gaze at her. To appease her, he tugged open his center drawer and rooted through paperclips and invoices until he found Benito Alvarez's registration.

"Here you go," he said, handing it across the desk. "By the way, who is this guy?" Based on what Colt knew of Alvarez—age sixty-one, widowed, one child, clean record, owner of B&A Home Health Services—he guessed Leah worked for the man, but some secret part of him feared Alvarez was more than just a boss. Colt added with a wink, "You didn't steal his Escalade, did you?"

Leah took the document but didn't meet his eyes. "If I did, you think I'd be stupid enough to tell the town sheriff?"

"Probably not," he conceded, pretending to search the drawer for her license. "You always were a smart girl."

A humorless chuckle shook her chest. "That's debatable."

"Hey, I wouldn't have passed Senior Chem if it

weren't for you." After Colt had transferred to Sultry High, the science teacher partnered him with Leah, who'd offered to bring Colt up to speed. Within a couple of weeks, they'd started meeting after school in his granddaddy's shed to make a little chemistry of their own. "You were a real good tutor."

The light flush that stained her cheeks told him she remembered all the study sessions where they'd never once cracked a book. Where he'd memorized each fragrant curve of her body instead of chemical equations. Where he'd lifted her onto a sawdust-coated worktable, stroked her into a frenzy with his fingertips, and then taken her virginity to the backdrop of a violent late-summer storm.

He remembered, too, and the mental echo of her gasps of pleasure made his pants suddenly snug in the front. He rolled his chair forward until his belly bumped the desk. For good measure, he did an algebra problem in his head.

"I don't remember it that way." Leah went quiet when her eyes darted to Emma. Clearly, she had more to say, but not in the company of a princess-in-training.

"Well, you put up with a dumb jock like me." Emma tugged on Colt's sleeve. He ignored her and added, "I was mighty grateful."

Leah seemed to warm at that, shrugging one shoulder and favoring him with half a smile. "You weren't stupid. I always hated that you thought so."

"Uncle Colt?" Emma interrupted. "I'm hungry."

"Just a minute, hon." He waved her away and focused on Leah. "You used to get so mad at me for saying that. Remember?"

"Uncle Colt?"

"Because it wasn't true," Leah insisted.

"Uncle Colt?"

"Tell it to my transcript," he countered.

"Uncle Colt?"

"There's more than one kind of smart," Leah pressed.

"Uncle Colt?"

"Only one kind that counts for anyth—"

"UNCLE COLT!"

Colt sucked a loud breath through his nose and closed his eyes while fishing inside his pocket for a dollar bill. Damn it, he was finally beginning to crack Leah's shell. If he could only get rid of Emma for a few minutes…

He pushed the money into her little fist. "Go find Miss Darla at the front desk. She's selling Hershey bars for the school marching band."

Emma's face brightened. "Reese's Cups too?"

He gave her another dollar. "Buy one of each."

"Thanks, Uncle Colt!" After hugging his arm, Emma skip-ran from the room and left them in peace.

Colt tried resuscitating the conversation, but when he returned his gaze to Leah, he found her studying him in open-mouthed surprise.

"You're letting her have chocolate," she peered at the old analog clock on the wall, "at nine in the morning?"

"What?" Colt shrugged. "It's not gonna kill her."

Those warm blue eyes turned frosty, and just like that, he lost her. She held out one hand. "Where's my license?"

Wait, what had he done wrong? A little candy never hurt anyone. And what did Leah care? Emma wasn't even her kid. Oh, all right, he knew it wasn't the best move, but…

"My license," she repeated.

"Can't find it." Scooting back, he pulled his drawer completely open and pointed inside to show her. "Want to stay while I keep looking?"

"Forget it. I'll just swing by the courthouse and get another."

"No, wait." He couldn't let her do that. Holding onto her license gave him a sliver of hope—no matter how slim—that she'd stay in town. "I think I gave it to Horace. When he comes off patrol duty, I'll ask him."

She heaved a sigh. "Fine."

"I'll track you down once I have it. You gonna be at Trey Lewis's party tonight?"

Her eyes flew wide. "Why? Are *you*?"

Colt wasn't book smart, but he had enough intelligence to understand that Leah hadn't expected him at the potluck. Nor did she want him there. He didn't hesitate to tell her, "No, I hate those kinds of things."

"Oh." Her shoulders relaxed a few inches. "Too bad. I'll bet he'd like to see you."

"I'll catch him another time. Small town, remember? We're bound to run into each other, probably before lunch."

Leah grumbled something that sounded like, "Tell me about it," and with a halfhearted wave good-bye, she made her exit.

Colt hoped he'd told a convincing lie. The last thing he wanted was for Leah to hole up inside her daddy's house again. She didn't know it, but Colt had big plans. Big, sneaky plans.

Tonight, he'd get Leah back in his arms or die trying.

# Chapter 5

LEAH STRAIGHTENED THE BODICE OF HER CHERRY-PRINT sundress as she crossed the dark parking lot, gravitating toward the sound of Toby Keith's "Red Solo Cup." The sharp autumn breeze brought goose bumps to her bare arms, but she resisted the urge to return to the car for her sweater. She knew from experience how sweltering the fellowship hall could get when filled to capacity, and judging by the distant din of laughter and conversation, the party was already in full swing.

The familiar scents of Lit'l Smokies and Hawaiian Punch greeted her beyond the hall's double doors, bringing back a flood of childhood memories—everything from her baptism social to the youth group mixer where she'd stolen her first kiss from Josh Schroder behind a dusty silk ficus tree in the corner. The ficus was gone, but little else had changed.

Like the old junior high cafeteria, dozens of long plastic tables and folding metal chairs claimed the floor in two parallel rows. Right now, the eggshell tile wasn't visible beneath hundreds of shuffling sandals and boots, but Leah knew Ms. Bicknocker kept it waxed to a high gloss that would reflect the overhead fluorescent lights during clean-up later. The decorating committee had peppered the walls with an assortment of photographs of the Lewises, and white paper streamers crisscrossed the length of the room, leading to a faded, well-used *Welcome Home!* banner that hung above the head table.

A prickle of envy tugged at Leah's heartstrings. As the daughter of the town preacher, this church had been her second home, its people a natural extension of her family. If she'd told anyone about her plans to return to Sultry Springs, would they have thrown her a party like this?

She doubted it. Daddy's congregation was too angry with her for "running away and breaking his heart." But they didn't know the real reason she'd left. They didn't know *her*. Nobody did, and it made her feel like a stranger in her own hometown.

She lost a few inches as she strode toward the punch bowl for a little high-fructose fortification. Just as she'd predicted, the air heated the farther she waded through the crowd. By the time she lifted a cup of fruity red punch to her lips, she wasn't surprised to find it warm and watered-down. Thank goodness she'd discovered this old summer dress at the back of her closet. She only wished she'd brought an elastic to lift the heavy waves of hair off her neck.

"Hey," June's voice called from behind. "You made it!"

Leah turned with a grin on her lips, which immediately fell once she caught a glimpse of her friend. *Oh, Lord.* June looked more bloated than a wet breadstick. Her taut, dewy cheeks could barely manage a smile, her fingers so puffy she'd removed her wedding band and looped it though a chain around her neck.

"Are you okay?" Leah asked.

"Mmm-hmm." June fanned herself with a discarded church program. "Why?"

Leah stalled. She couldn't very well say *You look like a tick about to pop*. "I noticed your hands are a little swollen. When's your next doctor's appointment?"

"Oh." With a nod, June touched her face and seemed to blush. It was hard to tell, because her skin tone already resembled the inside of a ripe watermelon. "I just saw him last week, so I won't go again for another month. I'm retaining water. It's probably time to lay off the Doritos."

"How's your blood pressure?" Leah didn't mean to be nosy, but after what happened to her mother, she couldn't help it.

"A little higher than pre-pregnancy, but the doctor's not worried."

"Any headaches or spotty vision?"

Laughing, June squeezed Leah's arm. "No, Nurse McMahon."

"Preeclampsia's nothing to mess around with," Leah warned. "Keep an eye on your blood pressure. And not with one of those machines at the drug store—sometimes they're not calibrated. Come see me if you can't get in with your doctor. I brought my cuff."

"Will do," June promised, tugging Leah toward the head table. "Come on. I want you to meet Trey and Bobbi."

As they wove between tables, Leah scanned June's swollen feet and ankles, wondering if she'd made a big deal out of nothing. Most women suffered from edema, especially in the third trimester. She certainly had. Birkenstocks were Leah's best friend during her last month of pregnancy.

*It's probably fine*, she decided. *June's doctor knows best*.

Once Leah quit obsessing and glanced up again, it was to the shock of two faces so gorgeous she expected to spot a Hollywood camera crew nearby.

"Hey there," said a blond-haired, blue-eyed beef-cake, extending a hand. "I'm Trey. You must be Pastor Mac's daughter."

"Leah." She grasped his palm and studied him as he pumped her arm up and down. He wore a Cubs baseball cap and an easy, genuine smile that made her like him immediately. Just when she thought he couldn't get any cuter, a pair of deep dimples appeared in his cheeks. If she looked up *All-American Boy Next Door* in the dictionary, she'd expect to find his photo there. He re-minded her of a young Brad Pitt.

"Easy, Golden Boy," chided the stunning redhead at his side. "You're gonna shake the arm out of her socket." The woman claimed Leah's hand in a firm grip and said, "I'm Bobbi. You probably don't remember me, but—"

"Sure I do," Leah told her. "Mrs. Eckleman's preschool class. We used to eat Play-Doh when she wasn't watching."

The group laughed at that, except for Bobbi, who only smiled and studied Leah with a critical eye. Having grown up in *Sultry Springs, population: 975 righteous souls*, Leah knew that look. Someone had filled Bobbi in on some juicy gossip, most likely having to do with her mysterious departure ten years ago.

By now, Leah was used to the judgment, but she didn't expect Bobbi to say, "So you're the girl who broke Colton's heart."

Leah froze as everyone around her drew a collective breath.

Luke Gallagher pinched the bridge of his nose and

whispered to his sister, "You just *had* to go there, didn't you?"

Leah shook her head in shock. *She'd* broken *his* heart? More like the other way around! Everyone in town knew what he'd done to her. Everyone! Mothers throughout Sultry County still recounted *The Shameful Misfortunes of Leah McMahon* to their teenage daughters in hopes of warning them away from the likes of Colton Bea. Had the jerk spun his own twisted version of their tale?

She gulped enough air to demand, "Is that what he's been telling people?"

Panic sparked behind Bobbi's widened eyes as she flashed a defensive palm. "No, no, no! Not at all. In fact, he told me you didn't do anything wrong. He said it was all his fault. I just meant—"

"Leah," Trey interjected, wrapping a casual arm around his wife to rein her in. "I forgot to ask how Pastor Mac's doing. Didn't he just have the ol' ticker fixed?"

Heat rose into Leah's face, and she shot Trey Lewis a glare that said she didn't appreciate the change in subject. "This wouldn't be the first time Colt's spread rumors about me. I want to know what he's told y'all."

"Hardly anything," Bobbi said. "It takes a crowbar to get information out of that man."

"Or a bottle of whiskey," Trey added. "Look, Leah, it's none of our business." He delivered a pointed look to his wife when he said, "And we agreed to stay out of it, didn't we?"

"*We* didn't agree to jack squat," Bobbi retorted before returning her attention to Leah. "I'm sorry if I gave you the wrong idea. I got to know Colton a couple of years ago. Your name came up, and I could tell how much he still cared for you. He's been looking for you a long time. That's all."

Leah had a hard time believing Colt cared for anything other than his motorcycle and his willy, not necessarily in that order.

The doubt must have shown on her face, because Bobbi promised, "Really. I have video footage I could show you from *Sex in the Sticks*. You can see how much he's hurting."

"Sex and the what?" Leah felt her eyeballs bulge. "Is that some kind of adult film?"

Trey laughed with a mouth full of punch and wound up sputtering fruit juice into his fist. He used the back of his hand to wipe red dribble from his chin. "Sounds like a porno, doesn't it?"

"No, it doesn't," Bobbi said, elbowing him in the side. "It's a documentary about me and Golden Boy" nodding at Trey, "finding love in this small town. In fact, we're wrapping up a special feature tonight." She pointed across the room to a mammoth, blue-haired Asian man with a camera perched on his shoulder. "Weezus is about to start filming."

"Filming what?" Leah asked, instinctively backing up a pace. She didn't want any part of this.

"Mostly the two of us," Bobbi said, then gesturing at the crowd, added, "and a few shots of our friends and family. You know, to show community support."

Leah took another step back. "I can't be on camera." The tremor in her voice didn't escape Bobbi's notice. Those relentless green eyes narrowed in scrutiny while Leah scrambled for damage control. "Uh," Leah added, pointing at her own face, "no makeup!"

"Uh-huh," Bobbi said, clearly not buying it.

With a nervous twitter, Leah pressed one hand over her stomach. "I'm starving. Think I'll grab some of Pru's famous German potato salad." She waved while continuing to back away from the group. "Great meeting you."

Before anyone had a chance to respond, she turned and began picking her way through a swarm of bodies. When she reached the hors d'oeuvres table, crowded with simmering crock pots and sandwich platters, she decided to continue to the dessert station at the far end of the room. No one could film her back there. But just to be on the safe side, she faced the wall and pretended to consider the assortment of fruits and candies spread out before her.

As she scanned the melon balls and brownie bites, she wondered how soon she could leave the party without appearing rude. She probably shouldn't have come in the first place, but Daddy's house was starting to feel small, and she needed a break.

*Fifteen more minutes*, she decided. *Then I'll—*

All thoughts froze when her gaze landed on a tray of Richman's éclairs.

Oh, holy Moses. Richman's éclairs!

Like dewy manna from heaven, a thin sheen of condensation made each pastry shimmer in the light. Thick layers of fudge icing had softened, oozing down the sides, just the way Leah liked it—the chocolaty flavor was so much stronger when it melted on her tongue. A faint scent of cocoa lingered in the air, titillating her senses, tempting her to surrender to a thousand-calorie devil in disguise.

With one hand, she pulled back her hair and bent at the waist to inhale a lungful of pure, unadulterated sweetness. It smelled so good, she closed her eyes and did it again. Her mouth watered in rapture. She simply had to have one.

When she stood, a new sensation interrupted her confectionary haze. She felt the heat of a large body close behind her, the bold scents of shaving cream and soap filling her head. More than that, an energy charged the air, a force so signature and electric she didn't need to turn around to identify the man who wielded it.

"Go ahead, honey," Colt whispered in her ear. "You know you want it."

She closed her eyes again as chills lifted the tiny hairs along the back of her neck. The floor seemed to soften and tilt beneath her feet, forcing her to grip the table's edge for support. Just as she opened her eyes to orient herself, Colt eliminated the space between them and settled one hand on her hip while he reached past her to grab an éclair. In that moment, every inch of her Judas body flashed hot in recognition of the touch she hadn't felt in over a decade. The pulse rushing through her veins didn't seem to care that Colt had ruined her life. Her tightening nipples didn't give a damn either.

Why couldn't she crave healthy things, like carrot sticks and accountants?

She swallowed a mouthful of desire and said, "Actually, I don't," then pointed to a fruit platter. "I'd rather have fresh strawberries."

The hard contours pressed into her back shook with silent laughter. "For a preacher's daughter, you sure lie a lot."

Using the table ledge as her guide, she scooted aside and put some precious distance between them. "I happen to like berries."

"Dipped in vanilla yogurt," he said. "I remember."

"Then what makes you think I'm lying?"

"'Cause I also remember the little noises you used to make every time you ate one of these." He tipped his éclair as if toasting her health, then brought it to his mouth for a bite. Stopping just shy of his lips, he added, "Like you were coming." Smiling, he shook his head at the memory. "Best sound in the world."

Refusing to acknowledge his lewd comment, she folded her arms and watched him devour his pastry. He'd undone the top buttons of his uniform, and he wore his hair loose tonight, shaking it back between bites. The action reminded her of all the times Daddy had complained, *That boy needs a haircut!* But she'd begged Colt to keep it long. Like his barely street-legal Harley, those silken locks had epitomized the lure of the forbidden.

Now she knew better. She might not be able to control her body's reaction to the drug that was Colton Bea, just like she couldn't help wanting to inhale a dozen Richman's éclairs, but she *could* control whether she acted on it. Sexual chemistry loaded the gun, but she wouldn't pull the trigger.

She plucked a strawberry from the fruit tray and shoved it in her mouth while Colt sucked fudge off each of his fingers.

"Mmm," he said, patting his flat belly. "How's your berry?"

Unripe and way too tart. "Perfect," she garbled around a bitter chunk. "Think I'll have another."

He caught her wrist as she reached for the table. "First, let's talk a minute about your license and papers. Out there," he nodded toward the lobby, "so we don't disturb anyone."

She shook free from his grasp and rubbed the skin around her wrist to extinguish the tingling sensation. "There's nothing to disturb. We can talk right here."

But naturally, Miss Pru chose that moment to flip on a microphone and ask the crowd to take their seats. The associate pastor joined her at the head table, clearly gearing up for a welcome home speech.

Leah gave a resigned sigh. "Fine."

She stalked into the dim lobby with Colt on her heels. When she reached the barrier of the double doors and turned to face him, she was surprised to see he'd nabbed another éclair.

"You're having *two*?" she asked.

"Hell, yeah." He shoved half of it into his mouth and spoke with both cheeks full. "You don't know what you're missin', honey."

The bastard was rubbing it in, pardon her language. "Sure I do. I'm missing twice my daily allowance of sugar and saturated fat."

Still chewing, he shrugged. "You only live once, Angel. Might as well make it count."

*Angel*. The seemingly innocuous nickname made her eye twitch. "Just give me my license."

"Don't have it," he said unapologetically, then gobbled the other half of his dessert.

"Then why are we here?"

"Hmm?"

"You said you wanted to talk about my license."

"Oh, yeah." He nodded and licked the chocolate off his lips. "I lied."

Leah hung her head. She didn't have the patience for this.

"I just need you to hear me out," he said, stooping to her height. "Please?"

Leah glanced at her watch. "You have ten seconds."

"Now, don't be like—"

"Nine."

"C'mon, Leah."

"Eight."

"Okay, I get it. Just listen—"

"Seven."

"Damn it," he snapped, dragging one hand through his hair, "I need to apologize, and it's gonna take longer than ten seconds!"

His booming voice caused a few heads to turn in their direction. After placating the onlookers with a repentant wave, he gripped Leah's upper arms and backed her toward the corner and out of view.

She shrugged free and held her ground, refusing to let him trap her. "I told you before, you don't have to apologize. I forgave you a long time ago."

He made a disapproving noise, half grunt, half snort. "There you go again with the lies."

"It's no lie. I couldn't hold on to that anger. It was making me crazy."

He seemed to turn that over in his mind, then conceded, "Okay, maybe you *think* you've let go, but you haven't." He shook his head and pressed a quick palm over her heart. "Not really. Not deep down."

She backed away from his reach, cornering herself. "Don't pretend to understand how I feel."

"It's common sense." With one step, he closed the distance between them. "I screwed you over, hard. You wouldn't be human if you weren't still pissed."

She didn't want to hear this, didn't want to dredge up those old feelings. "I'm not—"

"You know the difference between men and women?" he interrupted. Without giving her a chance to supply the obvious explanation, he said, "When guys get angry, we go a few rounds, and we're buddies again five minutes later. But not women. Y'all pretend like nothing's wrong, and you stuff that anger down so deep, it settles in your bones like a cancer." He held up one fist and flexed it in demonstration before pointing to the smooth edge of his jaw. "You need to get the poison out, honey."

"Are you suggesting we fight?" This was crazy, even for Colt.

He drew back as if offended. "Of course not. I've never hit a girl. I'll give you a freebie."

"A freebie?"

"As many as you want, wherever you want." Quickly, he clarified, "Just not below the belt. I might want kids someday."

Leah's stomach lurched as if he'd taken a free shot of his own. Her gaze dropped to the tips of his boots. She had no right to look him in the eyes. *You already have a child*, she wanted to tell him. *But he's someone else's son now, and I can't give you another*. She'd already delivered a fatal blow, straight to Colt's heart. He just didn't know it.

Her voice sounded small when she said, "I'm not going to hit you."

"Yeah, you are." Blocking her escape route, he braced both hands against the wall on either side of her body. "Remember why my folks sent me to live with my granddaddy?"

She nodded, trying not to show how much his closeness unsettled her. "They busted you for joyriding in a stolen pickup."

"That's right. They thought my friends were a bad influence, and a change of scenery would fix me. But they were wrong. And here's why." He leaned closer as if to share a deep, dark secret with her. "An asshole in Oklahoma is still an asshole in Texas. I wasn't interested in changing, and when I got here, it didn't take long to find my own kind."

"Tommy Robbins."

"Yep." He pulled back to give her some space, but didn't move aside. "The first thing I did was brag about what a badass I was—how I could lift as many skirts as cars. That's when Tommy threw down the gauntlet."

Leah didn't want to hear any more. She pushed against his chest.

"Nail the preacher's unattainable little angel," Colt continued, unmoved. "I accepted the challenge. I told him I'd have your panties off in less than a month. And I did, didn't I?"

"Stop it." She tried ducking under his arms, but he anticipated each move, stepping aside to block her. "Let me go."

"I still remember the day I announced my victory."

Leah's face flushed with anger. She pushed against

him, harder, but it was useless. He towered over her, asserting his dominance like the bully he was.

"I pulled Tommy aside in the locker room," he went on, "then told him I banged you in my granddaddy's shed."

"That's enough!"

"I had you wide open, literally begging for it." He closed his eyes and used a breathy voice to mock her. *"More, Colt. Please! Oh, god. Don't stop!"*

"Shut up!" She pounded one fist against his stone chest. "I mean it!"

"You were moaning like a wildebeest," he taunted. "And I reenacted all your little noises for Tom. He thought it was hilarious. I had him rolling on the floor."

Leah's pulse hammered in her ears, her body tense and feverish.

"After I left for my next class," Colt said, "the bastard stood on a bench and announced it to the whole football team. Didn't they cover your locker in condom wrappers the next day?"

Yes, they had. And every day afterward.

"Then your youth group found out and quit talking to you." He snorted a dry laugh. "I'm surprised they didn't stone you in the parking lot."

Did he really think this was funny? She'd given Colt her love—her body—and in return, he'd made her the running joke of the county. Leah decided she *could* hit him. She tensed her arm, pulled back, and slapped him across the face with a satisfying *thwack!* that stung her palm like a fistful of nettle. The force of the blow turned Colt's head, and as soon as he righted himself, she slapped him harder, with all her weight behind it.

He let out a low whistle, then rubbed his cheek. "Felt good, didn't it?"

Leah hesitated a few beats, her breathing choppy, heart pounding, before she admitted, "Yeah, kind of."

"Wanna do it again?" he offered.

She shook her throbbing hand and flexed her fingers. "No, I'm done."

"You sure?"

"Mmm-hmm."

"Okay." He unsnapped one of the compartments on his utility belt and produced a pair of handcuffs, then made a *turn around* motion with one finger. "In that case, I'll go ahead and take you in now. You're under arrest for assaulting an officer."

"*What?*" Surely he didn't mean it. "Is this a joke?"

"'Fraid not, honey." He took her by the shoulders and rotated her to face the wall. When she stiffened and jerked from beneath his touch, he warned, "Don't make me add 'resisting arrest' to the charges."

"You're serious?" she asked. "You're really going to do this?"

"Sure am," he drawled. "Now be a good girl and put your hands behind your back."

"I changed my mind. I want to hit you again."

He laughed while gathering her wrists. "Too late."

"This is low, Colt, even for you—and that's saying a lot."

Instead of answering, he fastened the handcuffs with a tenderness that surprised her, leaving the metal shackles so loose they fit like bracelets instead of restraints. Then he pressed a palm against her lower back and guided her outside to his cruiser. The crisp night air helped clear her mind, but didn't do anything to dispel the heat from his possessive touch. She hated herself for reacting to him. He'd just tricked her—again—and *still* her tummy fluttered with desire for this toxic man. Clearly, she needed therapy.

When Colt unlocked the front passenger door and held it open for her, she glanced at him in confusion. "Aren't you going to put me in the back?"

"Of course not," he said, disgusted. "The seat's made of plastic so we can hose it down. It's nasty and uncomfortable as hell."

Supporting her elbow, he helped her lower onto the front seat before closing the door and sauntering around the front end to join her. She thought it strange that he didn't fasten her seatbelt, nor did he start the car once he'd taken his place behind the wheel. Instead, he just sat there and fidgeted with his keys. If she didn't know better, she'd think he was nervous.

"What're we waiting for?" She shifted to the side to take the pressure off her bound wrists, bringing her within inches of Colton's thigh. No matter what she did, she couldn't escape him. Even the cruiser smelled of his coffee and aftershave, an intimate mingling of scents too homey for her liking. "Isn't this the part where you humiliate me in front of the whole town again?"

"No." He stared out the front windshield, expression unreadable. "This is the part where I explain myself."

"Enough with the games. Are you arresting me or not?"

"That's up to you." He turned to face her, the creak of leather amplified by the darkness. "I can take you in, or you can sit here and listen to what I have to say."

"And then you'll let me off?"

"Scot-free," he promised, holding up a solemn hand.

"All right, then." She'd listen, but it wouldn't change anything. "Get on with it."

"Just simmer down a minute." He huffed a sigh as if she'd done something wrong instead of the other way around. "I've had ten years to rehearse this, but it's not easy getting it out."

He paused for a few moments, running his fingers along the edge of a laptop computer attached to the console. An outbreak of applause from the fellowship hall punctuated the silence and seemed to spur him into action.

"What I said back there," he gestured toward the church, "about not wanting to change when I came to live in Sultry Springs…"

She nodded for him to continue.

"That wasn't the whole truth."

Leah rolled her eyes. "How shocking."

"New rule," he said with a warning glare. "You don't get to talk."

Ignoring the urge to thrust out her tongue like a six-year-old, she returned his glare with twice the fire and clamped her mouth shut with an audible snap.

"Damn it, this is hard for me." A frustrated groan rumbled from his chest. He took a moment to calm down, and when he finally continued, he stared into her lap. "I *did* want to change, but not until the day I met you."

Leah didn't believe that, but she played nice and kept quiet.

"You were so damn beautiful," he told her, "and you were so *good*. It's like you had this light inside you, and I thought if I could be with you, it'd make me good too."

He paused and shook his head absently. "By association, or something."

The sadness in his voice softened Leah's heart by a few degrees. She'd always hated the way Colt had put himself down. Despite her best efforts, she'd never been able to convince him he was more than a "stupid delinquent."

"I wanted to change for you," he said. "But I didn't know how. So I fumbled along, half-assing it, letting my friends think you were just another score." He glanced up and met her gaze beneath his long lashes, eyes dark with a sincerity that made it hard to breathe. "But it was never like that for me, not for a second. I loved you. I want you to know that."

Now it was her turn to look away. Unable to bear the intensity behind his eyes, she stared blankly at the tiny cherries dotting her dress. If he hadn't cuffed her, she would've run. She didn't want to hear that he'd loved her. It was easier believing he never cared.

"And that day in the shed," he continued, "I want you to know that had nothing to do with Tommy. I needed to be with you. It wasn't just teenage hormones or plain old lust. I needed you. It was like…" He sighed in frustration, splaying one hand as if to communicate what he couldn't say. "I can't make you understand, 'cause I don't even get it." Quickly, he added, "But that doesn't excuse what I did. I knew you wanted to wait for marriage, and I seduced you anyway. It was wrong of me to take that from you."

With one gentle hand, he cupped her chin and tipped it up, forcing her to take in his beautiful face, his eyes heavy with contrition. In a voice so sincere she almost couldn't stand it, he told her, "I'm sorry for that."

For the first time, she was glad he'd forbidden her to speak, because she didn't know what to say. All she could do was nod within the confines of his palm and fight back tears as he continued.

"After we had se—" he cut off and corrected, "after we made love, it felt like someone turned my body inside out. Like I was missing my skin. I loved you so hard, just thinking about you made me ache. It was wonderful and horrible, all at once. Some days I was afraid I'd crack in half if you looked at me the wrong way."

She remembered feeling the same—worried she loved him too much. People said love shouldn't hurt, but it did. The intensity of it hurt like nothing else on earth.

"I'm not gonna lie." Still caressing her face, he inched closer, until their knees touched. "It was scary as hell. I think I knew, deep down, that you wouldn't stay with a loser like me, and I panicked. I ruined everything so you couldn't dump me for a better guy." He took her cheeks between both hands and admitted, "I sabotaged what we had because I was a coward, and I didn't think I deserved you."

The backs of Leah's eyes stung as tears blurred her vision. She didn't want to believe him, and yet her heart surged with the hope that he'd once loved her. She held her breath and tried to force down a sob, but it bubbled up from deep in her lungs and broke free. Holding firm, he tilted their foreheads together.

"I still don't deserve you, Angel." He stroked her face with his thumb, wiping away a tear while his warm breath tickled her cheek. "But I'm all grown up now, and I'm not afraid."

He drew nearer, held her gaze as he licked his lips.

It was the last thing Leah saw before letting her eyelids flutter closed.

She didn't resist the soft brush of his mouth. Instead, she tilted her head back and opened to him with a whimper that betrayed the depth of her craving. He groaned in response, capturing her mouth with enough passion to liquefy her bones. When their tongues met, every cell in her body hummed alive with the memory of his kiss, even after all these years.

Her hands strained against the metal cuffs, fingers aching to touch his face and recall the features they'd once known so well. Unbound, Colt didn't hesitate to re-acquaint himself with every curve and pulse point along her throat, first with his hands, and then with his open mouth. He knew exactly where to lick and nibble, how to work the carnal spot at the base of her neck that'd always driven her wild. She tipped her head aside in a silent plea for more, and when he sucked her sensitive flesh, she moaned out loud as every drop of blood in her body pooled between her thighs.

He returned to her mouth before the moan had even left her lips, the rich, decadent sweetness of éclairs lingering on his tongue. She'd denied herself this taste for so long, and now she delved deeper, taking her fill until a distant voice of reason called out, *Not healthy*.

She ignored the voice. Colt's seeking tongue felt too good sliding between her parted lips. She was hungry, and she wanted more.

*Not healthy*, the voice called again.

She battled the voice. It had been too long since a man had worshipped her with his mouth this way—ten years too long.

*Not healthy*, her conscience screamed, refusing to be ignored.

With a groan of protest, she summoned all her strength and turned her face aside to break the kiss, then whispered, "Stop."

She braced herself for a graze of teeth at her jaw, a massaging hand at her breast, a wicked whisper of breath in her ear—the artillery of seduction Colt had used against her so well.

But instead, he rested his forehead on her shoulder and fought for breath, his hands sliding to her arms, gripping her as if struggling for control. His voice was thick with lust when he asked, "Is that really what you want?"

Afraid words would make her a liar, she only nodded.

He placed one chaste kiss on her head before pulling back. "All right, then. We'll go as slow as you want, Angel."

"Don't call me that," she whispered. "You don't know me, Colt. I'm no angel, and I'm not here to stay. This can't happen again."

"It's okay." He held up both hands in surrender. "All I'm asking is that you forgive me, nothing else."

"I told you, I already—"

"There's more."

Leah felt herself fading. She couldn't take much more of this. If confession really was good for the soul, Colt would beat her to the pearly gates by a mile. She let her head fall against the seatback and asked, "What now?"

"After you left and I couldn't find you..." He paused to clear his throat. "I'm not proud of the man I became after that. You've probably heard stories—there're plenty going around."

"It's none of my business."

"Well, I'm making it your business, because I want you to know I've changed."

Leah wanted to tell him it didn't matter—it was too late for them—but the words caught at the top of her lungs.

"Let me show you," he asked. When she opened her mouth to object, he added, "Just as friends. We were friends once, right?"

"For about a week. Then it turned into more."

"But we're older now."

"Not necessarily any wiser."

"Maybe not." He disarmed her with a lethal smile, his white teeth a flash in the darkness. "But I already told you I'm not afraid. Are you?" He raised both brows in a challenge. "How 'bout it? Can we be friends?"

"If I say yes, will you let me go home?"

He dangled his keys in the air. "Scout's honor."

"Fine, we're friends." He really knew how to wear a girl down. "Don't make me regret it."

"Never," he promised in a solemn tone. "Never again."

# Chapter 6

"Look! It's 'N Sync!"

Rachel yanked the T-shirt from Leah's closet and held it over her chest. She smoothed a loving hand over Justin's face and mouthed *Hello, lover*. As teens, she and Leah had both aspired to the title of Mrs. Timberlake, and that was long before he brought "sexy back."

"I remember when we went to this show," Rachel said with a nostalgic sigh.

"Me too," Leah said from her spot on the bed. "Because Daddy wouldn't let us go alone." Ever the diligent chaperone, he'd insisted on hanging alongside them in his pink Izod polo with the popped collar, waving his arms in the air and singing the wrong lyrics to "Bye Bye Bye." "Between his falsetto and your dancing, it's a miracle I didn't die of embarrassment."

"Hey, I had some bitchin' moves back in the day." Rachel performed a few hip thrusts and a stiff version of the Running Man while Leah broke into a fit of giggles. "Tell me that's not fresh-dope-ill."

"Wiggity-wack," Leah said. "You've still got it, fly girl. Your talents are wasted at the hardware store."

"You're right. I should ask the owner for a raise."

And she'd get it, too, because Rachel *was* the owner. The co-owner, anyway.

After taking a bow, Rachel slung the T-shirt over one shoulder and continued rifling through Leah's closet. "And look—your prom dress. It still has the tags on it."

She lifted a sapphire, floor-length taffeta gown for display, the one Leah had ordered for $79.99 plus shipping and handling from the JCPenney catalog. Back then, she'd considered eighty bucks a fortune—heck, it was kind of a fortune now—but she'd gladly parted with her babysitting money because she'd thought Colt would like it. Never mind that she technically wasn't allowed to dance; she'd intended on going to prom anyway.

But that was before the breakup...and the positive pregnancy test that followed.

Leah drew both knees to her chest. "I didn't have the heart to send it back."

The oversized bow at the waist sagged with age, but the dress still shimmered, rich and opalescent, when it caught the sunlight. Waves of hidden, poufy crinoline bustled beneath the fabric, beckoning, *Try me!*

Leah tipped her head and studied the bodice. "Wonder if it still fits."

Rachel tossed it onto the bed. "If you can still fit into your prom dress, the world finally has a reason to hate you."

"It's a risk I'm willing to take."

She stood and faced the wall to slip off her clothes, not out of modesty, but because she didn't want Rachel to notice the scar that bisected her from hip to hip. Leah's bestie had given her an unusual reprieve from questions regarding her ten-year absence, and she didn't want to disrupt the unspoken bargain of "don't ask, don't tell."

Stepping inside the gown made her feel like an instant princess, the silky fabric cool against her legs. She pulled up the dress and slid her arms through the spaghetti straps, then straightened the waist and backed toward Rachel.

"Zip me up, will you?" Leah swept her hair aside while sucking in her tummy. The touch of Rachel's icy hands made Leah flinch, but the zipper closed without a fight. Smoothing her hands over the wide pleated skirt, she spun to face her friend.

"It's a good thing I love you," Rachel said, "'cause that shit's not fair."

Leah swished around the bed to the mirror mounted on the opposite wall, her heart fluttering in anticipation of a glimpse. In seconds, she got one, but she didn't expect the wistful tug of disappointment that accompanied the sight of herself in the old gown.

Technically, there was nothing wrong. The material hugged her curves and flared out at the hips in a perfect complement to her figure. But the youthful style stood out in contrast against her strong features. Her face had matured since the last time she'd tried on this dress, cheekbones sharp, the hollows beneath carved from life's trials. The gown was clearly designed for a teenager, not a grown woman. It looked ridiculous on her.

That's when the realization hit like a kick to the chest—she'd missed prom. Really missed it. That night was gone forever.

She turned away from the woman in the mirror and asked Rachel, "Remember that character in *Pretty in Pink*, Andie's boss at the record store?"

"Mmm-hmm."

"She talks about feeling like something's missing from her life, and she decides it's a side-effect of skipping prom." Leah plopped onto the bed. "Now I finally get it."

"You didn't miss much, trust me," Rachel said.

Leah knew better. She'd give anything to travel back in time and experience that magical night.

"I mean it," Rachel insisted, "the whole night was hella awkward. I dumped Tommy after what he did to you, and so did half the girls dating the football team. Most of us went stag. Hardly anyone danced. I think I left at nine."

"Oh, no," Leah said, slumping over. "So basically, I ruined prom for the whole school?"

Rachel flapped a hand. "If anyone should feel bad, it's me. I took him back two weeks later. Should've known better." Shaking her head, she grumbled, "Guys like Tommy and Colton never change."

At that, Colt's words echoed inside Leah's head. *I'm making it your business, because I want you to know I've changed.* So who should she believe, Rachel or Colt? Could people really reform themselves, deep inside where it counted, or were personalities forged in concrete from a certain age?

Of course, it didn't matter because she and Colt were all wrong for each other. Even if she cared enough to try and trust him, she'd have to come clean about Noah. That could jeopardize the adoption. She'd never take that chance.

Leah blocked Colt's image and glanced at the sparkling blue fabric covering her legs. "Guess I should donate this old thing."

"What about in there?" Rachel asked, pointing at the closet. "The nineties called, and it wants all that stuff back. Your whole room is a time warp."

"I know." Daddy hadn't changed a thing—not the

faded pink bedspread, not the lava lamp bubbling away on the nightstand, not even the decade-old calendar on her bulletin board. "I'll box it up before I leave."

"Are we done pretending like nothing happened?" Rachel demanded abruptly. "Are you ready to talk to me now?"

Leah's heart chilled. She wasn't prepared for Rachel to repeal "don't ask, don't tell."

"Oh, come on," Rachel said when Leah didn't respond. "There's nothing you can't say to me."

"There's nothing to tell," Leah began, reciting the same tired lie she'd peddled all over town. "I had a fight with Daddy—"

"Stop!" Rachel yanked the concert T-shirt from her shoulder and threw it onto the bed. "Don't pull that. Not with me!"

Leah ducked her head and gazed at the scuffed hardwood. As much as she wanted to unburden herself with the truth, she couldn't put Noah at risk. She loved Rachel, but she loved Noah more. A whole lot more.

The bed shook as Rachel sat beside her. "I know you," she said softly. "And I know how much you loved your dad. You wouldn't have stayed gone unless you were in trouble."

"I can't talk about it." Leah dared a glance into Rachel's eyes. "I wish I could."

Rachel's brows lowered in concern. She studied Leah for a few seconds. "Now you're scaring me. I've had a lot of theories over the years. Sometimes I wondered if you ran away because you were knocked up, but now I'm thinking…" She trailed off, studying Leah's expression while tipping her head in contemplation.

Leah held her breath instinctively, frozen as if Rachel might read the truth on her face if she moved. *Nothing to see here.*

Rachel gasped, bolting upright. "Oh my god! That's it, isn't it? You were pregnant!" She clapped a hand over her mouth and darted a glance at the bedroom door. After pulling her palm away, she whispered, "Does your dad know?"

Leah should've denied the accusation, but she was too worried that if Rachel had put two and two together, someone else might've done the same. "Yes, but he's the only one who knows. Do you think anyone suspects? Was there talk after I left?"

"Plenty of talk, but most folks figured you'd pulled a typical 'preacher's daughter' and took off to embrace your wild side." She smiled in wonder and took both of Leah's hands. "I can't believe it. You're a mama."

Leah shook her head. This was nothing to celebrate. If the news got out, it could destroy Noah's world. "Rachel, no one can ever know. I put the baby up for adoption without Colt's consent. If he ever found out…"

"He won't find out," Rachel swore. "Not from me."

"You can't tell a soul."

Rachel pretended to zip her lips and lock them tight, but before throwing away the key, she yanked the "zipper" aside and said, "You know I want to see pictures, right? Do you have any?"

Despite the cold rush of anxiety still flooding her veins, Leah's mouth broke into a grin. Noah might not call her Mom, and she couldn't legally take him to the doctor or pick him up from school, but she always kept a digital photo album on hand. In that way, she was a true mother.

"Hand me my iPad," she said, pointing at the desk, "and get comfy, because there's a whole lotta cute in there."

———~~~———

Colt unloaded five bags of Weed & Feed onto the front stoop and turned to survey the patchy, briar-filled land-mine Preacher McMahon called a lawn. You'd think with all those parishioners, someone would cut the old guy's grass once in a while, maybe pull a few weeds and do some aerating. Lucky for Colt, the holy rollers of Sultry County thought breaking a sweat was the eighth deadly sin. It would take at least half a dozen trips to get this overgrown ruin in shape, which gave him an excuse to see more of Leah. Mowing, weeding, raking, reseed-ing—he could easily stretch out this job for weeks.

He glanced toward the backyard, wondering if the shed was locked. Either way, he should probably check in before getting started. A break-in scare wasn't the best way to get on Leah's good side, and he couldn't afford to lose footing with her. He'd made decent head-way last night—not as much as he'd originally hoped, but nothing to sneeze at. He'd kissed her, and more im-portant, she'd kissed him back. Not out of duress, either. If he hadn't cuffed her, she would've run her hands all over him; he could tell by the way she'd moaned into his mouth and massaged his tongue with hers.

He could've gone farther. A few more licks to the sweet patch at the base of her neck, and he would've had that dress shoved around her waist and her panties on the floor. Easy as pie. He still remembered how to drive her crazy. Every sensitive spot, each erotic zone was imprinted on his brain like a roadmap to sex. But not every path would lead to the promised land. He wanted more than one night with Leah; he wanted a lifetime of nights. Tricking her into bed wouldn't get him to his forever goal, so for now, he'd resist making love to her.

Of course, that didn't mean they couldn't fool around in the meantime. Nothing wrong with a few orgasms among friends, right? Before long, he'd get those panties on the floor. He'd dip his fingers inside where she was hot and slick, then close his mouth over her tight, pink nipples and torment her with soft suction and deep strokes until she shattered and cried his name.

God damn. Just thinking about it gave him a stiffie.

Wait. Why was he here?

Oh, yeah. The lawn. He needed inside the shed. He needed inside Leah even more, but first things first. After waiting for the blood to drain from his crotch, he punched the doorbell.

From the other side of the dented aluminum siding, he heard the preacher holler, "Pumpkin! Company!" followed by the soft thump of footsteps on wood planks. When Leah threw open the door, she was in bare feet and a frumpy bridesmaid's dress.

Colt couldn't help chuckling. He pointed to the limp bow hanging from her waist like a piece of overcooked linguini. Whoever the bride was, she sure didn't want any competition. But wasn't that usually the case with women?

Leah's fair cheeks flushed, blue eyes narrowed as she stood straighter in the dress. "What do you want?"

"Well, now, that's not very nice." He nudged the bottom bag with his boot tip. "Especially considering I'm here to help."

She noticed the Weed & Feed and chewed her bottom lip while glancing at the shaggy lawn. "Thanks, but we can handle it."

"Honey, you lie like a Persian rug." He reached out and tugged a lock of her hair. "I bet you'd look real good in tassels, too."

"I mean it," she grumbled, shoving his hand away. "I was going to take care of this myself."

"We're friends now," he reminded her. "And friends don't let friends drink alone or sweat alone."

"I don't drink."

"That's right." He tipped back his Stetson and told her, "Me neither—I quit the firewater a couple of years ago—but I can still make you sweaty. Now get in there and take off that bridesmaid's dress. Put on some shorts and one of those see-through white tank tops you used to wear in high school. Bra optional."

She studied the tips of her ivory toes. "It's not a bridesmaid's dress. I bought it for…" She trailed off and mumbled something he couldn't understand.

"For what?" He couldn't believe she'd actually paid money for the thing. "A costume party?"

Before Leah could answer, the Wicked Bitch of the West brushed past, slinging her quilted handbag over one shoulder. "No, douche nozzle," Rachel snarled. "It's her prom dress. The one she never got to wear, thanks to you." After one last death-glare, she turned to give Leah a kiss on the cheek. "I've got a town council meeting. Gotta block that Home Cheapo from going up."

"Give 'em heck," Leah said.

"I don't give anyone heck, but I'll give 'em hell." As

if to prove her point, Rachel flipped Colt the bird before riding off on her broomstick.

"It's no big deal," Leah said as she watched her friend walk away. "I just wanted to try on my dress one more time before I take it to the Goodwill."

"The Goodwill," Colt repeated. He let out a long, slow breath that left his chest deflated.

Senior prom. Quite possibly the worst night of his life.

He'd done a fairly decent job of blocking it out, but he remembered exactly where he'd spent that evening. In a seven-by-seven juvenile detention cell that reeked of rust, piss, and failure. Leah had dumped his sorry carcass, and he'd turned to his old buddy, Jim Beam, for comfort. But Jim had been a shitty friend with a lot of bad ideas. Go figure. Colt had ended up buck-ass-naked, riding a foam noodle in the mayor's brand new above-ground swimming pool. Instead of bailing out Colt, Granddaddy had let him rot in juvie for a week to teach him a lesson. For all the good it did. That weekend had set the tone for the next ten years.

He filled his lungs with warm Texas air and regarded Leah with fresh eyes, imagining her blond curls lifted in a twist, a light sheen of gloss on her lips, a cluster of roses and silky ribbon secured at her slender wrist. Maybe the dress's droopy bow wasn't so bad after all. He kind of liked the way it accentuated her waist and made him want to rest his palms there. And the color was perfect—a rich, deep indigo that seemed dyed to match her baby blues.

He wanted to say *It's beautiful*, but his voice was too thick with regret and longing to squeeze through his windpipe. In the recesses of his feeble teenage brain, he must've known his relationship with Leah wouldn't last until prom. Because even though he'd asked her to the dance, he'd never bought the tickets or rented a tux. He hadn't allowed himself to imagine what her dress might look like or how it would feel strutting into the school gym with the prettiest girl in Sultry County on his arm. In other words, he'd been a first-rate pansy.

But not anymore.

"Come here."

It wasn't a request, and she must have known, because she took his outstretched hand, gathered her heavy skirts, and padded down the steps onto the front walk. Gripping her fingers, he lifted one arm above her head and twirled her in a slow circle so he could see all of her.

The gown rustled as she moved, reminding him of dried leaves scraping the sidewalk. It was a good sound that evoked images of Southern belles and blushing brides. He took in the graceful curve of Leah's exposed back and wondered if she might've felt chilled on prom night. He pictured himself shrugging out of his tuxedo jacket and draping it over her shoulders. Tiny as she was, it would dwarf her, hanging halfway down her thighs. Kind of like the time she'd worn his football jersey to a pep rally. He'd always loved seeing her in his clothes. He'd enjoyed marking her that way, telling all the other guys who she belonged to. Which reminded him…

"You still got my class ring?"

Reflexively, she touched the hollow at the base of her throat, where his heavy ring used to rest on a silver rope chain. "It's packed up back home."

"I figured you'd pawned it." Colt drew her in for an impromptu dance.

To his surprise, she didn't resist. She rested one hand on his shoulder and placed the other in his leading grip. "Wouldn't have gotten much for it."

"Still, you could've thrown it out." He curled one palm around her waist and stepped close enough to feel the tips of her breasts against his T-shirt. The heavy petticoat beneath her dress pillowed against his thighs. "Or chucked it in the river."

She smiled up at him sweetly, but there was fire in her eyes. "Don't flatter yourself, CJ. It was just as easy to toss it in a box and move on."

That was the second time she'd called him CJ, short for Colton James. He suppressed a grin, but felt it deep in his gut. He was making progress. So to keep it that way, he shut his trap and pulled her body close.

Their feet never left the ground as they swayed to the drone of a distant John Deere, their movements barely discernible on the pavement. This was his favorite kind of dance, nothing more than an excuse for two lovers to hold tight to one another. Still, he wanted more. He wanted to feel Leah rest her head on his chest and mold herself to him. But as it was too soon for that, he took what he could get and enjoyed the warm sun on his shoulders and the scent of strawberry shampoo wafting up from her corn silk hair.

"Hold on," he warned before bending her backward in a dip.

With a throaty laugh, she arched her neck and threw back her blond waves, drawing Colt's eye to a quarter-shaped bruise at the top of her shoulder. He recognized it instantly, and this time, he couldn't hide the smile that pushed up the corners of his mouth.

"Why, Leah McMahon," he said, pulling her upright, "is that a hickey?"

"What?" She followed his gaze and pressed two fingers over the spot. "Of course not. How would I—" Cutting off abruptly, she flushed scarlet as she put the pieces together.

"Mmm-hmm," he said.

She slapped his bicep. "You jerk! You gave me a *hickey*?"

Colt brushed her hair aside to get a better look. He rubbed his index finger over the purple splotch, then shook his head and gave a *tsk-tsk-tsk*. "Back in town a week, and you're already letting strange boys suck on your neck. I hope your daddy doesn't find out."

Her brows lowered as she shoved against his chest, but he gathered her into his arms and took her hand to resume their dance. "Simmer down, honey. It's about time you had some excitement in your life." Bringing his lips to her ear, he murmured, "Want me to give you one on the other side to match?"

"You're like a disease, Colton Bea."

"Can't argue with that," he laughed. "And since there's no cure, you might as well quit squirming and dance with me."

She surrendered, releasing a puff of breath against his throat. One gradual inch at a time, she relaxed into his arms, and within a few minutes, they'd resumed their lazy two-step on the sidewalk.

"See?" he whispered above her head. "Isn't this nice?"

She didn't answer, but the fact that she hadn't already retreated into the house told him she agreed.

Closing his eyes, Colt let the sounds of birdcalls and lawn mowers fade into the background, imagining a slow song booming from the school's gymnasium speakers.

Maybe "It's Your Love," by Tim McGraw and Faith Hill. Nah, not that one. He hated pop-crossover country. Instead, they'd dance to a classic eighties ballad, like "There's No Gettin' Over Me," by Ronnie Milsap. Never mind that the hired deejay wouldn't have it.

As the daydream solidified in his mind, the scents of grass clippings and honeysuckle gave way to rubber basketballs and lemony floor wax, the cement beneath his boots softening into springy bamboo. The gym would be dripping in crepe-paper streamers and balloons, and knowing him, he would've spiked the punch with a ten-ounce bottle of Jack. It would've been *A Night to Remember*, just as the prom committee had promised.

Damn it all. It wasn't fair that they'd missed it. He wanted a do-over—to dance with Leah for hours, then sneak out the back door and park with her on a dark wooded path before taking her home to her daddy. Impossible as it was, he wanted to recapture what they'd lost.

He opened his eyes and pulled back to look at her. "Don't pitch the dress."

"What do you mean?"

"Keep it," he told her, stroking her satiny waist with his thumb.

She searched his face a while before asking, "Why?"

"I don't know." Because he felt cheated, that's why. "Just promise you won't give it away."

She didn't promise him anything, just turned her gaze toward the street to watch the occasional truck roll by. As the seconds passed, he wondered what she was thinking. Did the dress remind her of him? Was that why she was so eager to box it up, like the ring he'd given her all those years ago? Would she tell him there was no going back?

He never got the chance to find out, because as his shitty luck would have it, a set of tires screeched to a halt at the curb, forcing their attention to a mustard-yellow convertible Mustang with the top folded down.

"Hey!" a woman yelled from behind the wheel. "That you, Crazy Colt?"

He released Leah's hand and shielded his eyes to identify the driver and her passengers. Strippers, the whole lot of 'em. He could spot a dancer a mile away. Part of his job as deputy had been periodically inspecting the girls to make sure the right parts were covered, and he'd mixed business with pleasure on more than one occasion. A sick feeling took root in his stomach. This probably wouldn't end well.

"Remember us?" a passenger in the back seat asked with a seductive smile.

"No." Colt darkened his voice, leaving no room for doubt when he added, "Y'all get going."

The woman thrust out a pouty lower lip and said, "I'll bet you remember these, Big Daddy," then hiked up her top to reveal her enormous boobs, nipple rings glinting in the sunlight. Her friends threw back their heads and cackled wildly as the driver peeled out, filling the air with smoke and the stench of burnt rubber.

That sick feeling spread to his chest. What were the odds that he and Leah could pick up where they'd left off?

As it turned out, slim to none.

She gave him a look that would singe the beard off Grizzly Adams, hitched up her dress, and hiked into the house, slamming the door behind her.

Son of a bitch. That had sure gone south in a hurry.

One step forward, two steps back.

# Chapter 7

"IS THAT ALL OF IT?" A MIDDLE-AGED, BEARDED MAN IN stained coveralls used his sneaker to push a box of old clothes toward the wall. According to the oval patch affixed above his chest, his name was George.

"No, there's this too." Leah handed her prom dress over the counter, and George took it without making eye contact. He tossed it into a rolling bin overflowing with outdated sweaters, Sunday dresses, battered leather shoes, and a few graduation gowns.

"Need a receipt for your taxes?" He extended a trembling hand toward a ballpoint pen, revealing dirty fingernails and the inky ghost of a homemade tattoo across his knuckles.

"No." Leah hadn't filed a return since she quit serving frozen custard at the Taste-E-Freeze ten years ago. "But thanks all the same."

George still couldn't meet her gaze when he muttered, "'Kay. Have a good one."

Leah's heart gave a sympathetic squeeze as she watched George turn to sort through a crate of knick-knacks. He was clearly in withdrawal and looked miserable in his own skin. She wanted to tell George she'd pray for him, but decided it would only make him feel worse. Plus, God had stopped hearing her prayers a long time ago. Any intervention by her on George's behalf would probably do more harm than good.

She backed away from the donation counter and threw a final glance at her discarded dress, which had begun to slide from the top of the heap. Her body automatically tensed to catch it before it hit the gritty tile, but then she reminded herself that it didn't belong to her anymore. What did she care if the dress landed on the floor? Goodwill would render it for rags if it didn't sell, and she couldn't imagine who'd buy something so unstylish.

It was time to let go—of prom, of the past, of Colt. Especially Colt. She wouldn't gain anything by fantasizing about what might have been. And Rachel was right. Guys like that never changed. Yesterday's drive-by-skanking proved it.

Through her peripheral vision, she watched the gown drift to the floor as she strode out the front entrance and slipped on her cardigan.

The setting sun sliced through heavy clouds in a flash of orange and pink, just long enough to tease her with its warmth before disappearing again. Leah tugged her sweater lapels closed and knotted the belt at her waist. Fall had made its arrival, every bit as severe as it was abrupt. In less than twenty-four hours, the temperature had fallen from seventy to fifty. It was true what folks said about Texas weather: if you don't like it, stick around for a few minutes and it'll change. She shouldn't complain, though. This beat a Minnesota winter by a country mile.

She started Bruiser and drove to the Sack-n-Pay for a gallon of skim milk and a box of Cheerios, then headed to the drug store to refill Daddy's prescriptions.

"How's your dad?" the pharmacist, Mr. Phelps, asked.

"Fine," she told him. "He's up and around now."

He'd also lost twelve pounds, but she kept that private. She certainly wouldn't want him discussing her weight with the locals. "He starts cardiac rehab next week."

"Sultry Memorial?"

"Mmm-hmm."

"They have a good program there." He scanned two pill bottles and told her, "Eighteen ninety-nine."

"Oh, shoot." That was more than she'd expected. "He still hasn't met his deductible?"

Mr. Phelps squinted at the computer screen. "Not quite."

Leah reached into her purse, but she knew she wouldn't have enough cash to cover the bill. She'd only brought a twenty with her and had spent some of it at the grocery. But oddly, when she opened her wallet, she found nineteen dollars.

That couldn't be right.

She counted it again and got the same result. The cashier at the Sack-n-Pay must've given her too much change. She dug into her pocket for the receipt and solved the mystery. They'd forgotten to charge her for the Cheerios.

After paying for Daddy's medicine, she drove home to refrigerate the milk and grab some cash from the lock box hidden beneath the bed—not the most original hiding place, but anyone desperate enough to rob the town preacher needed the money more than she did. Then she hopped back inside Bruiser, flipped on her headlights, and returned to town.

Money in hand, she pushed open the glass door to the Sack-n-Pay and made her way to the single register that doubled as the customer service station.

Once she'd taken her place in line, she studied the

food inside each customer's cart. You could tell a lot about a person by the groceries they stocked. For example, the elderly lady in front of her was a health nut—all fresh veggies and nothing boxed or frozen. If only Leah could get someone like that to cook for Daddy.

When boredom took over, Leah glanced at the candy bars to her right and the assortment of gums and mints on display to her left.

Oh! Bubblicious still made Carnival Cotton Candy—her favorite flavor! She plucked one from the box and set it on the conveyor belt.

The elderly lady in front of her glanced at the gum and then back to Leah as if to say, *Seriously? Bubblicious? At your age? Don't you know that four out of five dentists recommend Trident?* And she was right. Leah snatched the pack off the belt and replaced it in the carton. The last thing she needed was another cavity, and she shouldn't be making impulse purchases anyway. But as it turned out, the woman grabbed a pack of Carnival Cotton Candy for herself and tossed it next to her collard greens.

Maybe it was for her grandkids. Or not. Either way, Leah couldn't buy a pack now without looking like a copycat, so she folded her arms and pouted inwardly. A few moments later, someone settled behind her and plunked a six-pack on the belt. Leah glanced over her shoulder and locked eyes with the one person she'd hoped to avoid more than Colt.

"Well, slap my grandma!" his voice boomed.

Tommy Robbins—quarterback, homecoming king, and the biggest asswipe in Sultry County, pardon her language.

"Or you could slap someone your own size,"

Leah suggested, and then remembered that Tommy's grandma *was* his size. Even grannies were bigger in Texas.

"Hey there, Tink." Tommy cocked his head and smiled so widely it crinkled the skin around his blood-shot eyes. Not a hint of sarcasm colored his tone when he said, "I heard you were back in town."

"Yeah," she said cautiously. "Just for a few more weeks."

"Well, good to see ya." He removed his Rangers ball cap and ran a hand through his shaggy blond hair before tugging it on again. "You're as pretty as ever."

She waited for the punch line. Tommy never doled out compliments unless there was a zinger attached. He'd tack on the disclaimer, *pretty damn ugly!* or *pretty pathetic!* and then bray like a donkey. But after a long, awkward pause punctuated by the crinkle of paper bags and a series of beeps from the cash register, she had no choice but to offer her tentative thanks.

Instead of razzing her, he hooked a thumb toward the toiletry aisle. "Hold my place in line, will ya? I forgot something."

"Sure," she said, still bracing for the impact that never came.

He held up a finger, promising, "Be right back," then jogged off and disappeared behind a tower of Coca-Cola twelve-packs stacked into a pyramid.

Leah stared after him, wondering why he was being so nice. From the stories Rachel told, he was still mean as a junkyard dog, especially after a few Lone Stars.

Maybe he'd mellowed with age. She shrugged it off and approached the cashier, who'd just sent the previous customer off with a smile and a wave. Once the old woman in front of her left, Leah reached back and retrieved her pack of Bubblicious.

"Before you ring me up," Leah told the girl while fishing the receipt from her purse, "I need to take care of this." She handed over the slip of paper.

"What's wrong?" The girl pursed her frosted-pink lips while studying the receipt.

"You forgot to charge me for a box of Cheerios."

"And…?" the girl said, clearly not understanding the problem with getting something for nothing.

"And I want to pay for it." Leah pointed at the gum. "And this."

An achingly familiar, deep chuckle sounded from nearby. She'd know that laugh anywhere. It had the unholy power to make all her naughty places go tingly.

"Only you," Colt muttered, setting his shopping basket on the conveyor belt without bothering to unload it. A peek inside revealed a rib-eye steak, a bundle of asparagus, two baking potatoes, a carton of coffee creamer, and a Gillette refill cartridge. Surprisingly tame contents, considering its owner.

Leah refused to engage him. "It was a big box," she told the checkout girl. "The biggest on the shelf."

"It's okay if you just wanna keep—"

"I need to pay for it," Leah insisted. "Or it's the same as stealing." She shouldn't have to explain things like this to people.

The girl sighed. "That's probably the eighteen-ouncer. I'll have to go grab one." She lingered as if giving Leah one last chance to change her mind.

"Want me to do it?" Leah asked.

"No, I got it." With an eye roll, she turned and trudged toward the breakfast cereals, two aisles over.

From the corner of Leah's eye, she saw Colt shake his head. He leaned one hip against the counter. "You really are an angel, aren't you?"

Not at all. If he only knew the things she'd done.

"You gonna keep givin' me the silent treatment?" he asked.

She stared straight ahead.

"'Cause I haven't seen those girls in years." He propped one elbow on the side of his shopping basket. "You can't hold things like that against me. You know I've got a past, and it's gonna pop up now and then. I told you I'm not proud of—"

"I don't care," she said. "And I told *you*, I'm no angel."

"Who else would go through all this trouble over a box of cornflakes?"

"Cheerios."

"Same difference." He crossed one boot over the other and drawled, "Face it, honey, you make the rest of us look bad."

"Stop saying stuff like that." She had no place atop the pedestal he'd built for her. "You don't know me."

"If you say so, hon." He grabbed a pack of watermelon Bubble Yum from the display and dropped it beside his coffee creamer. "But it's kinda hard to ignore your actions when they speak so loud."

Tommy and the checkout girl returned at the same time, one with a bright-yellow box of cereal in hand, the other using his T-shirt like a kangaroo pouch, revealing a slightly hairy beer gut as he hauled his items to the lane. Tommy turned sideways and sucked in his belly, slipping past Colt to resume his place in line.

"She'll take these too," Tommy said with a wide grin and dumped his haul beside her pack of gum.

Dozens of condom boxes spilled across the conveyor belt—Trojans, LifeStyles, Crowns, Kimonos, Naturalambs, Bravos, even Magnums. A box of Durex Her Sensation, "ribbed and studded for her pleasure," tumbled onto the glass laser-panel and automatically scanned with a *beep!*

It took a few heartbeats for Leah to absorb what had just happened, but once the humiliation set in, her face grew hot and her head started to buzz.

Then she wasn't at the Sack-n-Pay grocery anymore. She was in the senior hallway at Sultry High School, staring blankly at her locker, which had been "decorated" with a hundred multicolored condom wrappers. Laughter and hushed voices filled the air. Broken whispers of *I heard* and *she did it* and *Tommy said* and *with that new kid, Colt*. It was then that she'd learned Colt had used her. That their lovemaking hadn't meant anything to him beyond bolstering his reputation as the county stud.

More than embarrassment, she'd felt shame. She'd broken her purity vow—tossed away all those promises to God and herself, for Colt—and he'd made a joke of it. She'd tried so hard not to cry that morning, but the condoms had blurred into a rainbow as hot tears burned behind her lids.

"Miss?" the cashier asked, bringing Leah back to the present. "You really want all this?"

Leah shook her head and used a sweater sleeve to blot the moisture welling in her eyes. She turned to Colt, but he wasn't looking at her. He was glaring at Tommy with a fury that tightened Leah's stomach.

Colt's nostrils flared. He pointed to the condoms and told the cashier, "Darlin', get rid of that, will you?" Despite the cordial words, his voice was low and terrifying, like a distant rumble of thunder.

The girl didn't hesitate to grab a plastic grocery bag and scoop the boxes inside. Within seconds, they'd vanished from sight.

Tommy's smile fell as he rubbed the back of his neck. Judging by the way his shoulders crept toward his ears, he knew he'd made a huge mistake.

"Apologize," Colt told him.

Tommy nodded enthusiastically, eager to comply. "Sorry, Tink. I thought it'd be funny, that's all. But it probably wasn't funny for you."

"Not good enough." Colt rested a hand on the butt of his pistol in what Leah hoped was an empty threat. "I'm gonna give you one more chance."

Leah didn't like this. Confrontation made her uneasy, and she didn't want anyone to get hurt. "It's okay, really."

"No, it's not," Colt said to Tommy. "Dig deep, asshole."

"I'm sorry." Beads of sweat had broken out on Tommy's upper lip. "Real sorry. I shouldn't have done that. It was stupid. You know me—I'll do anything for a laugh."

"Okay," Leah said, trying to catch Colt's gaze, which lingered like grease fire on the back of Tommy's head. "I forgive you. Let's forget it ever happened, all right?" She needed Colt to back off. The air was so thick with tension, she could've packed it between her palms like a snowball.

Colt glanced at the cashier. "Close your eyes. You don't need to see this."

Instantly, the girl clenched her lids shut and rested her balled fists on the counter.

"See what?" Tommy asked in a shaky voice.

Colt warned, "I'm gonna hit you."

And he did, with a powerful right hook to the kidney that knocked Tommy forward and tore a sharp cry from his lips. Then Colt grabbed the counter for leverage, drew back, and pummeled him again in the exact same spot.

"Do we have an understanding?" Colt asked, panting with rage. He flexed his fingers, resisting the obvious urge to keep going.

Agony distorted Tommy's features while he gripped the ledge and gasped for air. He wiped a trail of spittle from his chin and whispered, "Please, Leah. I'm sorry."

The suffering in his voice ripped through her in a stab of sympathy pain that reached all the way to her toes. With shaky fingers, she found her wallet and pulled out a five-dollar bill. She slapped it on the belt and ran out the front door.

She kept running until she reached the far end of the dark parking lot, then turned in a clumsy circle to look for her car. With only a handful of vehicles on the lot, you'd think she could identify the one that belonged to her, but she couldn't. She felt disoriented, like she'd just woken from a dream and wasn't sure if her surroundings were real. She pressed both palms over her eyes and took a deep breath to calm down.

*Bruiser*, she said to herself. Her car had earned that nickname because it was ugly and purple. All she had to do was find the only purple hatchback on the lot. She could do that.

"You okay?"

She gasped at the sound of Colt's voice. "No, I'm not okay!"

From two parking spaces away, he held up both hands to placate her. "He's not gonna mess with you again."

"Is that what you think?" she demanded, her pitch rising on the last note. "That I'm upset because of Tommy's idiot prank?"

Colt didn't answer, but his expression said exactly that.

"It's you!"

"Me?" he asked in disbelief, touching his own chest. "What'd I do?"

"Wha—" she began and cut off. Did he *really* not understand what he'd done wrong? That beating people was an unacceptable way of dealing with life's problems? She'd always hated violence, and he knew that! "You just kicked the shit out of someone!" Quietly, she added, "Pardon my language."

Colt shrugged. "He had it comin'. Maybe if I'd done that ten years ago, he wouldn't—"

"No." Leah marched toward her car. "That's not how I live, Colt. That's not how civilized people deal with conflict."

In a few long strides, he met her at the driver's side door. "You don't get it. Guys like Tommy don't respond to that *turn the other cheek* bullshit. They've gotta be taught the old-fashioned way. The foot-up-the-ass way."

She glared right into his aquamarine eyes. "That *bullshit* is the basis for everything I believe. So ex-*cuse* me for holding myself to a higher standard."

His gaze iced over, jaw clenching as he backed up a pace and snapped, "My apologies. We can't all be saints like you." Then he turned and stalked back into the Sack-n-Pay without another glance in her direction.

Leah stood there, keys in hand, lips parted in disbelief. How dare he turn this around and make her the villain? She was no saint, and she kept telling him so. Besides, it didn't take a martyr to realize that pounding on people was wrong. Colt was wrong. End of story.

But as she climbed inside Bruiser and fastened her seatbelt, she couldn't deny the heavy ache that radiated along her breastbone. Darn if it didn't feel a lot like guilt. Leave it to Colt to break all the rules and somehow foist the emotional fallout on her.

―――

"Is your daddy's heart still broken?"

Leah smiled at the empathy written all over Noah's face. *This* was her son, not the cranky prima donna who'd hung up on her the last time they'd chatted. If anything could improve a lousy day, it was her sweet boy. She brought the iPad to the sofa, where Daddy sat working on Sunday's sermon—his first since the surgery.

"No," she said. "The doctors fixed it. He's right here. Say 'hey.'" She turned the screen toward Daddy and heard Noah chirp, "Hey, Mr. McMahon."

Daddy waved. "Nice to meet you, Noah. You can call me Grandpop, if you want."

There was a pause on Noah's end. Leah checked to make sure the connection hadn't frozen, and found Noah's black brows knitted together. "I already got a Grandpop. He's my mama's daddy. He lives in Duh-looth."

"Duluth?"

"Yeah."

"It's all right, Bud." Leah stuffed down the all-too-familiar surge of envy she'd never managed to tame over the years. She knew Diane was her son's mother, but the reminders stung. Maybe it was time to accept that they always would. "You can call him Pastor Mac, just like everyone here does."

"Pastor Mac," Noah said, trying it on. He flashed that adorable gap-toothed grin and declared, "It sounds cool, like mac-n-cheese."

"Then it's settled," Leah said. "Now tell me what's new since the last time we talked."

His eyes brightened, lifting the corners of his mouth and warming the deepest recesses of Leah's soul. Nothing compared to the joy of seeing him happy. If scientists could trap that feeling in a pill, they'd rule the world.

"Can you keep a secret?" he asked.

"You bet I can." She extended her little finger. "Pinky swear."

He hooked his pinky toward hers and gave a solemn nod. "Me and Daddy are givin' Mama an extra-special surprise for Christmas."

"Ooooh," Leah crooned. "I love surprises. Is it homemade?"

He shook his head. "Even better!"

"Better than a homemade present? That's every mama's favorite kind."

"She's gonna love it. Daddy promised."

"Well, don't keep me in suspense. Tell me what it is."

"Okay." He leaned closer, practically vibrating with anticipation. "We're takin' her to Paris for Christmas!"

"Paris?" Leah asked.

"Yep. That's in France. And we're stayin' for two whole weeks!"

Leah's heart dropped into her lap. She couldn't quite manage to catch her breath. The whole family would be gone for the holidays, which meant she'd miss her cherished Christmas Eve visit with Noah. She looked forward to that outing all year—it was their only tradition, just the two of them. They'd spend the morning ice skating, then sip hot chocolate aboard a real train modeled after the Polar Express. That day was a gift, and now it'd been snatched away.

"That's great," she lied, fighting to keep the sadness from showing on her face. "I'll miss you, but I hope you have fun."

"Yeah," was all he said before Diane called him away for dinner. He offered a hasty good-bye and disconnected. Then he was gone, just like that.

Leah stared at her iPad screen, seeing nothing.

She had no recourse. The adoption, while considered open, didn't specify any visitation rights. Legally speaking, Jim and Diane didn't have to let her see Noah at all. They could cut her off whenever they wanted, without so much as a photograph or a letter to document his growth. She'd carried and delivered Noah, loved him like no one else, but her time spent with him hinged on the whims of others.

It wasn't fair.

She swallowed hard and tried not to cry. From beside her on the sofa, Daddy set his Bible and notepad aside and wrapped an arm around her shoulders, pulling her in for a hug. There was extra love in his embrace, a tight squeeze he reserved for her darkest moments. He probably knew how she felt. She'd called him every Christmas Eve to relay the details of her "date" with Noah. Sometimes she'd sent pictures too. She rested her cheek against him, taking comfort in his warmth and the familiar scents of spearmint mingled with Aqua Velva.

She expected Daddy to offer some uplifting words of encouragement, to remark that this wasn't the end of the world or remind her there'd be a dozen more holidays to celebrate with Noah. Instead, he told her, "There's an old saying that a man becomes a father when he meets his baby for the first time, but a woman becomes a mother when she finds out she's pregnant."

Leah nodded against his shoulder. She'd heard that one.

"But that wasn't true for me," he continued. "I loved you from the instant your mama told me we were expecting."

She wasn't sure where he was going with this, but she said, "Thanks, Daddy. Love you too."

He kissed the top of her head. "You did a brave thing, giving Noah to the Ackermans—the most loving, self-less thing a person can do. I don't think I could've done the same. I'm not strong enough. But, Pumpkin, part of giving up is letting go."

She sat upright and turned on the sofa to face him. "Let go? He's my son."

Daddy took her hand and gave it a gentle pat, the way people did when trying to soften bad news. "But, he's not, hon. And..." *He never will be*. She knew how that sentence ended. Daddy didn't have to say it aloud.

"He's part of me. No piece of paper can change that."

"I know." His eyes found Mama's portrait, and Leah couldn't help thinking his advice was a little hypocritical. He'd never let go of Mama, and she'd been gone for ages. "You gave Noah a great life," he said. "Maybe it's time to make one for yourself." He released her hand, but held her gaze. "Here, at home, with the people who love you."

The word *What?* formed on her lips, but never materialized. Was he actually suggesting she move to Texas and leave Noah behind? He couldn't really think she'd do that.

Daddy seemed to read her thoughts. "Nearest airport's only an hour away. You could still keep your visits with Noah. Only difference is you'd be here in the meantime, not there, waiting on the sidelines and wishing your life away."

The only argument she could think of was, "All those plane tickets would add up."

"Then I'll help."

The idea of leaving Minnesota chilled her to the core. She'd moved there at seventeen—it was nearly all she knew. And even though she couldn't see Noah more than once a month, she liked being near him.

"Sultry Memorial's always looking for nurses," Daddy went on. "Wouldn't take long to get your license current." When she didn't answer, he said, "Just promise you'll think about it."

She nodded. "I promise." But she wouldn't have to think very long.

"I just wanna see you happy, Pumpkin," Daddy said. "It's all any parent wants."

She knew that. And how. Only moments ago, Noah's

happiness had filled and defined her. Her little boy was safe, content, and loved, which was all a mother could want for her child.

So why did she feel empty?

# Chapter 8

LEAH PROPPED A HIP AGAINST THE BACK OF A WOODEN pew and admired the grouping of vibrant orange potted mums decorating the podium. No silk flowers today. The hospitality committee had upgraded to the real thing in honor of Daddy's return to the pulpit. More than that, a certain enthusiasm charged the air; she could hear it in the exuberant chatter of voices and the eager bounce of dress shoes. It made Leah smile. Daddy's flock had missed him—he was well-loved here. In fact, half the congregation still refused to meet her gaze as punishment for all the "suffering" she'd caused him.

The organist played "Praise Him, O Praise Him" in quarter-time while suited gentlemen escorted their ladies into the sanctuary, some of them towing little girls in Mary Janes. A young boy dragged his loafered-feet down the aisle, tugging at his shirt collar. Leah couldn't help but laugh under her breath. He reminded her of Noah, and as she often did, she wondered what he might be doing right now.

He wasn't in church—she knew that much. Longtime agnostics, the Ackermans had decided to raise Noah without the influence of religion. It was their right, but she wished they'd at least take him to services on Christmas and Easter. Just the bare minimum, so he'd know the difference between Madonna, the blessed virgin, and Madonna, the *like* a virgin. Of course, that

SURRENDER TO SULTRY 119

wasn't her decision to make, so she shouldn't judge. Remembering Daddy's advice on letting go, she tucked Noah's image to the back of her mind and tried to live in the moment.

She turned and spotted poor, puffy June filing inside ahead of Luke and Bobbi. Trey loped in a second later with a Latino teen in khakis and a white button-down polo. The boy wore his long, black hair in a low pony-tail, reminding her of a young Colton. But she didn't want to think about *him*. Four days had passed since the Sack-n-Pay incident, and she hadn't caught a single glimpse of his russet face. It seemed he'd finally decided to leave her be, something that made her feel unexpect-edly irritated, though she refused to ask herself why. Instead, she met June at the last row, closest to the rear entrance, where her group had begun to settle.

Leah waved at Bobbi, but kept her distance. She didn't like the way Bobbi studied her in that critical, journalistic way. The woman smelled a story; Leah could tell.

Trey took a seat beside his wife and flashed a sunny, dimpled grin. He gestured to the teen at his side. "This is Carlo, my apprentice."

"Oh, cool," Leah said, leaning over to shake the boy's hand. "What trade?"

"Building and repair," came the reply. He didn't elaborate, but he offered a smile every bit as infectious as his mentor's.

Luke clapped the boy's shoulder. "Best guy on our crew."

Carlo shrugged away the compliment, his face beam-ing. "I'm glad your dad's better," he told her.

"Yeah," Trey added, "we're not usually church-going

folk, but we wanted to be here for Pastor Mac's big comeback."

"I'm glad you came out." Leah turned her attention to June. "Especially you. I'll bet you'd rather be on the couch with your feet up."

She'd just bent to give June a hug when she noticed someone new step through the double doors—a tall, broad-chested man with raven hair brushing his shoulders. It took a few moments for her to recognize him as Colt, and even then, she didn't believe her eyes. In his black suit, starched white shirt, tie, and sunglasses, he looked like one of the Blues Brothers, minus the fedora hat. She'd never seen him so dressed up before. Or inside a house of worship. What the apple fudge was he doing here?

He slipped off his shades, dropped them inside his breast pocket, and fastened that jade-blue gaze on her. Her tummy did two double flips. Lord help her—she was toast.

While she stood frozen in place, he strode over and placed an innocent kiss at her jaw, then pressed something into her palm. She glanced down to find an opened pack of Carnival Cotton Candy Bubblicious and twenty-six cents.

"You left this behind," he said in a smooth, deep voice that washed over her and settled low in her abdomen. "And you forgot your change."

She pocketed the coins and held up her gum. "There's a piece missing."

He shook his head and told her, "Two," before chewing a few times and blowing a wide, pink bubble.

"Colt!" she chided, popping it with her index finger. "We're in church."

"I know, Angel." With a wicked grin, he sucked the deflated bubble into his mouth and asked, "Want me to testify?"

"This isn't funny—"

Bobbi interrupted, "Is that Crazy Colt?"

Leah gritted her teeth. She was getting really tired of hearing that nickname.

"Well, lookie here," Colt said, turning toward Bobbi, who stood and inched her way along the pew to give him a hug. "It's the Bodacious Gallagher."

"It's the Bodacious *Lewis* now," Trey corrected from his seat.

Colt and Bobbi embraced, holding on a bit too long for Leah's comfort. From the look of Trey's creased forehead, he wasn't pleased either. When they parted, Bobbi took Colt's face in her hands and said, "You look great. How're you feeling?"

"Fine," he replied, but Leah knew better. She'd noticed his careful footsteps and the way he sometimes kneaded his lower back with the heel of his hand.

Bobbi sat back down, and Colt nodded at Carlo, extending one fist for a bump. "Little Hammer," he said, snickering in what was clearly an inside joke. Then Colt noticed June for the first time, and his eyes went wide. "Whoa," he said, pointing at her mammoth belly. "Any day now, huh?"

June's narrowed gaze said she wasn't amused. "I'm not due till the end of January."

"*What?*" Colt leaned to the side to study her more closely. "Is it twins?"

You could cut a tomato on the sharp edge of June's voice. "No."

"You sure?" Colt asked. "'Cause those ultrasounds don't catch everything. I've heard one baby can hide behind the other."

Luke swept a protective hand over his wife's tummy. "It's not twins, dickhead."

"Language!" June hissed with an elbow to Luke's ribs.

Luke rolled his eyes and crossed himself, never mind that none of them were Catholic, and Leah decided to break up the mini-reunion before anyone came to blows. She waved good-bye and threaded one arm through Colt's, tugging him away from the group.

"Okay," she whispered, "you should go before the—"

Without letting her finish, he interlaced their fingers and led her down the aisle to a middle row with two vacant seats on the inside. He half-ushered, half-shoved her in, then followed and sat down, trapping her between his massive body and that of his step-grandma, Prudence Foster-Bea, whose knees touched the pew in front of her. If Leah wanted out, she'd have to climb over Colt's lap, and the smug, smiling jerk knew it.

Colt patted the oak beside him. "Looks like the service is gonna start soon. You'd better settle in."

"You're really staying?" she asked.

"I didn't get all spiffed up just to bring you a pack of gum, honey." He rested his ankle on the opposite knee and stretched an arm along the back of the pew, making himself right at home. And leaving very little space for her. But if Colt thought he'd manipulate her into an impromptu cuddle fest, he had another thing coming. She lowered to the pew's edge and sat straighter than a schoolmarm, managing not to make contact with anyone.

That's how she sang the opening hymn, and afterward, bowed her head for the invocation. It's how she made her offering when the collection plate came around, and clapped her hands to congratulate the new baptisms. It's how she listened as Daddy thanked the fellowship for their prayers during his recovery, and detailed the upcoming Bible Study social. But by the time Daddy began relaying the story of the Prodigal Son, Leah's unnaturally stiff posture had given her a backache. Her muscles trembled, her thighs burned, and she was forced to admit that she couldn't keep this up much longer.

Faking a yawn and a stretch, she snuck a glance at Colt, who never took his eyes off the pulpit. If she didn't know better, she'd think he was actually paying attention. As slowly as she could stand, Leah slid her tushie to the rear of the bench and rested against the seatback, silently groaning with relief. She relaxed against Colton one muscle group at a time—first her shoulder against his chest, then her leg pressed to his thigh, and finally her neck molding to the strong arm wrapped around her from behind.

Just as she'd feared, Colt was warm and solid and smelled of bold aftershave. He seemed to relax into her, too, tipping his head a little nearer and stroking her hair with his fingertips. Mercy, he felt so good. Even the brush of his trousers against her bare calf made her all twitterpated.

She had to get it together if she stood any chance against Colt's wiles. Leaning forward a moment, she gathered her hair to one side so he couldn't play with it. Not much, but at least it was a start.

"…my own sweet Leah…"

She flinched at the echo of her name though the speaker system.

"…who returned to me a couple of weeks ago," Daddy said. "And like the man in the parable, I welcomed her home with wide-open arms and a joyful heart—because a father's love is eternal. I know that my Father will receive me into the Kingdom of Heaven with that same spirit of forgiveness, because His love is eternal too."

Leah stared at her folded hands, feeling the weight of a hundred gazes on her shoulders.

"But the elder son didn't share his father's enthusiasm," Daddy went on. "He resented his brother for leaving, and refused to pardon his sins. He let moral superiority keep him from true happiness, and that's a sin in its own right." Daddy gripped the lectern and fell silent for a few seconds. "Brothers and sisters, aren't you glad the Lord doesn't hold grudges like that?"

Leah understood what her father was doing—sending a clear message for his sheep to play nice and accept her back into the fold. She wondered if his desire to keep her in town had something to do with this, but she quickly criticized herself. Daddy loved her and wanted her to be happy. He didn't have an ulterior motive.

"Whose actions will you emulate?" Daddy asked the congregation. "The older son, hardened by bitterness and anger, or our Father, who's willing to wipe the slate clean for all of us?"

At those words, Pru reached over and gave Leah's hand a hearty pat, a message of acceptance that was likely the first of many to come. She expected Colt to do the same—to use any excuse to touch her—but he pulled his arm free and leaned forward, resting both elbows on his knees. His withdrawal left more than just the back of her neck cold.

He pulled a donation envelope and mini-pencil from the rack in front of him and sat back to scrawl a message, keeping it covered so she couldn't see. When he'd finished, he tossed the envelope into her lap.

*The preacher got me all inspired. Guess I'll forgive you for the other night.*

What? He'd forgive *her*? What an arrogant jackass! She snatched a pencil of her own and replied, *I don't think so!!! I'll forgive YOU for the other night!* She passed it back.

A moment later, he wrote, *Awesome. Now that we're all made up, let's have dinner.* When she stared at the paper without responding, he yanked it back and added, *Friends have dinner all the time. It's no biggie.*

She knew better. Dinner with Colt would send the wrong message, so she told him, *That's a bad idea.*

*No, it's not,* he argued. *Drunk, naked cow-tipping is a bad idea, especially when there's a bull in the field. (Not that I'd know, or anything.)*

Her mouth twitched in a smile. *No.*

Colt shrugged and folded his arms, then focused on the sermon. Or pretended to.

After the benediction, Daddy made his way down to greet them. He extended a hand to Colt, who gave it a firm shake.

"Nice to see you here, Sheriff," Daddy said. "I don't think you've made it to one of our services before."

"No, sir," Colt answered. "But I reckon I'll come around next week too."

Daddy rocked back on his heels, pleased at the prospect of a new convert. "How'd you like to join us for supper?"

Leah's brows shot up her forehead. "I'm sure Colton has plans." She locked eyes with him. "Isn't that right?"

"Not at all." A shit-eating grin curved Colt's mouth, pardon her language. "I'd love to come over, especially if Leah's cooking."

"She sure is," Daddy told him. "Chicken and dumplings, with angel food cake for dessert."

"Angel food?" Colt's grin grew impossibly wider. "That's my favorite kind."

She had a feeling he was referring to more than cake.

"Great," Daddy said, patting Colt's arm. "See you at six."

———※———

Colt could get used to this.

He finished his second bowlful of chicken and pastry, then pushed back from the table to help Leah clear the dishes. She'd changed from her Sunday skirt and blouse into a pair of loose cotton pants and the same oversized Vikings sweatshirt she'd worn to the station last week. She looked so dag-blasted cute in her little socked feet and her hair up in a ponytail. It made him want to snuggle with her on the sofa to watch football. Or better yet, peel off her clothes and make love on the sofa with the game playing in the background. Oh, yeah. That was perfection, right there.

In that moment, he glimpsed a snippet of their future together—a thousand lazy Sundays just like this—and he liked what he saw. If he could only get her to share that vision…

Leah pulled a couple of tubs from the refrigerator and asked him, "You want strawberries and whipped cream on your cake?"

He wanted whipped cream on the nipples hidden beneath her sweatshirt, but he wasn't stupid enough to say so. "Yes, ma'am."

"Me too, Pumpkin," the preacher said from his spot at the table.

Colt pulled three dessert plates from the cabinet while Leah sliced the angel food cake. She kept sneaking sideways glances at him while she ladled diced berries and Cool Whip onto each serving. Her gaze wasn't spiteful, but it wasn't too kind, either. More like curious. He wished he knew what was going on inside that pretty blond head.

She slid her daddy's plate across the tabletop and sat down to eat. Colt joined her and dug right in. His first bite didn't disappoint. Between the cake, berries, and cream, it was the perfect mingling of tangy and sweet, much like Leah herself.

He toasted her with his iced tea. "I forgot what a good cook you are."

She lit up at that, though she tried to hide it. "Did I ever cook for you before?"

"Sure." He slipped off his suit jacket, then loosened his tie and unbuttoned his shirt collar. When Leah's eyes found the patch of skin at the base of his throat, he undid a couple more buttons and watched her cheeks flush. He'd bet his bottom dollar she remembered every morsel she'd ever fed him. He decided to test his theory. "You made cranberry-almond cookies for me when I moved to town. And when I got mono, you brought me chicken noodle soup."

"Turkey and wild rice," she corrected, proving him right.

Colt bit back a smile. "No, I'm pretty sure it was chicken noodle."

"You're wrong."

"Sure about that?"

"Of course. I don't make chicken noodle. It's too pedestrian." To clinch it, she added, "And it wasn't mono. You had strep."

"That's right." He lightly slapped the tabletop. "I remember now. My throat was on fire, and that soup felt real good going down."

She gave a satisfied nod and licked a smudge of whipped cream off her top lip.

"Well, Angel, you put half the cooks in the county to shame."

"Amen to that," her daddy said. "If I had my way, we'd do this every Sunday."

Colt shot the preacher a questioning look.

"I'm trying to convince Leah to stay on," the old guy explained, "instead of going back to Minnesota at the end of the month."

Colt practically gave himself whiplash turning to face her. "That's a great idea. The hospital's understaffed. They're always looking for good nurses."

Her daddy pointed at him. "That's exactly what I told her!"

Leah tried shutting them down with a flash of her palm. "I said I'd think about it, nothing more."

"C'mon, hon. Anyone can see your daddy needs you," Colt said. "Plus, it's a darn shame to leave so soon after *the Lord* called you home." He couldn't keep the sarcasm out of his voice. Part of him wanted Leah to know he didn't buy into her bullshit. The other part had stopped caring why she came back to town, so long as she stayed here.

She dipped her spoon into a pile of Cool Whip and then sucked it clean. "I have a life in Minnesota."

"Nothin' you can't rebuild here," the preacher said. "Unless you plan on getting back together with Ari."

*Ari?* Colt's fist tightened around his glass of iced tea. Who the hell was that?

"My ex-fiancé," Leah explained with a dismissive wave. "And no, I'm not."

"You were engaged?" Colt felt the blood in his face drain into his suddenly throbbing heart. He didn't want to believe Leah had loved another man enough to say *yes* to spending a lifetime with him. Colt had messed around with a lot of women over the years, but he'd never cared for any of them. He'd never wanted to put a gold band on anyone's finger. He glanced at Leah's hand, sick at the thought of her wearing some other guy's ring.

"Yep," her daddy said. "To a doctor."

Holy flaming sack of shit. A doctor? Like he could compete with that. The ring was probably freakin' enormous—a real sparkler. The kind he couldn't afford. Colt didn't want to know any more, but he couldn't stop torturing himself. "Why'd you break it off?"

"I didn't," she said.

The doctor had dumped *her*? Did that mean she still loved him? And why on earth would anyone let Leah go? She was damn near perfect. "What happened?"

She got quiet and darted a glance at her daddy. Then she scooped a big spoonful of strawberries and ate them real slow. When she'd finished chewing, she swallowed, cleared her throat, and announced, "I can't have children."

Colt wasn't sure what to say to that. *Sorry* seemed to fit, but he'd grown tired of hearing that word after his accident. Nobody liked being on the receiving end of pity.

"I had some health problems when I was younger," she went on, "and I needed a hysterectomy." She shrugged one shoulder and jabbed a chunk of cake with her spoon. "At first, Ari was okay with it, but then he decided he wanted kids."

Colt wished he could punch the good doctor in the nuts. "There's more than one way to start a family." Leah would make a great mother. A blind man could see it. At any given moment, there were a dozen children in Sultry County that needed fostering. The same was true in Minnesota.

"He's entitled to have biological kids if that's what he wants." She set down her spoon and pushed her plate aside. "Nothing wrong with that."

"Yeah, there is—when his DNA's more important to him than his wife." Colt snorted in disdain. "Good riddance. He probably would've made a crap husband... beggin' your pardon, Pastor Mac."

"It's all right, son," the preacher said. "I'm inclined to agree." He looked at his daughter. "I didn't know the whole story till now."

"I'm allowed to keep some things private," Leah told him. "Besides, I've only been home a couple of weeks. I haven't had time to catch you up on everything."

"Well, this is one more reason for you to stay," her father said. "What's there to go back to?"

"My life, that's what," she gritted out.

Leah clenched her jaw and stared down her daddy. The old guy did the same, and the two of them had words without saying a thing. Clearly, they'd had this argument before. Colt didn't understand what was so great about Minnesota or why Leah would want to return. Knowing her, she was just being stubborn. The worst thing he could do was push—then she'd really dig in her heels.

"It's all right," Colt told her. "It's a big decision. Sleep on it a while."

And while she was sleeping, he'd double his efforts to keep her in Sultry Springs. If there was any chance they could have a life together, he'd grab the opportunity with both hands and go down fighting to keep it. Anything it took—the end would justify the means. Maybe it was time to get sneaky again. Lucky for Colt, that came easier than breathing.

# Chapter 9

Leah had barely stepped inside from dropping off Daddy at cardiac rehab when a familiar rumble sounded from the driveway and rattled the windowpane. She pushed aside the living room curtain and squinted against the morning sun at Colt, who'd just kicked his Harley to standing. Leah was impressed. He'd promised to roll in bright and early to help work on the lawn, but she hadn't expected him to arrive before the paper. When he tugged off his helmet, his turquoise eyes found her at once. He nodded hello, and as it always did, her tummy greeted him with a wild flutter.

God bless, it was getting worse—her body and mind were officially at war. With each passing day, she felt her resolve slipping, and if she wasn't careful, her body would win the final battle in a brazen victory. In retrospect, it probably wasn't a good idea to have him over with Daddy gone.

Despite her worries, she couldn't help snickering at the way Colt's fingertips tenderly brushed the Harley's seat as he walked away, like a lover who couldn't bear to part from his better half. No mistress could compete with that hog. How many women had it outlasted? Leah didn't even want to know.

She slipped on her sneakers and met him on the front stoop. While she pulled her hair into a ponytail, Colt moseyed up, hands wedged in his back pockets, looking finer than any man had a right to be.

His gaze traveled the length of her body for a few static beats, and after he'd had his fill, he said, "Honey, I could sop you up with a biscuit."

Leah waved him off. He'd said the same thing after church yesterday when she'd changed into sweats, and she didn't look any better today in yoga pants and a long-sleeved T-shirt.

"I'm serious," he insisted, leaning to the side to admire her butt, then shaking his head in appreciation. "Whoever invented those stretchy pants deserves free beer for life. They cling to all the right places."

Leah hid a smile and skipped down the front steps. "We'd better get started." She didn't want to encourage him. Besides, she'd never been able to take a compliment. "I've gotta pick up Daddy in a couple of hours."

"I see you're still a slave driver," he complained. "I'll never forget all the chemistry facts you made me memorize in my granddaddy's shed."

"Oh, yeah?" She doubted it. They'd pulled a couple all-nighters in that shed, but they hadn't done a lick of schoolwork. Just a lot of licking. "What's absolute zero?"

"Zero Kelvin," he replied without a moment's hesitation. "The coldest it gets." With a wink, he added, "Basically, the opposite of you in those ass-huggin' drawers."

She paused on the front walk, feeling her eyes widen. "Wow. I'm impressed."

"Don't be." He nudged her with his elbow. "That was an easy one. The answer's right in the question."

"Okay, what does TNT stand for?"

"Trinitrotoluene, but that doesn't count either," he said, heading toward the backyard shed. "I have to know that stuff for work."

"Well then, what's the definition of a solid?"

"Something with definite volume and shape." A grin split his face. "Again, like you in those britches."

She shoved his shoulder playfully, but it didn't budge him. "Time to admit you're smarter than you think."

"Didn't I say you were a good tutor?"

She sniffed a laugh. "You must've absorbed it through osmosis, because we didn't do a lot of talking."

He went quiet for a few strides, letting the crunch of half-dead grass beneath his boots replace their conversation. Finally, he said, "I wish we had."

"Had what?" she asked.

"Done more talking." They reached the old metal shed, and Colt unlatched the door. "Maybe if I hadn't rushed things, you wouldn't have gotten in trouble and run off like you did."

Leah's heart jumped. *In trouble* could mean a lot of things. Her first thought was that he'd found out about the pregnancy, and she couldn't hide the fear in her voice. "What do you mean, gotten in trouble?"

He froze, one hand curled around the aluminum door, then studied her for a long moment. The sheriff in him had clearly noted the change in her inflection, and Leah cursed herself for panicking.

"Your daddy found out we slept together, and you two had a fight." His voice was slow and careful, thick with new doubt. "Or at least that's what you've been telling people. Is there more to the story?"

She swallowed hard and shook her head.

"One of these days, you're gonna have to quit lying to me, Angel." An emotion flashed in his eyes, something that looked a lot like hurt. "I'm on your team."

Leah felt heavy inside. She half expected to sink a few inches into the grass.

"Was it me?" Colt asked, staring into the darkness of the shed. "I always figured there was something else going on, but maybe it was me all along."

"No." She couldn't let him think that. It wasn't fair to him—none of this was fair to him. She rested one hand lightly on his back. "It was more complicated than that. I just don't like talking about it."

He glanced at her. "Promise?"

"Pinky swear." She extended her little finger.

The ghost of a grin tipped his mouth as he regarded her pinky. He hooked his finger around hers and gave a shake, then led the way inside the shed.

He didn't bring up the subject again, but she could tell he wanted to. They busied themselves in an effort to diffuse the uneasy silence—Colt stacking bags of Weed & Feed inside the seed spreader while she gathered trowels and rakes. It stayed that way for the next several minutes, until they'd hauled the supplies to the front yard.

"So," Colt began while tearing open a bag of feed, "how long have you been a home health aide?"

After the personal topics they'd unearthed during the last couple weeks, his attempt at small talk felt unnatural, but Leah thought about it and replied, "About six years."

"And you always lived with your patients?"

"Mmm-hmm."

"Where'd you stay before then?" Casually, he shook the bag of granules into the seed spreader, then asked what he'd probably been wondering all along. "Who took you in when you left home?"

She should've known this wasn't innocent small talk. "And why Minnesota?" he added.

Growing up in Sultry Springs had taught Leah a thing or two about how inquiring minds worked, so she'd already prepared an answer. "I wanted to get as far away from here as the Greyhound would take me, which turned out to be Minnesota." She knelt at the main flower bed and used her trowel to uproot a cotton-tipped weed the size of a small cornstalk. "I spent a couple nights at the women's shelter, then found a church. That's where I met Benny. He took me in and offered me a clerical job—scheduling appointments, answering phones, things like that."

"Benito Alvarez?" Colt asked. "The guy whose Escalade you're driving?"

"The guy whose Escalade I'm *parking*, yes."

She'd mostly told the truth...omitting the seven months beforehand when she'd lived with the Ackermans. Instead of crashing at a women's shelter, she'd met Jim at the bus station, and he'd driven her to his house in the 'burbs. She'd met Benny after the birth, when she was at the lowest point of her life. That's when she'd sought comfort at church. She'd never had the courage to attend services while pregnant—she was afraid of what the congregation might think.

"He was real good to me," she said, getting a little misty. "Gave me a job and a home and never asked for anything in return. He's the one who encouraged me to try my hand at nursing." She sat back on her heels, smiling at the bittersweet memory. "We were driving to work one morning, and I asked him to stop for a squirrel on the side of the road. She'd been hit by a car, but not hard enough to kill her. I scooped her up in a box and we drove her to the vet."

"Did they save it?"

"No," Leah said. "But they put her down so she didn't suffer. I sang to her when she passed. Benny said anyone with a soul that gentle was a born healer."

"I'm glad you found Alvarez," Colt said, folding the empty bag and handing it to her. "Sounds like he was a second daddy to you."

"Mmm-hmm." She took the bag and tossed it onto the front stoop. "He's Ari's father. That's how the two of us got together."

Colt made a disgusted noise from the back of his throat. "You mean Dr. Pecker?"

A burst of laughter shook Leah's chest. She couldn't keep a straight face when she told Colt, "That's not nice."

"Well, no shit. He's a total wanker."

"I promise, he's not."

Colt's only reply was a disbelieving grunt.

"Really." Ari had his flaws, but they'd been friends once. She didn't want Colt thinking ill of him, though she didn't know why she cared. "He was in residency while I was getting my license, and he took the time to help me study, no matter how—"

A whir of plastic interrupted her as Colt began pushing the seed spreader in a meticulous line parallel to the sidewalk. The tight set of his jaw told her he didn't care to hear any more. Refusing to meet her gaze, he marched onward until he'd coated several rows of lawn. Just when Leah returned her trowel to the dirt, the whirring stopped and Colt heaved a sigh.

"Do you still love him?" he asked.

She pushed the blade into the ground and levered back. "I don't know."

"Do you think about him?"

She lifted one shoulder. "It's kind of hard not to when you bring him up like this."

"You know what I mean."

Leah added another weed to her pile and released a quiet sigh. Yes, she understood. Colt wanted to know if it was Ari's face she saw behind her eyelids when she rested her head at night, or if the memory of his touch gave her chills from a thousand miles away.

Not even close. She didn't think of Ari that way, never really had. Only one man held that kind of power over her, and it was the one currently scowling from behind a dusty seed spreader.

"No," she admitted. "He doesn't cross my mind all that much."

With a satisfied nod, Colt resumed his work. If she'd lied and said she still loved Ari, it might keep Colt at arm's length, but she couldn't do that to him. She'd wronged him so much already.

She watched him a while and noticed a slight unevenness to his gait, not quite a limp but it would be in a few hours. The muscles along his back bunched beneath the snug-fitting fabric of his T-shirt, and when he reached the end of each row, he'd stop and press both thumbs along his lower spine. As much as she wanted to mind her own business, she hated seeing him in pain.

"When did you quit physical therapy?" she asked over her shoulder while attacking another weed.

He continued working and raised his voice over the clamor. "I dunno. About as soon as I started walking again, I guess. Didn't see the point in going back. All the lady did was watch me stretch and suffer, maybe holler at me every now and then. I figured I could do that by myself at home."

That didn't surprise her. Men like Colt—old-school tough guys who liked being in charge—generally disliked a stranger contorting their bodies and bossing them around. Leah'd never had a patient quit on her, but only because they'd lived under the same roof and there was no escape.

"Well, you need to go back," she said. "I can tell you quit too soon."

He dismissed her with a *harrumph* and tried lengthening his stride to conceal the discomfort, but his slowing pace proved she was right.

"Come here," she said, standing and brushing dried grass from her knees. When he glanced at her with a question in his gaze, she motioned for him to join her. "Show me where it hurts."

He smiled through the pain. "We gonna play doctor?"

"We're going to play nurse. That means you show me yours, but I won't show you mine."

"That hardly seems fair."

She grabbed one hip and shifted her weight to it. "You coming or not?"

"You always this bossy, Nurse McMahon?"

Tired of his obstinacy, she marched over and joined him, stepping close enough to take in the scents of crisp fall air and shaving cream that clung to his skin. He smelled completely male, not a hint of styling products or perfumed dryer sheets. Leah tried to ignore the thrill that charged her body at the thought of touching his. She could be a professional about this.

"Go ahead and take off your shirt," she said as sternly as she could.

His lips twitched. "Right here in the front yard? Don't you wanna go inside?"

Inside with a half-naked Colt? Bad idea. "Right here. We'll make it quick."

"Kinda chilly this morning," he complained, never mind the sheen of perspiration along his tawny forehead. "Can't we do this in the den?"

"Nice try." She lifted his shirt hem to take a peek at his lower back, noting a raised scar marring his flesh. She bent at the waist for a closer look. "Surgery?"

"Uh-huh, last year." In one fluid motion, he grabbed a handful of cotton and tugged the shirt over his head, then turned to face her. "For nerve damage."

"Nerve da—" she began before the sight of him knocked the wind from her lungs, leaving her in an open-mouthed, testosterone-induced walking coma. She might've even drooled a little bit—it was hard to tell.

Saints alive. She'd seen him semi-nude before, a decade ago when he was lean and strong, but more boy than man. He'd made her heart pound then, but there was no mistaking the changes that'd broadened his shoulders and bunched the contours of his chest—his tight male nipples now encircled in the barest sprinkling of raven hair that matched the trail leading down his flat abdomen and dipping below the waistband of his jeans.

This was no boy. She wondered if the rest of him had grown in proportion, but she quickly shut down that train of thought. She'd barely been able to accommodate all of him at seventeen, so how could—

"I know it's not pretty." Colt rubbed the scar that

puckered the skin between his rib cage. He must've mistaken her silence for disgust. Lord have mercy, he couldn't have been more wrong.

"Don't be silly." Leah cleared her throat and moved in to skim her thumb over the faded ridge of his largest scar. He was so smooth and warm beneath her palm that she had to fight the urge to run her hands all over him. She met his gaze and asked, "Internal bleeding?"

"Uh-huh." He took her hand and guided it to another scar, low on his belly. "Here too."

She pulled free, no longer able to bear the contact. It was too much. "You need some vitamin E capsules. Snip off one end and then rub the oil over your scars."

"I thought that was your job."

Refusing to be baited, she stepped behind him and settled her palm at the base of his spine, then used the pads of her fingertips to gently probe the stiff muscles clenching his vertebrae. She was so distracted by the hard planes of Colt's upper back that she had to close her eyes to process what her fingers were trying to tell her.

"You're out of alignment," she said against his heated skin. "Big time. Probably to the point where you've aggravated a nerve."

"Alignment?" he asked skeptically. "You gonna try and sell me on a visit to the chiropractor? 'Cause I don't believe in that stuff."

"Well, you should, because you'll be miserable the rest of your life in this condition." She used her thumbs to press outward, testing the firmness in his knotted muscles. "Not that a visit would do you any good."

"Right. Because they're quacks."

"Wrong. Because your muscles are so tight they'd

just pull you back out of alignment again. You've got to loosen up first—apply heat, do some stretching, get a few therapeutic massages from someone who knows what they're doing." Before he had a chance to ask, she added, "And no, I'm not offering my services."

"First the oil and now this. You're not impressing me with your bedside manner."

She ignored his teasing. "How flexible are you?"

He glanced over his shoulder, scanning her from head to toe. "Not as flexible as I remember you being."

"I'm serious. Show me how far you can bend over."

He released a burst of laughter and stepped away, holding up both hands. "Honey, no man wants to hear those words."

Leah clamped her lips together in an effort to stifle a laugh, but a puff of air broke free in an ungraceful guffaw. After her chest quit shaking, she pointed to the ground. "I mean it. I need to see how bad it is so I can decide which routine to prescribe."

Reluctantly, he obeyed, and just as she'd expected, he couldn't reach more than halfway past his calves.

"There's your first problem," she said. "I'll show you some stretches before you leave. That's priority number one—getting those muscles loosened up. You need to apply heat too. I don't suppose you've got a hot tub."

"No, but the next best thing is just ten minutes from here."

"What's that?"

"The springs."

"Oh! That's perfect." She couldn't believe she hadn't thought of it herself. "Some people say the minerals promote healing."

She expected him to balk at that, but he nodded in agreement. "I'm on duty tomorrow, but I get off at six. Want to meet me there?"

Leah hesitated, holding statue-still. A steamy evening rendezvous with Colt was a bad idea, but the most deliciously bad idea she'd ever struggled to overcome. She had to virtually wrestle her own tongue to the ground to tell him no. "But you go ahead. Hot baths and heating pads will work too."

He shook out his T-shirt and tugged it over his head, then pushed both arms through the sleeves. "How 'bout this—I'll be there every night after supper. If you can meet me, fine. If not, no worries." After refastening the ponytail at the base of his neck, he said, "But I do like seeing you."

She liked seeing him too, but didn't say so. Instead, she turned and knelt on the ground to pull another weed. Colt took the hint and resumed his work on the lawn. They each worked in silence for a while, and when Colt finished spreading the seed, he took a knee beside her and grabbed an extra trowel. His large hands plunged the blade into the ground with ease, uprooting five weeds for every one of hers. Once he'd worked his way through his side of the flowerbed, he took a break and sank back on his heels.

"Can I ask you something?" he said.

"Sure." She blotted her temple with one sleeve.

"It's been bugging me since that night at the Sack-n-Pay." He sat in the grass and stretched out his long legs, crossing them at the ankles. "Why would you go through all that trouble to pay for a box of cereal but cheat Uncle Sam by not filing taxes all those years?"

Wow. Colt sure didn't hesitate to tackle the tough questions, did he? She started to ask how he knew, but figured the answer was plain enough. The night of the Lewis homecoming, Bobbi had said that Colt searched for her a long time. He'd probably started by asking one of his law enforcement buddies to scan the IRS database.

"I didn't want to be found," she said, brushing off her hands to take a break. "So I let Benny pay me under the table, but I tried to make up for it in other ways. I still gave my twenty percent, just not to the government."

A shake of his head said he wasn't surprised. "How'd you do that?"

She drew both knees to her chest. "Anonymous donations to schools, parks, libraries, animal shelters, scholarship funds…that sort of thing." Sure, what she'd done was technically illegal, but the way she saw it, she'd cut out the middleman. Her way was more efficient.

Colt chuckled and pushed to standing, then extended one hand to help her up. "And you had the nerve to tell me you're no angel."

"I'm still telling you I'm no angel." She took his hand, and he easily pulled her to her feet. "Giving away money is easy. That doesn't make me a good person."

"Right, but you know what does?" He tapped her forehead with his index finger. "Your borderline crazy drive to do the right thing. Trust me, honey, you're one of the good ones."

"You don't know me, Colt." How many times would she have to say it before he believed her?

Her insides felt heavy again, like in the shed. Images of Noah's face—so much like his father's— filled her mind, and she couldn't stand Colt telling her what a good person she was when she'd given his son to strangers.

*Maybe it's time to tell him*, she thought. He wasn't the same wild-as-weeds boy who'd seduced her all those years ago. He was the town sheriff now, stable and responsible. *Which is why he can't find out*, a secret side of her warned. He might try to take Noah from the Ackermans  the only parents he'd ever known. Colt had legal connections. What if he contested the adoption? Would he stand a chance in court? If so, it could devastate Noah. Did she really want to risk it?

"Hey, did you hear me?" Colt nudged her back to reality.

"Sorry, I zoned out."

"I'm gonna grab some coffee and a couple of doughnuts. You want anything?"

"No," she said. "I had grapefruit and egg whites for breakfast."

Colt rolled his eyes. "Of course you did." He dug his keys from his pocket and strode toward his Harley. "Be right back."

As he drove toward town, she watched the jet-black ponytail whipping his shoulder blades, the masculine set of his body as he mastered the powerful machinery between his legs and steered it out of sight. He was stunning, and she wanted him—she couldn't deny it. But they didn't stand a chance after what she'd done.

For the first time in her adult life, Leah wished she were seventeen again. If she could go back, she'd do so many things differently.

# Chapter 10

"HONEY, I'M HOME."

Leah was washing her hands at the kitchen sink when Colt returned from the store and strode through the back entrance without knocking. He set a white paper bag on the counter, followed by a Big Gulp, then removed his sunglasses and tucked them in his front pocket. After she'd rinsed the suds from her fingers, he used one hip to bump her aside so he could lather up too. The gesture was so natural, like he'd breezed through her door before and would do it again a thousand times in the future. Like he belonged here. Truth be told, it kind of felt right, and that scared her.

She dried off with a dish towel and pointed to his Big Gulp. "That's quite a caffeine addiction you've got there. Did you drain the whole pot?"

He turned off the water and grabbed the towel from her hand. "The Harley's not too practical for making coffee runs. I use an oversized cup and fill it half way so it doesn't spill."

"I didn't think about it until you left," she said, "but I could've brewed a pot here."

"It's okay." He lightly flicked the towel at her backside before slinging it over the oven handle to dry. "I wanted to surprise you anyway."

Leah didn't like surprises—she had terrible luck with them. "What'd you do?"

"Simmer down, hon." He tore open the bag and pulled out a bundle of waxed paper, then unfolded the ends to reveal two slightly smooshed Richman's éclairs. "Turns out the Harley's not too good for doughnut runs either. But they're fresh out of the oven—the newest batch in the bakery."

Oh, Lord. She believed him. Even with half the icing smeared onto the waxed paper and cream filling oozing out both ends, the golden pastries looked light enough to melt on her tongue. She pulled in a breath of sweetness and her mouth watered in response. Why did Colt have to tempt her like this?

"That was nice of you," she said, still gazing at the sinful offering. "But I already ate."

"I'm sure you can make room for more." Carefully, he lifted an éclair with both hands and held the fragile bits together. He sank his teeth into one end, closing his eyes in rapture while he spoke with one cheek full. "Mmm. That's pure perfection, right there."

Leah swallowed reflexively. Maybe one bite wouldn't hurt.

It was like he'd read her mind. "Wanna share this one?"

"I shouldn't…"

"Aw, c'mon, hon." He lifted the other end toward her mouth. "Live a little."

She leaned in a fraction, but quickly changed her mind. On second thought, she couldn't do this. Leah knew herself. One bite wouldn't be enough—it'd lead to another and another until she'd scarfed down her whole pastry. His too. Then she'd wind up driving to Richman's every day like an addict jonesing for a fix. Moderation didn't work for her any more than it'd worked for her daddy. It had to be all or nothing.

She shook her head. "I can't."

Colt scowled at her. "Give me one good reason why."

His scrutiny rubbed her the wrong way, making her feel like a child. She backed up until her rear end met the countertop. "I don't have to give you anything."

"What's your problem?" He closed the distance between them, trapping her between his body and the counter. "You love these."

"You're the one with the problem." Why did he care so much whether or not she ate a stupid doughnut? It wasn't any of his business. "Just back off."

"God damn, you're the most stubborn woman I've ever met." He brought the éclair to her lips and demanded, "Just take a friggin' bite already."

He was pissing her off now, pardon her language. Who did he think he was—bursting into her kitchen and ordering her around? "I said no!" She drew back and shoved his outstretched arm, sending the pastry flying right into her face, where it stuck to her cheek for a split second before tumbling down her arm and to the floor.

Leah gasped in horror. A glance at her brand-new white shirt revealed a chocolate smudge staining the sleeve. When she touched her face and pulled back, a thick layer of icing coated the pads of her fingertips. She fired a glare at Colt and smacked his chest with her clean hand. "You just couldn't listen, could you?"

Colt glanced at the fallen pastry, then back at her. "I'm sorry." But his laughing eyes made him a liar.

"It's not funny!" But a tiny giggle snuck up from her chest and made her a liar too. "Look at what you did." She waggled the evidence at him, then held out her arm. "And I'll never get this stain out."

"I'll buy you another shirt." He took her hand to inspect the mess.

"Never mind. It wasn't expensive." She tried pulling
free, but he held tight.

Then, in an abrupt move that changed everything,
Colt licked her middle finger and took it into his mouth,
shocking her with a jolt of pleasure that made her gasp.
At her reaction, he drew her finger in deeper with a tug
of hot, wet suction that sent chills skittering over every
inch of her body. He slid his lips to the base of her fingernail and sucked his way back down again, locking his
wicked gaze with hers in a silent dare to tell him to stop.

That was the moment she should have yanked free
and ordered him to leave, gathered her wits, and listened
to her conscience, which screamed *Not healthy!*

But she didn't budge, and she didn't speak.

Instead, she skimmed her index finger invitingly
along his upper lip and let him take that one too. He
doubled his efforts, closing his eyes to savor the taste of
her skin, gliding his lips up and down over her knuckles
and using his tongue in a torrid swirl that she felt every-
where. She couldn't believe the intensity in this simple
act. With nothing but two fingers in his mouth, Colt did
things to her body she'd never felt with any other man.

After he'd sucked every trace of icing from her pink-
polished nails, he used his thumb to spread the chocolate
from her cheek downward, creating a trail from her jaw
to the top of her shoulder. Again, he paused, giving her
a chance to stop him. Again, she said nothing, answering
with a tilt of her head.

Colt wasted no time in cleaning up the mess he'd
made. Taking hold of her ponytail, he pulled back her

head and molded his body to hers as he lapped unmer-
cifully at her throat. Leah rested both elbows on the
countertop and savored the intoxicating sensations of his
gifted tongue and the burgeoning erection pressed to her
belly. She sighed into the air, softly at first, then deepen-
ing to a low moan when he used his teeth to scrape the
top of her shoulder. He latched onto her neck and sucked
hard, and her knees went slack, forcing her to grip his
shoulders for support.

He wrapped both palms around her waist and hoisted
her onto the counter before parting her knees and stepping in between. "Lift your arms," he ordered in a husky
voice that made her stomach drop into her panties. She
obeyed, and he peeled off her shirt and tossed it aside,
then unfastened her bra and shucked it to the floor in
one brisk motion.

On instinct, she covered herself. She barely filled her
B-cups, nothing like the women Colt was used to. She
couldn't compete with their voluptuous bodies, and she
felt too exposed in the harsh sunlight streaming through
the kitchen window.

"Don't." He gathered her wrists and pinned them
behind her back, securing them in one hand while he
used the other to gently cup her right breast. He gazed at
her in wonder and whispered, "You're perfect, Angel."

Leah shook her head as her cheeks burned. Nothing
about her was perfect—not her itty bitty chest, or her
short legs, and especially not the scar that joined her
hipbones like a macabre version of connect the dots.
She wished they were in her bedroom, under sheets and
blankets, so she could cover her flaws.

"I mean it," he said, kneading her more firmly. "I've

fantasized about these for the last ten years." He reached for the waxed paper and dipped his thumb into a dollop of cream, then massaged the cool filling into her nipple, bringing it to a hard point. "I've always wanted to do this to you. No one else but you."

Leah groaned, bowing back to lift her nipple to his mouth, hungry for the same hot suction he'd used on her fingers. He teased her at first, swirling his tongue around and around the pebbled tip before licking up the center. She kicked off her Keds, then locked her ankles behind his back and shamelessly rocked against his stone chest. When he drew her deep into his mouth, she did it again, desperate for friction to soothe the hot ache growing between her thighs.

"Do you believe me?" he asked, and blew cool air over her glistening nipple.

"Yes," she breathed.

At that, he released her wrists and she leaned back, bracing herself on the counter to grind harder against him in a brazen drive for release. Somewhere in the recesses of her mind, she knew she should feel embarrassed for rubbing on him like a cat in heat, but she didn't give half a damn. If anything, she only quickened the pace.

"Hold on," he said while putting a few inches of cold space between them. When she whimpered in protest, he tucked one hand inside the front of her pants and said, "I wanna feel you come."

His fingers slid beneath her bikini briefs and tangled with her blond curls while his mouth latched on to her neglected nipple. Just when she thought it couldn't get any better, he dipped a thumb inside and spread warm lubrication along her sensitive folds, petting her until she grew so achy she feared she might burst. He isolated her swollen bundle of nerves between two fingers and slid them back and forth in a liquid saddle that had her moaning loud enough to stop traffic. All the while, he drew teasingly on her nipple. She arched her lower back and clenched her thighs around his body to move in time with him, faster and faster, until she felt her inner walls tense for release.

"More," she cried, closing her eyes to savor the pleasure washing over her.

He gave her what she needed, stroked her harder while thrusting a finger deep inside, where she shuddered around him in fierce spasms. Her lips parted in a muted scream, head tipped back as she gripped the counter ledge and rode his hand with a wild fury she didn't know she possessed. Wave after wave crested before the last one left her sated, and her body finally went limp.

The tremors had barely ceased when Colt pulled her to sitting, grabbed her by the thighs, and carried her to the table. "We can do a lot better than that, honey."

Leah shook her head, still drugged and gasping for air. "I don't think that's possible."

He swept a pile of mail to the floor and laid her down on the cool oak, then peeled off her yoga pants. "Watch me do the impossible." He spread her legs and fit himself to her, gliding the steel ridge of his erection in slow circles over her aroused flesh.

"Oh, god," she swore. "Maybe we can." She planted both heels on the table and rose to meet him, greedy for more. She hooked her thumbs beneath the waistband of her panties and tried tugging them down. "I want you inside me. Hurry."

He groaned in approval but quickly stilled her hands. "No."

"Why?"

"You're not ready."

"Yes, I am." And she showed him with a decadent arch of her hips. "Touch me again and see."

"Shit, baby." He pinned her wrists to the table and lowered onto her body, resting his forehead on her chest in an obvious struggle for control. But for what, she didn't know. She'd just offered herself to him. He didn't have to wait another second. "You're not makin' this easy for me," he whispered.

It didn't get any easier than this. She wrapped one leg around him and said, "I want you, Colt. I'm ready."

After releasing her wrists, he propped himself on one elbow and gazed down at her beneath lids heavy with lust. "You're ready here," he said, using the heel of his hand to massage the dampened fabric of her panties. Just as she'd closed her eyes and started to writhe against his palm, he withdrew and rested it above her heart. "But not here."

"I am," she insisted. "I promise."

"No, Angel." He cupped her cheek. "I got you all worked up, but when it's over and you come back down, you'll be sorry it happened. Just like last time." Something in his eyes shifted, sadness mingled with desire, and she felt a tug at her belly. "I don't think I could take it if you regretted making love with me again."

Leah didn't know what to say—he'd stunned her into silence.

He skimmed his hand down her face, along the outside curve of her breast, over her waist and hips to her cotton bikinis, where he pulled them back up. "We can fool around all you want, but these have to stay on until the time's right." His gaze moved over her features as if worried for her reaction. "Until you're sure. Okay?"

She only nodded, unable to speak over the thickness in her throat.

This wasn't the Colt she remembered—the arrogant boy who'd seduced her in that hot and dusty shed ten years ago. This Colt was all man—and a *good* man, at that.

She stroked the smooth edge of his jaw and pulled him in for a soft kiss, a tender brush of lips to show how much his actions warmed her heart. In response, he opened to her, using his tongue to trace her lower lip in an invitation that she took. She delved inside where the flavor of éclairs lingered on his mouth. She'd come to associate his kisses with the taste of vanilla cream and chocolate icing. And much like those pastries, one nibble wasn't enough.

She pulled him harder against her, making love to his mouth if not his body, absorbing all the sweetness he had to offer. And he offered nearly everything he had, sliding his tongue between her parted lips as he crushed her beneath his weight and ground his hips against her in a slow, delicious rhythm.

He broke the kiss to take her earlobe between his teeth, rolling to the side just enough to slip his fingers once again beneath the cotton of her briefs. Using his thumb, he traced her stiff bud while probing deep with his index finger. She spread wider for him and arched her back, willing him to go further, and then he twisted that finger to face the ceiling and massaged an erotic zone she didn't know she had. Her toes curled in response while an animalistic noise rose from the back of her throat.

With his mouth still at her ear, he whispered, "Can the doctor make you moan like that?"

Her lips parted, but she couldn't breathe over the dizzying sensations. She brought both knees to her chest in a silent plea for more, and he rewarded her by adding a second finger and pumping in and out of her throbbing center in a slow, sensual dance. He sank deeper with each stroke, filling and stretching her while she rocked her hips for more.

"Can he do this to you?" he asked. "Can he make you so wet you drip into his hand? Listen to this." He angled his pistoning fingers to amplify the sound of her arousal. "I can hear how much you want me. Did you ever want him like this?"

She thrashed her head from side to side. "No. Never." She knew she was at his mercy, and she didn't care. Flat on her back, wide open on her daddy's kitchen table, begging for Colt's sinful touch, and she didn't care. "You're the only one."

"Remember that." He kissed a trail to her shoulder and bit down, still moving inside her. "Tell me you'll remember."

She answered with a moan, and he withdrew his fingers.

"I'll remember!" she shouted, eyes flying wide, desperate for him to keep going.

He chuckled darkly and moved to the end of the table, taking a seat on the chair between her legs. Then he grabbed her by the thighs and pulled her to the wooden ledge, propping her heels on his shoulders. "I know you will. I'm about to make sure of it."

With one hand, he hooked the cotton fabric aside,

then bent to his work and used his tongue on her, circling and teasing in whisper-light licks that only served to heighten the dull ache spreading low in her belly. She grasped the table's edge with both hands and let her knees fall out to the sides while he resumed pumping inside her with his fingers. Her moans grew urgent and half-hysterical. She couldn't survive much more of his scintillating torture.

"Colt," she murmured, "please."

He groaned, vibrating against her before drawing her into his mouth with a strong pull of suction that had her sobbing with pleasure. He worked her relentlessly, took her higher than she'd ever thought her body could go, then catapulted her into the sun. The erotic pressure continued to build inside her until she thought she'd die from it, and then he twisted his fingers again and found that magical spot, and her whole world blew apart.

Her inner walls tightened like a vise around his fingers and released, tightened and released, in a quaking orgasm so powerful she almost couldn't bear the ecstasy. Her cries filled the kitchen and reverberated off the walls, sounding distorted to her own ears. She'd never felt anything this strong. On and on it went, until her leg muscles went slack and her heels slipped from Colt's shoulders. He stayed with her until the end, when the shudders finally stopped and her cries quieted.

She lay on the table, heart pounding so hard she felt it in her toes. While she fought for breath, Colt withdrew his fingers and left her with one last, gentle kiss between her thighs. As soon as she could draw oxygen and form a coherent sentence, she told him, "I'll remember."

He laughed at that and pulled her into his lap, where

she straddled his thighs and linked her arms behind his neck. There, he fed her sweet, lazy kisses and danced his fingertips along her spine. A few minutes later, she became aware of the erection still straining the front of his Levi's. Every bit the man, he'd seen to her needs and ignored his own. But she intended to rectify that—to give *him* something to remember—starting right now.

—⁓—

Colt was in heaven.

He'd just made Leah come like a freight train—the hardest orgasm of her life, he was sure of it—and now he held her pliant body in his arms, stroking her silken skin and savoring the steady thump of her heart beating against his chest. How many nights had he wished for this? God only knew. He could hardly believe it was really happening, but her salty flavor lingered as evidence on his tongue. The air was still thick with the tantalizing scent of her arousal. He pulled back to glance at her, so beautiful with her mussed hair and her flushed cheeks, drunk on the satisfaction he'd given her. In that moment, she was all his.

It didn't get any better than this.

She reached down to stroke him through his jeans, then worked the button on his fly and whispered in his ear, "Your turn."

Okay, maybe it *could* get a little better than this.

After she'd lowered his zipper, she stood from his lap long enough to help him push his pants and boxer-briefs to his knees. He was hard enough to split stone, but when she curled her soft palm around him and stroked his length, he grew incredibly harder. He bit his lip to contain a curse and tipped his head to rest on the seatback, then closed his eyes, focusing on the gentle friction of their joined skin, occasionally thrusting up to meet her hand. Suddenly, her weight lifted from his lap, and he opened his eyes to find her kneeling at his boots, a sight he didn't like one bit.

"What're you doing?" he asked in a voice that made his feelings clear. He didn't want Leah on her knees. It was degrading. Over the years, he'd let dozens of women service him that way. They'd dropped to the floor and sucked him off in closets and bathrooms, dressing rooms and backyards. It was a way to get his jollies without giving anything in return. He couldn't do that to Leah. She was his angel—she was above it.

"Isn't it obvious?" Grasping his base, she licked the underside of his rounded tip like a kid with a snow cone.

His eyes rolled back and his cock twitched, despite his best efforts to ignore the repeated laps of her tongue. "Get back up here."

"Why?" Her baby blues widened in a way that made his heart heavy. "Am I doing it wrong?"

"Hell, no."

"Then why do you want me to stop?"

"Honey, you're doin' everything right. I just don't like you down there on your knees."

She licked him, long and slow up the center, then grinned. "Did you have another position in mind?"

First the panties and now this. She was making it awfully hard for him to do the right thing. Hard in more ways than one.

Before he could protest any further, she began stroking him while massaging the skin behind his balls, and pure pleasure wiped his mind clean, making it impossible to think about anything but the cocktail of sensations between his legs. He closed his eyes again and leaned back in his chair, helpless to stop her. He'd done all he could. The head on his shoulders wasn't the one making the decisions anymore.

She took him into her mouth one slow inch at a time, pulled back, and then slid her lips further down his slippery shaft. When she couldn't take him any deeper, she used one hand to stroke his base, twisting her grip while clamping her lips tighter around him and quickening the pace. A whimper escaped his chest while the pit of his belly coiled, the tension mounting until he knew he'd go in seconds. And to think she'd worried she was doing it wrong. She worked him like a pro.

He couldn't help pumping his hips to meet her, whispering her name and pleading *Don't stop, baby. Please don't stop.* When his body tensed for release, she gripped him impossibly harder, took him impossibly deeper, and grabbed his backside with her other hand, digging her nails into his flesh. He didn't want to come in her mouth, but he couldn't control the hot surge about to erupt. She was too good. With a final thrust, he muffled a cry and let go, legs kicking out with rapture as she swallowed everything he gave her in wave after wave of his climax. It seemed to go on forever, but she didn't relent. She held on until he quit pulsing, then released him with a gentle suction that made him groan.

"God damn," he panted in awe, glancing down at her. "I don't wanna know how you learned to do that."

The way she smiled up at him—all coy and naked, her lips swollen from mouthing his erection—was anything but angelic. She licked the corner of her mouth and told him, "I could say the same thing about you."

"Come here." He held out his arms to her, not bothering to pull up his drawers. Soon she'd have to pick up her daddy, and he wanted to spend every spare minute holding her. She settled in his lap and laced her fingers behind his back, resting her cheek on his shoulder while he stroked her hair. Seriously, it didn't get any better than this.

After a few minutes of blissful silence, she trailed one index finger down the side of his neck and whispered, "That was amazing, but you know we can't do it again, right?"

Colt's heart pinched and he fought to keep the hurt from showing on his face. He'd expected her to pull away, but not so soon. Thank goodness he hadn't caved in and made love to her. She'd be halfway to Minnesota by now.

He faked his most unaffected shrug and said, "Whatever you want, honey," then added with a wink, "but you'll never be able to eat at this table without getting hot and bothered."

She dropped a kiss on the tip of his nose. "Lucky for me, Daddy likes to eat in front of the TV."

The moment ended far too quickly. She stood and retrieved her discarded clothes, then went to her room to fetch a clean shirt while he fastened his pants. When they cleaned up the kitchen, she tossed both éclairs into the garbage without taking a single bite, which bothered him more than it should have. She loved those things—always had—so why did she avoid them now? He wanted to see her indulge, to gobble one like a child.

That's why he'd bought them. Maybe next time she'd let go of whatever was holding her back.

And there *would* be a next time. He'd have to be patient and wait for Leah to come to him, but she'd come. She was his—she just didn't know it yet.

# Chapter 11

DRY GRAVEL CRUNCHED BENEATH COLT'S LAREDOS as he left his cruiser and picked his way across the trail leading to the springs. His movements disturbed the placid night air and sent a handful of critters scurrying into the tangled underbrush that sprouted along the water's edge. Colt smiled and unbuckled his utility belt. The presence of critters was a good sign—it meant he had the place to himself again.

He hadn't crossed paths with anything on two legs since his first visit a few nights ago, when he'd surprised a group of teenagers. Once they'd caught a glimpse of the gold star on his Stetson, they'd grabbed their six-packs and hightailed it the hell out of there. Word must've gotten out that the sheriff had taken to soaking in the springs after work, because they'd stayed away ever since. All the better. Now he could skinny dip without an audience.

The sun hung low in the sky, throwing shadows over the jagged ground and casting the mineral pool in a mystic greenish-blue glow. Surrounded on three sides by a red stony ridge, the space boasted more privacy than half the backyard pools in town. He enjoyed it out here, especially since the fall air had turned crisp, and he wondered why he hadn't come out more often in previous years. Probably because it was too peaceful—no blaring juke boxes or giggling women to drown out his thoughts.

He continued past the shallows to his favorite spot in the back, where time had eroded a natural bench of limestone beneath the water's surface. Once there, he stripped down and slung his clothes over a small boulder, then set his utility belt within reach of the pool, just in case he needed to draw his weapon. The odds were slim, but why risk getting caught with his pants down?

He sat on the gravel ledge and dangled his legs in the water to acclimate his skin to the hot change in temperature, then lowered to his chest and settled on the stone seat below. The air stank of sulfur, but it was worth it when the muscles along his lower back unclenched and his body melted into the earth behind him. He groaned in relief. This was a perfect way to spend the evening.

Almost.

There was room for one more body on the stone seat beside him, and he'd felt her absence each night like a rib stolen from his chest. He hadn't expected Leah to join him right away, but after their sizzling oral escapades last week, waiting for her to come to him was proving more than he could bear. He wanted her again—all of her this time. But she'd made it damn near impossible to get close to her again.

When he'd arrived at her house the last couple of mornings to tend the lawn, he'd found her gone, tagging along with her daddy to his hospital appointments. It was her not-so-subtle way of avoiding him. Aside from the Sunday service, he'd run out of excuses to be near her, and as much as Colt wanted to trust his instincts and play it cool, it wasn't easy. Still, he had to be careful. He never thought he'd get a second chance with Leah, and he wasn't about to blow it by pushing too hard. She'd seek him out—he had to trust that.

In the meantime, he tried to focus on the stretches Leah had shown him. He brought one knee toward his chest until he felt a pull at the base of his spine, then held it to the count of sixty and repeated on the other side. In just four days, he'd limbered up enough to notice a small difference. He couldn't quite touch his knees to his upper torso yet, but it wouldn't be much longer. He'd even scheduled a couple massages at the chiropractor's office. He didn't exactly enjoy getting rubbed down by a big, hairy dude, but he couldn't deny it had helped. And even though he didn't buy into that back-cracking shit, he decided to give it a try as soon as his muscles loosened up. What the hell, it was worth a shot, right?

He'd just finished his second set of stretches when his cell phone rang from inside his utility belt. After shaking the water from one hand, he unsnapped the pouch and glanced at the screen: *Shooters Tavern*. He swiped a finger across the glass and answered.

"Hey, Colt," June Gallagher shouted above a symphony of background noises he'd known well in a past life—shouts and laughter to the backdrop of a steel guitar. "Can you hear me?"

"Barely," he told her. "What's up?"

"I need you to come down here and pick up Rachel Landry. She's had too much to drink, and she's looking to start trouble. It's dollar draft night, and things are already cra—"

"Not my jurisdiction," he interrupted. Shooters was outside Sultry County lines; otherwise they wouldn't be allowed to sell booze. June knew that. "You're gonna have to call the locals."

"But if I do that, they'll arrest her."

"Isn't that the point?"

"No!" June yelled like he'd done something wrong. Probably hormones. A guy couldn't say anything right around a pregnant lady.

Colt reminded her, "You just told me Rachel's three sheets to the wind and spoilin' for a fight."

June huffed a sigh into the phone. "Think about it. She's Leah's best friend…"

Colt understood the implication. If he swooped in and rescued the sour shrew, it might earn him a few brownie points. He doubted it would do any good. Besides, the thought of Rachel Landry cooling her heels in the Hallover County tank made him smile.

At his hesitation, June added, "C'mon. Rachel's good people—you know that."

"She wouldn't piss on me if I were on fire."

"I know you two don't see eye to eye, but I've never seen her act like this. I think something's wrong. I tried calling Leah, but I couldn't reach her."

Colt felt his resolve slipping. He couldn't stand Rachel, but if she was in real trouble, he didn't want her doing something stupid and making it worse.

"Can't someone drive her home?" he asked.

"Trey already offered, but she won't go, and we're not allowed to restrain her."

"Fine." It sounded like Rachel was in a tizzy. "I'll be on my way in a few."

"Thanks, Colt."

He grumbled a reluctant "No problem" and disconnected.

So much for his near-perfect evening. For most good ol' boys, hitting the local bar after work was the most natural thing in the world, but Colt hated Shooters. He'd managed to avoid the watering hole since his accident two years ago. There was nothing wrong with the place—June and Luke had done a fair job renovating it—but he'd spent too many drunken nights there, made one too many mistakes within those walls. It was at the pool tables in the back of the bar where he'd picked up Barbara Lee, the lunatic who'd knocked some sense into him—from behind the wheel of her Ford Taurus.

Damn it, Rachel had better appreciate this. But knowing her, she wouldn't.

He hauled himself out of the springs and used his hands as a makeshift squeegee to dry off. Which didn't work. His uniform clung to his damp skin and chafed the insides of his thighs, pissing him off even more as he stalked back to the cruiser. By the time he arrived at Shooters and parked out by the Dumpster, he was madder than a box of weasels.

He pounded three times on the back door, figuring June was in the office instead of tending bar. Luke Gallagher was a crotchety son of a bitch, but a good guy, and he wouldn't want his pregnant wife on her feet all night long.

As it turned out, Colt was right. June answered, wearing a haggard expression and a knee-length maternity dress stretched tighter than a gnat's belly over a fifty-gallon drum. Each time Colt saw her, he didn't think June could get any bigger, but somehow she kept expanding. Colt didn't give a damn what anyone said— there were two babies in there. Maybe three.

"Thanks for coming," June said, stepping aside to let him in. "She's back here with me." Averting her eyes, she added, "Kind of."

"Kind of?" That sounded ominous. He noticed a violent thunk coming from somewhere nearby, like boots kicking the wall, and he wondered if Rachel was throwing a tantrum in the office.

June ducked her head and glanced down the dark, narrow hallway leading to the bar. "Luke and Trey locked her in the closet with the plastic cups and the cocktail napkins. We figured she couldn't hurt herself in there."

Colt shook his head and started toward the closet. "I'm gonna pretend I didn't hear that." The thumping grew louder as he approached the door. Rachel was going apeshit in there. He pointed at the brass latch. "Go ahead and release the beast."

June slid aside the bolt while Colt held the knob firmly in both hands. "Okay," he said, "now get back in the office. She might come out swinging." Once June had waddled safely into the next room, Colt opened the door and braced himself for impact. Good thing, too, because one hundred and thirty pounds of nearly dead weight fell into his arms. He widened his stance and tried to lift with his legs, not his back, but a shock of pain licked his spine.

Rachel gripped his shoulders and stared at his uniformed chest, then slurred, "Oh, good. The law's here. Occifer, I want 'em all arrested." She stank like cigarettes and sour whiskey. "They nevvver lemme finish my drink, an' I paid forrrr it."

There was no way she could walk to the cruiser on her own. Colt wrapped one arm around her rib cage and bent low to scoop beneath her knees. He hoisted her up and warned, "You'll pay for it big-time if you puke on me."

It took a few seconds for the lush to realize who was holding her. She wrinkled her forehead and peered at him with wide, unfocused eyes. "Heyyyy," she said accusingly, "it's you." She tried poking his chest with an index finger, but missed the mark and knocked his windpipe instead, making him cough. "I hate your face, Colton Bea."

He turned that face aside to cough again. "June," he called, "get the door."

"Guys like you 'n Tommy 'n Marcus," Rachel went on, "you think you're the shit."

June let him out into the parking lot. "Thanks again, Colt."

"...that just because you're good-lookin' or rich, you can do whatevvvver you want..."

"Next time, call the Hallover boys," Colt told June. "A night in the tank might do her some good."

"...you're lying liars, all three of you..."

Rachel's head flopped against his chest as he strode toward the car, but that didn't stop her from bitching about some guy named Marcus, who she claimed was a "lizard-licking donkey sucker." Colt didn't know the guy, but he felt kind of sorry for Marcus. Whoever he was, he had no idea of the hellfire he'd unleashed.

Colt set Rachel on her feet, but kept one arm around her waist while he pressed his key fob and opened the back door. No way he'd put her in front. She was going to spew for sure.

"Wait," she said, shoving aside a lock of her brown hair and scowling at the cruiser. "Am I underrrr arrest?"

"Unh-uh. But don't tempt me." He pushed on Rachel's head to keep her from clocking it on the roof, then helped her settle on the plastic bench seat. "You're going home."

She let out a small gasp and begged, "No! I don't wanna go home!"

For some reason, the drunks never did. "It's either that or the county jail."

"Jail, then."

Colt massaged his temples. He had no intention of hauling in Rachel. For one, he was outside Sultry County lines, and even if she'd given him cause to arrest her, all that paperwork would tie him up for the rest of the night. "Forget it. I'm taking you to your mama."

"Please," Rachel whispered. Her voice had turned thick, and Colt glanced down to find her eyes welling with tears. "I can't go back there and face her. Not yet."

"Aw, now, don't do that." He shook a finger at her wobbly chin. Colt couldn't stand to see a woman cry. It was the easiest way to get out of a ticket with him—fifty bucks wasn't worth having to listen to all that sniveling. "No crying."

Her face contorted and her whole body shook. She clamped her lips shut and made a few choking noises, then let it all out, bawling in loud, open-mouthed sobs, complete with dribble trickling down her chin. Black goop from her lashes began leaking down her cheeks, and she didn't even bother to wipe away the muck. Damn it. He'd never seen Rachel cry, not once in all the years he'd known her.

Colt tore off his Stetson. What was he supposed to do with her now? There really was something wrong. Plus, she needed to sober up, but the diner and the coffee joint were both closed.

"P-p-p-pleeeeeease?"

"Fine," he grumbled. "I won't take you home yet."

"Tha-tha-th-tha…" Before she could thank him, he shut the door and turned his face to the sky to pull in a deep breath.

What a shitty night this turned out to be.

—∿∿—

Leah gazed at the full moon and filled her lungs with sweet autumn air. What a beautiful night!

She clicked on her flashlight, slung her towel over one shoulder, and started down the narrow path to the springs, reminding herself she wasn't doing anything wrong. Colt enjoyed her company and she enjoyed his, simple as that. There was no harm in spending a little time together while she was in town. That didn't mean they had to take things farther, and it didn't make them a couple.

But when Leah arrived at the springs and saw that Colt wasn't there, her heart sank. She swept her flashlight beam over the water three more times as if to summon him through sheer determination. When he didn't magically appear, she stood there a while longer, rooted to the ground by disappointment.

Well, shoot. Where was he?

—∿∿—

Colt pulled a mug from his kitchen cabinet and filled it with fresh black coffee while Rachel rinsed her mouth in the sink. To her credit, she hadn't gotten sick in the cruiser. She'd waited until she reached his front porch, then tossed her cookies on his rattan *Welcome* mat. At least she seemed to feel a little better. She wasn't crying or slurring anymore.

"Here, drink this." He set the steaming mug on the table and pulled out a chair for her. "I'm gonna go hose off that mess."

She blotted her face with a paper towel. "Mm-kay. Sorry 'bout that."

"Better the porch than the living room." If she'd lost it inside the house, he'd have to pull up the carpet, because no way in hell was he getting on his hands and knees to clean up the contents of Rachel Landry's stomach.

Colt flipped on the front lights and uncoiled the garden hose. After he'd finished spraying down the mat and the surrounding wood planks, he returned inside and washed his hands. He changed his clothes, too, for good measure. When he joined Rachel in the kitchen, she was quietly sipping her second cup of coffee, gazing at her lap in obvious embarrassment. The last thing Colt wanted to do was have a heart-to-heart with her, but he needed to know she was okay. Rachel may have given him the single-finger salute more times than he could count, but June was right—she was good people. More or less.

He sat down opposite her at the table. "Did you and your mama have a fight?" Lord knows he wouldn't last five minutes living with his folks. They got along okay, but a man needed his space. "Is that why you don't wanna go home?"

She shook her head and gnawed on her bottom lip.

"You told me you couldn't face her," Colt said.

"You're not pregnant, are you? If so, you're off to a bad start with the cigarettes and the whiskey."

Peering into her coffee, she opened her mouth to answer him. But her voice came out low and pitiful in a way that made her sound like a little kid. "I couldn't stop him. Marcus Steele is putting up a Super Home Cheapo right outside town."

Colt drew a breath. That was worse than an unplanned pregnancy. He knew what it would mean for her family—Landry Building and Supply didn't stand a chance against the Home Cheapo. Nothing did. Mom and Pop shops like theirs couldn't compete. No matter how supportive the locals claimed to be, folks always gravitated toward the lowest price.

But Rachel had a spot on the town council. Colt figured that would've helped her block the big chain.

"I promised Mama I'd find a way to keep 'em out," Rachel went on, "but I couldn't do it. The bastards were too smart. Or maybe I was too stupid."

"What happened?" he asked. "I thought the council had to vote on anything that big."

"They do. Any retail store larger than five thousand square feet has to get approval before they can build." She glanced up at him. "But Steele got around it by splitting the supercenter three ways."

Colt raised his brows in a silent question.

"He's putting up three stores on the same lot," Rachel explained. "One for lumber, one for general hardware, and one for home goods. All right next to each other. And as fast as he builds them, they'll probably be open in the spring."

"Damn." What a dirty trick. "I'm sorry to hear that."

Colt remembered Rachel's words from earlier that evening. "You're right—he's a lizard-licking donkey sucker."

She laughed into her cup. "Steele's a clever son of a bitch, I'll give him that."

Colt leaned forward and folded his arms on the table. "What're you gonna do?"

"I'm not going down fighting," she said, wiping at the caked mascara beneath her eyes. "There's no point. I'll help Mama close down the store and sell off what we can before the Cheapo opens. The sooner the better—we won't have a lot of time. Daddy left her with enough savings when he passed, so she should be okay."

"What about you?" Colt asked. Rachel had worked in her parents' store since high school. When her daddy died, she'd taken over for him and married that loser, Tommy Robbins, instead of going away to college.

"I'll be okay too." She slouched, wrapping both hands around her mug. "I'm already living at home, so it's not like I've got much to lose. I'll figure out something." She drew a deep breath through her nose and held it a while, then let it out real slow. "I just don't know how I'm gonna break it to Mama."

If Mrs. Landry didn't know about the supercenter yet, she would soon. Nothing stayed quiet in this town. "She should probably hear it from you."

"I know."

Colt stood from the table and took Rachel's half-empty coffee cup. "Then let's get you home. She's only gonna worry if you stay out any later."

Rachel gave a weary nod, and Colt wished there was more he could do. She pushed to standing and took a sudden interest in her fingernails. "Thanks." She turned away and added, "For not locking me up and stuff. Maybe I don't completely hate your face."

Smiling, Colt set the mug in the sink and grabbed his keys. "You're not goin' soft on me, are you, Landry?"

She answered him with her middle finger.

*Yeah*, Colt thought, *she's gonna be all right*.

# Chapter 12

RACHEL PULLED A PLASTIC *GOING OUT OF BUSINESS!* SIGN from the store's shelf display and brushed her fingers over the glossy red lettering. "I always hated having to sell these—it meant someone's dream was dead. Never thought I'd need them myself." With a wistful sigh, she grabbed half a dozen more and passed them off to Leah. "At least we've got plenty in stock."

"You sure about this?" Leah asked. The flimsy signs felt like lead in her hands. She glanced over her shoulder at Rachel's mom, whose fingers flew over the keys of the same antique cash register her grandfather had christened with a wheat penny the day he'd opened this shop. Even though Mrs. Landry's voice sounded rough as asphalt from crying, she smiled and invited her customer to come back soon. But come back for what, the clearance sales? After bargain shoppers had picked the place clean, what would replace it, if anything? Was this the beginning of the end for Main Street?

A lump rose in Leah's throat. There was history here—years of memories in these narrow aisles. When couples married and bought their first fixer-uppers, they came to Landry Supply for everything from floor tiles to drawer pulls, and if Mrs. Landry didn't have it in stock, she'd special order it with free delivery. Leah had never thought about it before, but this humble store had helped transform every house in Sultry Springs into a home. It seemed wrong to let Marcus Steele win so easily.

After blotting her nose with a crumpled tissue, Rachel shrugged. "What're we gonna do? It's not like we can hogtie Marcus to my bumper and drag him down a gravel road." Before Leah could answer, Rachel went on, "Then strip him naked and dip him in the creek until he's covered in bloodsucking leeches." With an evil grin, she added, "Or spray him with deer pheromones and tie him to a log, bent over, so the bucks can violate his sorry ass all night long."

Leah couldn't help but giggle. Clearly, Rachel had given this some thought.

"That would take too much work," Leah said, faking a lazy shrug. "If you really want to get back at him, you should order a bunch of embarrassing stuff in his name, like male enhancement pills and a penis enlarger pump."

Rachel's eyebrows rose as a smile uncurled across her lips. "I like where you're going with this. I could subscribe him to some freaky-deaky magazines too."

"Along with some blow-up dolls...of sheep!" Assuming those even existed. "But mail it to his neighbor's house instead of his, so they have to hand-deliver it to him!"

Rachel lowered her voice and mimicked a British man, never mind that Steele Industries was headquartered in New York. "I say, Marcus, old chap, here's your deviant sexual paraphernalia. Let me know if those male enhancement pills work."

The mental image sent Leah into a fit of laughter. She braced herself against the wall, and when her belly started to ache, she collapsed onto a pile of sacks of concrete, doubling over in chortles. Rachel joined her, and together they giggled until they could barely breathe.

"Oh, god." Rachel wiped beneath her eyes and rested her head on Leah's shoulder. "I'm so glad you're here, Tink. I don't think I could do this without you."

Leah was glad too. If she couldn't stop the store from closing, at least she could lift her friend's spirits. "You're the strongest person I know, babe. You're going to be okay."

"Yeah," Rachel said, "I think I am."

"And now you can embrace your true destiny."

Rachel lifted her head and gave a questioning glance.

"As a back-up dancer," Leah explained. "Didn't I say your talents were wasted here?"

"Oh, totally. Just in time too." Rachel pushed to standing and performed a clumsy hip roll. "I heard they're making another *Magic Mike*."

"Sweet. I want to see what you'd do for a twenty."

"Be careful what you wish for," Rachel teased, hooking two fingers around her shirt lapel as if to tear it open. "'Cause I'll show you."

Leah shielded her eyes. "I take it back. All I've got on me is a ten."

"Never fear. A ten will get you plenty."

From nearby, a man cleared his throat and interrupted the striptease. "Uh, Rachel?"

They glanced down the aisle at old Mr. Phelps, the pharmacist, who studied them with a puzzled expression.

Rachel straightened and smoothed both hands over her shirt. "Hey, Mr. Phelps. How can I help you?"

He gestured out the front window to his store across

the street. "Just heard the news, and I wanted to stop by and tell you how sorry I am. Anything I can do?"

"Thanks, but no," Rachel told him. "Mama and I decided to go out on top."

Mr. Phelps nodded slowly, a flicker of fear sparking behind his bifocals. He and the other Main Street merchants were probably worried about their own fates. Rachel must've seen it, too, because she reassured him, "The council's already made sure this won't happen again. Any commercial outfit, no matter how big or small, has to make it past a committee now."

"Oh. Well, I suppose that's good." His withered form relaxed. He glanced at a display of emergency generators, turning the subject away from bankruptcy and heartbreak. "Been meaning to pick up one of these. Guess now's as good a time as any."

"We're getting ready to mark everything down," Rachel said. "If you wait till tomorrow, you'll save—"

"No," he interrupted, "I want one now. Big storm comin' later. I'll probably lose power, and I've got lots of orders to fill."

Leah gave him a smile. There were no storms on the horizon today, and anyone with a radio or television knew it.

Over the next few hours, other locals trickled in, claiming they wanted to get a head start on their Christmas shopping. They stocked up on power tools and paint supplies, each refusing the discount Rachel offered them. The community support warmed Leah's heart, and she couldn't stop Daddy's words from turning over in her mind: *Maybe it's time to make a life for yourself—here, at home, with the people who love you.*

Had she been too quick to dismiss the idea? Daddy and Rachel needed her. Could she say the same for anyone in Minnesota? She wasn't sure.

At noon, Rachel and Leah escaped to the stockroom, where two sack lunches awaited, complete with sandwiches, barbeque potato chips, and Mrs. Landry's oatmeal butterscotch cookies.

Rachel wore a smile as she tore into her turkey club and took a seat on a Rubbermaid bin. She asked with one cheek full, "So what'd you do last night? When I called, your dad said you went out, but he didn't say where." She popped open a Coke and took a deep pull. "June tried reaching you too. She only called Colt as a last resort."

Leah picked at the corner of her Ziploc baggie. She was in no mood to hear a laundry list of Colt's faults or endure a lecture about how men never changed. "I'll tell you," she decided, "but you have to promise not to give me any shit for it…pardon my language."

Rachel held up one hand in an oath. "No shit."

"I drove out to the hot springs to meet Colt, but he wasn't there. I guess by that time, he'd left to pick you up at Shooters." They must've missed each other by minutes.

"Oh," was all Rachel said before taking another bite of her sandwich.

"That's it?" She hadn't seriously expected Rachel to honor that *no shit* promise. "Just *oh*?"

"None of my business who you sneak around with," Rachel mumbled. "Besides, maybe he's not as bad as I thought."

"Whoa." In Rachelspeak, *not so bad* was a screaming endorsement—with pompoms waving and back flips. What had happened between those two last night? "Since when do you think Colt is anything less than the antichrist in cowboy boots?"

Rachel pointed her turkey club at Leah's nose. "Don't make a big deal out of it. I'm mature enough to admit when I'm wrong. All I'm sayin' is he's not so awful. That doesn't mean I want to braid Colt's hair and sing 'Kumbaya.'"

"Fine. Forget I asked," Leah said, grabbing her cardigan. "I'll get it from the horse's mouth." She'd planned to drop in on Colt and thank him, anyway. "I'm going to the sheriff's office real quick."

Rachel didn't take the bait. "Mm-kay. Have fun."

"I will." She pushed her arms through the sleeves as quickly as she could without snagging her watch. The mere prospect of seeing Colt had her insides all fluttery and her limbs twitching to run.

After gathering her sandwich and bottled water, Leah slipped out the back door and made her way around the side of the building to the sidewalk. To show her body who was boss, she slowed her pace and focused on the scents of grilled chicken and car exhaust, an oddly pleasant combination, and the cheery sounds of carols drifting though the pharmacy's open door. When the breeze kicked up, she tucked her water bottle beneath one arm and buttoned her sweater. Compared to Minnesota, where the first snow had already fallen, fifty degree weather should feel like a tropical vacation, but it didn't. Funny how quickly she'd acclimated to the mild Texas weather. If she stayed here much longer, she'd get spoiled…if she wasn't already. This wasn't an easy place to leave behind.

With Thanksgiving only days away, holiday

decorations were out in full force. Bright red bows adorned the tops of the streetlights, each one connected by strands of plastic garland leading to "The Square," where the town spruce would soon take up residence beside the fountain. As a little girl, she'd always looked forward to the tree-lighting ceremony. Daddy would say a few words asking folks to "remember the reason for the season," then offer a quick prayer before the mayor threw the switch. Afterward, families would line the sidewalk to watch the parade—nothing big or fancy, mostly an excuse for business owners to throw Tootsie Rolls to the children and mark Santa's arrival at the general store. If she closed her eyes, she could almost hear the high school band playing "Rudolph the Red-Nosed Reindeer."

God bless, she'd missed celebrating the holidays here. Just thinking about what she'd serve for Thanksgiving dinner put a spring in her step. She only wished Rachel and her mom would be in town to share it with them. Nothing beat a full table, bustling with laughter and conversation, except a friendly game of touch football on the front lawn afterward. Too bad Daddy wasn't ready for that yet.

A nasally voice from the street interrupted her reverie. "Hey there, Miss McMahon."

She glanced over and waved to a young deputy who'd rolled down his cruiser window. He crept along in time with her steps, slowing the line of cars behind him. She wondered how he recognized her, because they'd never met.

"You doin' okay?" he asked. "Need a hand, or a ride, or somethin'?"

"No, thanks. I'm good. Just taking a walk."

"Okay." He pointed to a black name badge she couldn't read from the sidewalk. "I'm Matt. Just holler if you need anything—anything at all." Then he grinned and added, "Be careful not to stub your toe," before rolling up his window and resuming his patrol.

*What?* He didn't even know her. What a strange man. She made a mental note to ask Colt about him, then jogged across the courthouse parking lot to the adjoining sheriff's building.

After taking a moment to fluff her hair, she climbed the front steps and tugged open the door, where she met Darla Jameson's wide brown gaze from the other side of the reception counter.

"Hiya, hon." Darla pushed a pen behind her ear and waved her red-tipped fingers. She wore a silky black top that fit her like a second skin...with an unlined bra underneath. And apparently, it was quite cold in here. If that wasn't bad enough, Darla's heart-shaped locket dangled an inch above a line of cleavage deep enough to hide an elephant. Did she always dress like this on the job?

From out of nowhere, a surge of envy knocked Leah's breath loose, and she had to mentally slap herself before she could return the greeting. She and Darla had never run in the same circles, but they weren't enemies. Leah had no reason to feel jealous of the busty blond bombshell... except for the fact that she worked directly under—

"Colt!" Darla shouted across the lobby. "Look who's here!"

Yes, Colt. She wondered if Darla had worked *under* him too. She turned and found the good sheriff, shoulder-to-shoulder with two deputies, decorating a battered artificial tree that had probably been around since the original Christmas. Colt had slung a rope of lights around his neck, and when his eyes met hers, his face glowed brighter than every bulb on the strand, his wide, answering smile wrinkling the tawny skin above his cheekbones. And he wasn't looking at Darla. He made Leah feel like the only woman in the room. Heck, in the county.

"What a nice surprise," he drawled, slow as honey and deeper than night.

Leah imagined herself melting into a puddle, right there on the checkerboard tile. Her Ziploc baggie plunked to the floor, and for the second time, she struggled to breathe. The war was over—her body had triumphed over her mind in a full-on blitz. It had shown *her* who was boss. How did Colt do it?

While she stood there like a lawn jockey, he detangled himself from the lights and joined her, then picked up her sandwich. He peered through the plastic and asked, "Turkey?"

"Uh-huh," she stammered. "And ham. Rachel's mom made it."

"Looks good."

She could only nod.

"If you're in the mood to share," he said, "we could eat in my office. Or if you want, we can go—"

From behind him, a deputy dropped a glass ornament and swore loudly.

"Hey!" Colt whipped off his Stetson and pointed it at the man. "Watch your mouth, all you bastards. There's a lady present."

Darla huffed and folded her arms beneath her gargantuan breasts. "What does that make me? I've been dodging your f-bombs for years."

Colt tossed his hat back on his head and gave Darla a teasing grin. "Aw, c'mon. You know you've got the dirtiest mouth in here."

Leah's stomach tightened. Just how familiar was Colt with that dirty mouth? Maybe it was time to quit pretending and admit the truth: Colt had plucked Darla more times than a West Virginia banjo. Leah squeezed her water bottle and tried not to picture them together—that was the old Colt. He'd apologized for his wild days, even though it was none of her business. He'd changed. She needed to remember that and leave the past where it belonged.

The offending deputy apologized to Leah while stretching high to place the tree topper—a Kermit the Frog hand puppet—on the highest branch.

"That's your topper?" Leah asked them, looking to the faces around her for some insight into the joke. Nobody was laughing.

Colt scratched the back of his neck and studied his boots.

"We used to put an angel up there," Darla said. "A long time ago. She was real pretty, with a white gown and hair down to her waist. But Colt made us pack it up when he got elected."

Colt's warm hand appeared at Leah's lower back. He muttered something about the separation of church and state while steering her toward his office. Once he'd maneuvered her well out of earshot, he admitted, "It made me think of you."

She wanted to tell Colt she'd had a living, breathing reminder of him for the past nine years, but she couldn't do it. Not until she was certain he'd leave Noah in peace. She shook those thoughts out of her head and said, "Well, at least buy a star. I like the Muppets and all, but Kermit looks ridiculous with a tree branch up his butt."

Colt ushered her inside his office and cleared a pile of paperwork from the chair opposite his desk. The masculine scent of his aftershave lingered in the tiny room, at once familiar and comforting. She'd missed that smell, especially when it came directly off his heated skin.

"I think I'll unpack the angel." He brushed his fingers casually down the back of her hair as she sat down. "No star could outshine her."

Her cheeks heated. "Want half my sandwich?"

"Sure."

She noticed him lower to his rolling chair without grimacing or bracing his hands on the desktop. He'd made pretty good progress. "You've been doing your stretches," she said, tipping her water at him.

"Every night, just like I promised. Been getting massages too. And you'll be happy to know I have an appointment with the chiropractor, even though I still don't believe in that mess." He pulled a handful of napkins from his side drawer, reminding Leah of her long-lost driver's license. But before she had a chance to ask him about it, he slid half the turkey club across the desk and stunned her with a hungry gaze that had nothing to do with lunch. "I won't be out at the springs tonight," he said, keeping their eyes locked. "Just in case you'd finally decided to meet me."

This time, more than just her cheeks heated. She

broke the static contact and took a bite of her sandwich, not tasting a thing. Once she swallowed, she peeked at him again. "I did come out. Last night."

"You did?"

"Mmm-hmm. But you were already gone."

He sat back, seemingly pleased to hear it. "Sorry I missed you."

"It wasn't by much." Which made her remember the real reason for this visit. "Thanks, by the way. For taking care of Rachel. I know she's never been your biggest fan, and if she was drunk, she probably didn't go easy on you."

Colt finished his half of the sandwich in two massive bites, then gave a dismissive shrug much like Rachel had done. "Wasn't so bad."

Leah laughed dryly. "Did you two rehearse lines? That's exactly what she said about you."

"She doing okay?"

"Pretty much. She and her mama are headed out of town for Thanksgiving. I think it'll be good for them. You know, get out of Dodge for a while, away from the reminders." When he nodded in agreement, she asked, "How about you? Are you going to Oklahoma for the weekend?"

"Nah." He removed his hat and set it on the desk, then refastened his ponytail. "Avery and Emma are riding up with Granddaddy and Pru. I'm scheduled for patrol."

That surprised her. Wasn't the biggest perk of being the boss the freedom to take off whenever you wanted? "You mean the sheriff has to work on Thanksgiving?"

He laughed and gestured toward the county jail at the rear of the building. "Wouldn't you know it, the criminals don't observe federal holidays. But I don't mind. Gives the other guys a chance to be with their families."

If her heart hadn't already melted, that would've done it. "That's sweet of you."

"Besides, I'm only working a half day."

She imagined Colt all alone in his kitchen, cooking up the steak and baked potato she'd seen in his Sack-n-Pay basket a couple weeks ago. "You know," she said, "it's just me and Daddy this year, so I'm only cooking a breast instead of a whole turkey. But there'll be plenty to go around if you want to join us."

A flicker of happiness flashed behind his aquamarine eyes. "You sure?"

"Absolutely."

"Then it's a date."

The word "date" made her feel equal parts cautious and giddy. She didn't know how to label what was going on between the two of them, but *dating* wasn't it. In an effort to make the invitation more casual, she told him, "You can bring the mashed potatoes. Dinner rolls too. And don't expect anything fancy. I'm too nervous to use Mama's china, so we'll eat off the Corelle."

"Hell, I'll bring paper plates if you want," he said. "But do we get to eat at the table?"

"Of course." Where else would they eat Thanksgiving supper?

"Good." A sinful grin lifted the corners of his mouth. "'Cause I do love eatin' at that table. Everything tastes so damn good on there."

Leah stared into her lap and bit her lip to hide a smile, feeling bashful but not the least bit ashamed for what they'd done. She wasn't sure if inviting Colt back into her kitchen was a wise idea, but she knew this: she didn't regret it. For once in her life, she'd given Colt more than she should, and she wasn't sorry.

"Let me take you to lunch," he said. "We can hit the diner, or I can fix something at my place. I'm not half-bad in the kitchen."

No doubt. But she was pretty sure lunch at Colt's house wouldn't involve food. And judging by the wolf-ish set of his grin, he wouldn't stop at third base this time. Was she ready for that?

*He made you sorry before*, a small voice warned. *And you never saw it coming.*

She ignored the words and reminded herself to let go of the past. She'd made mistakes too—far worse than playing kiss-and-tell in the boys' locker room. One day, she'd have to confess the truth about Noah, and how could she expect forgiveness from Colt if she wasn't prepared to offer it in return?

But despite her bold resolve, she declined his lunch offer. For whatever reason, she wasn't hungry anymore.

# Chapter 13

ONCE THE BUTTER MELTED AND DANCED IN THE skillet, Leah tossed in a cup of diced onions, instantly filling the kitchen with a loud sizzle and a savory aroma. She added the garlic and celery, then left them to sauté while she fished inside the refrigerator for the spicy ground sausage that would make this recipe pop. Was it heart-healthy? No. But her mouth watered at the mingling of bold flavors, and a few bites wouldn't hurt anyone.

"Smells good," Daddy hollered from the living room. "What'cha making?"

"Mama's stuffing." Which she hadn't planned on serving until a couple of days ago. The same was true for the pecan pie in the freezer. She tried telling herself these last-minute additions to the menu had nothing to do with her desire to impress Colt, but a smile ghosted her lips when she imagined how he'd go back for seconds and thirds, then whisper that not even his step-granny's cooking held a candle to Leah's. The way he savored each bite—eyes closed, leaning back in his chair with one hand over his heart—made her feel special. And who didn't like feeling special? In fact, maybe she should whip up some sweet pumpkin butter for the rolls.

From the living room, Daddy turned on the Macy's Thanksgiving Day Parade loud enough for her to overhear that the Snoopy balloon had sprung a leak and was headed for a full-body collision with Spider-Man. The reporter's enthusiasm for each float was infectious, quickening Leah's pulse and filling her mind with images of Christmastime. When the festivities segued into a JCPenney Black Friday jingle, Daddy joined her in the kitchen.

"Anything I can do?" he asked, leaning casually against the fridge.

Leah slid him a glance. Something was up. Daddy had always considered himself allergic to cooking, hence the drive-through diet that'd landed him in the hospital. If his congregation hadn't stepped up after Mama died, Leah would've grown up on Hamburger Helper and Spam sandwiches. She pointed to the stove and said, "Sure. You can brown the sausage while I marinate the turkey," but she didn't expect him to stick around long.

He cut off one end of the sausage tube, then squeezed it into the skillet while Leah gathered the seasonings she needed from the pantry. For several minutes, he focused on his task, silently pushing a wooden spatula back and forth across the pan. He cleared his throat a couple of times as if to speak, but hesitated and went back to work.

Something was definitely wrong.

"You okay?" she asked.

He licked his lips and stared at the sausage. "I've been thinkin'…"

"I *thought* I smelled something burning," she teased.

Her attempt to loosen him up didn't work. It took him two more tries before he finally said in a rush, "I think it's time Colton knew the truth about Noah."

Leah's stomach tried to escape her body by way of her throat. She tried to stay calm while fetching the turkey breast from the fridge, but she plunked it onto the counter loud enough to rattle the porcelain cookie jar beside the sink.

"Absolutely not. It's too soon."

"Just hear me out," Daddy said over the sizzle and crackle of sausage fat. "That's all I'm asking."

"Won't make any difference. I know what's best for my son."

Daddy shrugged. "If your mind's already made up, then there's no harm in hearing me out, is there?"

"Suit yourself." She busied her hands unwrapping the turkey, unable to look Daddy in the eyes any longer.

"Look," Daddy said, "we both know Colt acted the fool. I watched him do it. Every time he fell down drunk or got in a fight, I told myself we'd done the right thing. He even streaked the mayor's inauguration—buck-naked, wearing a wrestler's mask—but everyone knew it was him because he's got angel wings tattooed on his backside. What kind of father sets an example like that?"

Leah glanced at him, wondering where Daddy was going with this. His story only proved that neither she nor Colt were ready for parenthood back then.

"I kept on following the talk about Colt," Daddy went on, "even though I preach against gossip. I couldn't get enough." He pointed the wooden spatula at her. "You know why I did that?"

She shook her head.

"Neither did I, till recently." He broke their gaze as if ashamed. "I think I knew—deep down in my soul—that keeping your secret wasn't right, and I needed to justify what I'd done. All those dirty stories about Colt's drinking and hell-raising and running around made me feel like I'd committed the lesser of two evils." He turned his attention back to the skillet. "But two wrongs don't make a right."

"No, they don't," Leah agreed. "But it's not that simple. The right thing for Noah wasn't the right thing for me and Colt."

"But he changed," Daddy said. "Years ago. The gossip dried up, and all my excuses died with it. I tried ignoring Colt, but I couldn't ignore my conscience. Because I didn't just wrong that boy, Pumpkin." With rounded shoulders and a face full of contrition, he added, "I wronged you too."

Leah's fingers froze around the cellophane. Wronged her? Daddy had never been anything less than loving and supportive. "What do you mean?"

"When you came to me all those years ago," he said, staring at the stovetop, "and asked for help running off to Minnesota, I should've told you no. You were young and scared—you didn't understand the gravity of giving away that baby. I was the adult. It was my job to make the right choice."

"I knew what I was doing," Leah insisted. "And it *was* the right choice—for Noah."

Daddy shook his head. "You were only seventeen. And my reasons for letting you go weren't as pure as I led both of us to believe."

She didn't understand. "Then why'd you do it?"

"I was worried about my reputation," he admitted. "What would the congregation think if they found out my teenage daughter was pregnant by the town degenerate? Would the elders believe I was fit to run the church if I couldn't even run my own family?" He hung his bald head.

"I made my decision out of pride, not what was best for you or that baby. And certainly not what was best for Colt."

Leah stared at her daddy for several long beats.

His pride? *That* was why he'd agreed to send her away? A spark of anger flushed her cheeks when she imagined what might have been. If Daddy had insisted on keeping her home, she never would've placed Noah with another family. She'd have her boy in her arms right now. Everything would be different.

*Including Noah*, her conscience reminded her. *He'd be different too. You and Colt weren't ready. What would your immaturity have done to him?*

Just like that, her anger died. It might be easier to blame her heartache on Daddy, but everything had happened for the best. She had to believe that.

"Noah's better off for it." That's what mattered most.

"Maybe," Daddy said. "Maybe not. But it wasn't our choice to make. Colt should've had a say."

Leah rinsed her hands in the sink, then dried them and gave Daddy's shoulder a gentle pat. "We both did the best we could. We can't go back."

"I know." He turned off the burner and shifted the skillet away from the heat. "But we can set things right. Colt's a good man. I think it's time to tell him the truth and face whatever consequences come from it."

Leah understood his burden—for almost a decade, she'd felt the cold weight of guilt like a layer of ice around her heart. But she'd gladly bear the pain for the rest of her life if the truth put Noah at risk. She returned to the sink and absently gazed out the window to the carport. "Colt's got legal connections. What if he tries to take Noah away?"

Daddy countered at once, as if he'd anticipated her argument. "No judge in his right mind is gonna remove a nine-year-old boy from the only family he's ever known."

"You can't guarantee that."

"I quit lying to myself, hon." Daddy gripped her upper arms and turned her to face him. "Now it's your turn."

Leah tugged her brows down low. "What's that supposed to mean?"

"Are you really scared that Colt's gonna rip Noah away from his parents?" Daddy demanded softly. "Or are you more afraid that Colt won't forgive you for what you've done?"

Her jaw dropped. How could he possibly think her motivations were that selfish?

"I've seen the way you look at him," Daddy said. "Ask yourself if all this talk about keeping Noah safe with the Ackermans isn't your way of avoiding the real issue—you don't want to lose Colt."

"That's not it!" she insisted.

"You sure about that?" The question was rhetorical. She knew he wouldn't listen, no matter how she answered. "Just give it some thought. Really search your feelings."

Great, now he was channeling Obi-Wan Kenobi.

"If you and Colt are meant to be," Daddy said, "then he'll find a way to move past it."

*I wouldn't forgive me*, she started to say, but changed her mind because she didn't want Daddy thinking all she cared about was Colt's forgiveness.

"Eventually, you've got to tell him." Daddy lifted her chin and gave her a sad smile. "The longer you wait, the worse it'll be for both of you."

But what about the Ackermans? She'd lied to them, too, when she'd claimed not to know who fathered her baby. If Colt hired a lawyer and raised Cain, would they retaliate by cutting her off from Noah? They could do it—she didn't have any legal rights to see her own son.

*Neither does Colt*, she chided herself. *You've never cared about his rights. Maybe this is what you deserve.*

*No.* She closed her eyes and shook her head. She couldn't believe that. Her motivations had always been pure—Colt and the Ackermans wouldn't punish her so hurtfully for wanting to give Noah the best life possible.

At least she didn't think they would. She had no way of knowing for sure.

Daddy left her with a kiss on the temple and returned to the living room, where boisterous, cheery parade noises rang out in contrast to her now-dark mood. In a daze, Leah measured spices and oil, mixing a sloppy marinade, as her mind reeled with impossible questions.

Was Daddy right—should she tell Colt now and rip off the Band-Aid? Daddy had a point when he said it would only get harder with time, and in all honesty, a judge probably wouldn't remove Noah from his home, not at his age. But a persistent burning inside her chest warned her to reconsider. Something about the hypothetical confession felt wrong, and not just because she feared losing Colt's friendship. Her thoughts traveled in circles, and by the time she slid the turkey in the oven, she was more confused than ever.

So much for her perfect holiday.

"Thanks, Colt." Avery fisted the lapels of her ratty pink bathrobe and slumped against the doorjamb. She coughed and then immediately winced, pressing a hand against her lower belly. After a long groan, she murmured, "I hope you didn't have big plans."

Big plans? Nah. Just winning over the love of his life before she got bored and returned to her rich ex-fiancé in Minnesota, that's all.

At his hesitation, Avery nodded at Emma and said, "Just take her with you."

From beside him on the front stoop, Emma tugged his jacket hem, bouncing to the rhythm of her shouts. "Tur-key day! Tur-key day!" She beamed up at him. "It's turkey day, Uncle Colt! Can we have chicken nuggets? I want a Happy Meal, but not with a boy prize. I want the girl prize, the My Little Pony with the pink tail."

"Uh-huh," Colt said absently. "Whatever you want, hon." He raised his hand to indicate his sister's waxen, dewy forehead. "You sure this isn't contagious? The preacher's still recovering, and I don't wanna risk his ticker by giving him a virus."

"Trust me, there's no way he can get this," Avery promised. She leaned in and whispered, "I got a raging bladder infection from this banana-flavored lube Mike used last weeken—"

"Holy shit!" Colt covered his ears and shut his eyes, desperately trying not to picture his sister fooling around with her boyfriend's banana, or any of his other parts for that matter. Why couldn't she save those details for her friends? "For the millionth time, that skeeves me out!"

"Ho-ly shit!" Emma chanted with balled fists. "Ho-ly

shit!" She stomped her feet, triggering the lights inside
her sneaker soles.

Avery narrowed her eyes and shot him the death
glare. Great, so he couldn't swear around the kid, but
mentioning sex toys was hunky-dory? Talk about
screwed-up logic.

"I need to go to the bathroom again," Avery said, then
bent to give Emma a kiss. When Avery stood, she reminded him, "No caffeine and go easy on the sugar, okay?
I don't have the energy for a bedtime battle tonight."

"Got it." Colt gave Emma's brown ponytail a gentle
tug. "Ready to roll, monkey face?"

"Are we goin' to McDonald's?" The front door
clicked shut, and Emma wrapped her sticky fingers
around his hand, skipping down the steps toward his
cruiser. "The one with the ball pit?"

"Nope, someplace even better."

"Better than McDonald's?" she asked, as if such a
thing weren't possible. "But they have sundaes." She
scrunched up her brow and added, "And a slide that
makes my hair stick up when I come down it."

Ah, yes, The Shocker. Colt remembered that godforsaken
instrument of torture from the few times he'd taken Emma
out for lunch. "Remember my friend Miss McMahon?"

"The one with the pretty princess hair?"

"Yep." Angel hair, but whatever. "We're going to her
house for dinner. Doesn't that sound like fun?"

While he opened the car door for her, Emma considered his question, sucking her bottom lip and staring at
her rhinestone-studded jeans in deep thought. After he'd
installed her booster and helped fasten the seat belt, she
asked, "Will there be other kids there?"

"Well, no. But that means you get Miss Leah all to yourself." He'd give anything for that privilege.

The prospect didn't seem to float Emma's boat, but Colt didn't much care. He shut the door and jogged around the cruiser's front end, then smiled, realizing how long it'd been since he'd managed a run, albeit a slow one. He hated to admit it, but Leah was right about the chiropractor. If one adjustment had made this much of a difference, he couldn't wait to see how he'd feel after a few more.

After only twenty seconds, the inside of the cruiser smelled like peanut butter, Emma's signature scent. Colt began to wonder if she dabbed a little Skippy behind her ears and on the insides of her wrists each morning before she got dressed.

"Can we take your motorcycle instead?" Emma asked, planting her dirty sneakers on his glove box.

He pointed at her feet in a silent message, and she dropped them to the floor. "Your mama would string me up by my heels. Besides," he hitched a thumb toward the back, "I'm bringing mashed potatoes and rolls. How're we gonna carry all that on the Harley?"

She tapped her chin and stared out the window at a field of tall brown cornstalks. "I know!" she declared. "We'll put 'em in backpacks. I've got a Dora one, and it holds lots of stuff."

"Okay," Colt said, playing along. "But there's still the issue of your mama killing me when she finds out I put you on my bike."

Emma shrugged. "That's easy. We won't tell her."

Poor Avery was going to have her hands full with this one. Hell, she had her hands full now—Colt shuddered to imagine Emma as a teenager. With any luck, she wouldn't turn out too much like her uncle. Otherwise, Avery should go ahead and invest in a distillery, maybe stock up on Valium too.

"No deal," he told her. "Your mom and I are on the same team, monkey. We don't keep secrets from each other."

Emma switched gears right away, filling the silence with knock-knock jokes that made no sense but cracked her up regardless. By the time they parked on the driveway behind Bruiser and made their way to Leah's front door, Emma was so slap-happy she'd laughed her own ponytail loose.

He tried gently tugging her hair back in place while Emma punched the doorbell, but that only made it worse. Her head resembled a windblown haystack when the preacher answered the door.

"Well, who do we have here?" Pastor Mac said to Emma with a wide grin.

She responded with an enthusiastic, "Uncle Colt said I get Miss Leah all to myself!"

Colt chuckled and lifted his Pyrex dish in Emma's direction. "Hope you don't mind. My sister's under the weather, so she canceled her trip at the last minute."

"Course not." Pastor Mac stepped aside and opened the door for them. "The more the better. Leah made enough food for half the county."

Colt led the way into the living room, where the air was thick with the aroma of pecan pie and roasted bird. Even better, Pastor Mac had turned on the Texas A&M game. No Thanksgiving felt complete without a little pigskin action. Colt had just started to check the score when Leah padded in from the kitchen and tore his attention away from football. National pastime or not, no man in his right mind would prefer watching a huddle of sweaty athletes instead of Leah.

At the sight of her, his chest went all hot and prickly. She'd pulled her long waves into a twist with a tiny flower pinned behind one ear, and she wore the same knee-length black dress as her first day in town, but paired with a long silver necklace and matching earrings. A dusting of pink blush on the apples of her cheeks accentuated a timid smile that Colt returned in full force. Lord, she looked lovely. He was glad he'd taken the time to return home after his shift to change into khakis and his best sweater, otherwise he'd feel like a fool sitting beside her in his uniform.

"Here," she said, reaching for the bowl of mashed potatoes. "Let me take that."

Colt handed off the dish, and once Leah's arms were occupied, he snuck a lingering kiss on her jaw, right below her earlobe. He made sure to whisper, "Angel, you look good enough to eat," before pulling back and noticing the goose bumps that had puckered her skin. He wished they were alone so he could spread those chills all over.

She blinked a few times, then noticed Emma. Leah's eyes widened in surprise, but she didn't hesitate to crouch down and greet the crazy-haired-peanut-butter princess. While the girls gushed over each other's clothes, Colt reclaimed the potatoes and took them into the kitchen along with the rolls. Once there, he helped Pastor Mac arrange all the covered dishes in the center of the oak table and left him to carve the turkey breast. When Colt returned to the living room, Emma was seated on the floor in front of the sofa, head tipped back while Leah smoothed her unruly mane with a wide paddle brush and refastened her ponytail.

Once the up-do was complete, Emma faced her stylist and patted her head with explorative fingers. "Can you fix it like yours?"

"I will after supper," Leah said, standing from the sofa. "I worked hard on all that food, and I don't want to eat it cold."

Emma jutted out her bottom lip, but didn't argue as she dragged her feet into the kitchen. Everyone settled at the table—Leah and her daddy at opposite ends with Colt and Emma together on one side. It felt wrong watching the preacher sink into the same chair where Colt had feasted on the old guy's daughter, and he wondered how often Leah thought of that day. If she remembered now, she didn't show it. She kept her eyes downcast as she took Colt's hand for grace.

He grasped her cool fingers and discreetly brushed his thumb along her wrist while taking Emma's left hand. With her right, Emma linked fingers with Pastor Mac, who blessed the meal.

After *amen*, Emma announced, "That's not how my mamma says it. And she does this when she's done," then crossed herself backward.

"Avery went to Catholic school," Colt explained while spreading Emma's napkin in her lap. "Well, I suppose I did too, but only for a couple of semesters." He didn't mention they'd expelled him after he got busted behind the cafeteria with both hands under the cheer captain's skirt.

"There's no wrong way to thank the Lord for His

bounty," Pastor Mac said to Emma while he handed the platter of sliced turkey to Colt.

"For paper towels?" Emma asked.

Colt snorted a laugh. "Bounty just means a lot of something."

"Oh."

He speared a chunk of breast meat and set it on his niece's plate. She wrinkled her nose and objected, "I don't like turkey. I want chicken nuggets." Then, turning those wide brown eyes on him, added, "You promised, Uncle Colt."

He hesitated and darted a glance at Leah, who studied him silently from above her glass of iced tea as if waiting to see how he'd handle the situation. "Uh," he began, turning back to Emma, "Miss Leah's a real good cook, hon. Maybe the best in Texas. You don't want—"

"I don't like turkey!"

Colt recognized the edgy whine in Emma's voice, the one that said she'd stayed up too late playing her Nintendo DS and woke up with the sun to watch SpongeBob reruns. Trying to reason with her would only make it worse. If he wanted any peace, he'd have to trek to the nearest McDonald's for that pink pony. It was worth the trouble for an hour or two of silence.

He started to push away from the table when Leah nudged him hard with her foot. He froze and gave her a questioning glance.

"We have a rule in this house," Leah said, mostly talking to Emma, "that I only make one supper, and that's what we eat." She swept a hand toward the cluster of covered dishes. "We've got turkey, stuffing, mashed potatoes, gravy, green bean casserole, baked apples, and rolls. Out of all this, there's got to be something you like." When Emma drew a breath to argue, Leah cut her off. "And if not, I won't make you eat it. But this is our supper, and your Uncle Colt deserves to sit down and enjoy it."

Colt gaped at Leah until she nudged him again and he added, "Uh, yeah. I'm not going anywhere."

Emma's brows formed a V and she went boneless, slouching down in her chair and glaring across the room. Leah ignored her and asked Colt to pass the turkey. When a few minutes passed and nobody paid Emma any heed, she began kicking the vacant chair across from her.

"Emma," Leah said firmly, holding a forkful of stuffing an inch from her lips. "If you don't stop, you'll have to leave the table. And that'd be a shame, because I really wanted to talk to you about which Disney princess I'd trade places with if I could." She shrugged as if it made no difference to her either way and slid the bite into her mouth.

And, hot damn, if that didn't do the trick. Emma didn't exactly bounce to attention, but she quit kicking the chair and straightened her spine. Colt filled her plate with a few bites of everything before doing the same for himself, on a much larger scale, and passing each dish to the left. After a few minutes, Emma picked at a buttered roll while sliding sideways glances at Leah.

"Which one would you pick?" Emma asked, then bit off a chunk.

When Leah answered, "Ariel," it was in a chipper voice, like the battle of wills had never happened. "I've always wanted to be a mermaid. How about you?"

"Jasmine," she said with a cheek full of bread. "'Cause she's got her own flying carpet and a pet tiger. I think it'd be cool to have a pet tiger."

"She has a monkey too," Leah added. "Don't forget Abu."

"Oh, yeah. That's double cool."

As far as Colt knew, they might as well have been speaking Dutch, but he grinned and tried to follow along while he savored his supper. The turkey was perfect—not dry like most white meat—and the stuffing was so dadgum delicious he wanted to make love to it. Leah had skills, that was for damn sure. And not just in the kitchen. She handled Emma like a pro. She'd make a great mama one day.

When the preacher suggested they go around the table and share what they were grateful for, it didn't take Colt half a second to come up with his answer. He faced Leah and drawled with a teasing smile, "Old friends and Richman's éclairs."

He expected her to blush or giggle, maybe offer a witty comeback, but her answering grin wavered and a shadow seemed to pass behind her pale blue eyes. He'd seen her with this far-off look a few times since she returned to town, and he wondered for the thousandth time what made her so sad.

A frightening possibility came to mind. What if she was heartsick over that asshole doctor? If she loved him enough to accept his proposal, it might take a while to get over him. Colt only hoped the guy wouldn't take her back, because while Colt didn't deserve Leah, her ex deserved her even less.

Leah had just begun to speak when an obnoxious

chiming from the sideboard interrupted her. Colt glanced over his shoulder and found the source of the noise, a black iPad with the words *swipe to unlock* illuminated on the screen. Figuring Leah had a call, Colt reached for the tablet so he could hand it to her.

"No!" she shouted, leaping from her seat so fast she knocked over her glass of tea. Liquid rushed the length of the table while ice cubes plunked to the floor, but she ignored the mess and bolted to the sideboard to snatch her iPad and silence it.

What the hell was up with that?

She must have sensed his confusion, because she offered a shaky laugh and tucked the device inside one of the sideboard drawers. "I never take calls at supper. It's rude."

Colt's bullshit detector had never led him astray, and it was blaring a red alert so loud it distracted him from the tea dripping into his lap. He was no dummy. Leah didn't want him to know who'd just called, and that could only mean one thing: it was the doctor. And if the two were talking again, it probably meant they were toying with the idea of getting back together.

Absently, he scooted back and helped Leah dab at the mess until they'd soaked up the tea and resumed their supper. But it wasn't the same after that. An awkward silence hung over the table like a pestering cloud of mosquitoes. Emma must have sensed it too, her prattle a bit less animated than it'd been a few minutes earlier. She didn't even ask if she could play Angry Birds on Leah's iPad, which showed epic restraint on her part.

After dinner, Colt helped Leah clear the table and hunt down matching lids and plastic containers for the leftovers while Pastor Mac ushered Emma into the living room for a game of Chutes and Ladders. While they worked together, Colt tried to lighten the mood with an occasional joke or a casual brush of fingers along the back of Leah's neck. But each step closer somehow pushed him farther from his goal—she'd soften to him and then go wistful again. Colt's instincts told him to step up his game or risk losing what ground he'd won over the past few weeks. He'd been kicking around an idea recently; maybe it was time to put that plan into action.

"Hey." He stopped her en route to the fridge and took the green beans. "I've got the day off tomorrow. Let's do something."

When she pressed her lips together, he knew she was thinking of an excuse to say no.

"I've been working on a surprise," he went on. "I know you don't like surprises, but I promise this is a good one."

She stared at her tiny bare feet, a lock of blond hair springing free from her twist. "I don't know…"

Tucking the strand behind her ear, he set the leftovers on the counter. "Look at me," he said softly, then tipped her chin with his thumb. "I just want to spend some time together. That's all. No shenanigans, and I'll take you home whenever you want. You've got nothing to worry about, I swear."

She seemed to turn that over in her mind, chewing the inside of her cheek while searching his face.

"You can trust me," he added with an encouraging nod.

That didn't help. If anything, it made her hesitate further, forcing him to bust out the big guns.

"Please, Angel?" He bent at the knees, lowering until their eyes met. With one hand, he cradled her face while settling the other at her waist. "Just a few hours? That's all I'm asking."

A few seconds later, she agreed in a whisper, "All right. But I wish you'd stop calling me that. I've done things, Colt. You don't know—"

"We both made mistakes." He kissed one cheek and then the other. "If there was a prize for biggest screw-up, I'd take home a trophy so wide you could swim in it. But that's in the past. Let's focus on the now, okay?"

She nodded, but wouldn't meet his gaze. He didn't care if another man was on her mind. At least she'd agreed to come out with him, and that was an opportunity Colt wouldn't waste. He'd worked too hard and come too close to give up without fighting for Leah's heart. Time to turn it up a notch and make her forget Dr. Dickweed ever existed.

His whole future hinged on tomorrow night.

"I'll pick you up at six."

# Chapter 14

"I'm going to tell him tonight," Leah said into her iPad while scanning her closet for the right outfit to wear. Not that it mattered. Colt wouldn't give a crap whether her belt matched her shoes once she smashed his heart and ruined any chance of a future between them. "I can't put it off any longer."

Rachel paused on the other end of the line. "Probably for the best. Are you nervous?"

Leah laughed without humor. "You could say that." She'd had to tuck a paper towel in her back pocket so she could blot her sweaty palms every five minutes. And she kept forgetting to breathe. She'd darn near passed out twice this morning. "I'll feel a lot better once it's over and done with."

"I bet," Rachel said. "Wish I was there to help. Call me and let me know how it goes. I'm channeling all my good mojo in your direction."

Leah needed more than good mojo. She needed a full-on miracle, complete with a resurrection because her heart was pounding hard enough to bruise a rib and puncture both lungs.

The doorbell rang, and Leah pushed aside her bedroom curtain to peer at the front stoop. She spotted a distended belly, two puffy bare legs, and a pair of flip-flops straining beneath swollen feet. "June's here," she told Rachel. "Gotta go."

"Good luck," Rachel added before disconnecting.

When Leah answered the door, it was to June and a bonus visitor, Bobbi Lewis, who'd managed to hide behind her sister-in-law's considerable girth.

"Mornin'." Leah greeted them with a tentative smile. Bobbi always made her nervous, and today was no exception.

But instead of picking apart Leah with her shrewd gaze, Bobbi wrapped an arm around June's shoulders and asked, "Can we come in for a minute?" Now that Leah paid attention, she noticed the concern on Bobbi's face.

"Of course." Leah led them into the living room and motioned to the sofa. Daddy had left to meet his associate pastor for coffee, so they had the house to themselves. "You want something to drink?" She ran through a mental list of beverages suitable for an expectant mother. "Milk? Herbal tea, maybe? Or I can put on some decaf."

"No, thanks." June gripped the armrest and gradually lowered herself into an open-legged sitting position, then cradled her belly with both hands as if her body couldn't support the added weight. The poor thing needed an elastic pregnancy belt. "I'm here to take you up on your offer, if it's still okay."

A moment passed before Leah recalled what she'd offered her friend. "Oh, you want me to check your blood pressure?"

"If you don't mind," June said. "The doctor's office is closed and it's twenty minutes to Sultry Memorial."

"You feeling okay?"

"Yep."

"Any vision problems or tingling in your hands?" Leah asked.

"No, I'm fine." June patted her tummy and nodded at Bobbi. "Bo's giving me a hard time, and I just want some peace of mind, you know?"

"Absolutely." Pregnancy had a way of drawing out each woman's inner neurotic. Once the seed of worry was planted, it only took moments to blossom into full-blown panic.

"Well, look how swollen she is," Bobbi said, pointing at June's ankles. "That can't be normal."

"Let me get my bag and we'll see." Leah returned to her bedroom for her stethoscope and cuff, then settled on the sofa beside June and took her blood pressure. A couple of minutes later, she announced, "One ten over seventy. Perfectly normal."

June grinned at her sister-in-law and chirped, "See?" while Bobbi continued pointing at the irrefutable evidence.

"Are you watching your sodium?" Leah asked. "And staying off your feet?"

"Mmm-hmm."

Though there was no logical reason behind it, Leah couldn't shake the feeling that Bobbi was right. "Check with your doctor on Monday, just to be safe."

June thanked her and settled back against the couch, clearly in no mood to hoist herself to standing anytime soon. "How about you? What're you up to today?"

"Did you hit the Black Friday sales?" Bobbi asked, still standing by the door.

Leah took a seat on the arm of Daddy's recliner. "I'm more of a Cyber Monday kind of gal."

"Me too," Bobbi said. "It takes a lot more than fifty percent off to get me out of bed before dawn."

Leah imagined most women wouldn't get out of bed at all if they were married to Trey Lewis, but it seemed inappropriate to say so. Bobbi must have known she was thinking naughty thoughts, because those green eyes scanned her face for several long beats.

"You all right?" Bobbi asked. "You look ready to jump out of your skin."

No, she wasn't all right, and Leah didn't have the energy to pretend otherwise. She decided to tell the truth—half of it, anyway—since the whole town would find out soon enough. "I've got a date tonight with Colt."

Bobbi gasped and covered her mouth with one hand, then wildly shook the other while she jumped in place. A lot of squealing followed. She was so excited that Leah didn't have the heart to tell her this first date would also be the last. Then the questions and comments came from both sides, each in rapid fire succession.

"That's awesome!"

"I knew it!"

"Where's he taking you?"

"What time?"

"What're you wearing?"

Leah couldn't stop herself from smiling as she held up a hand to silence them. All the estrogen in the air made her feel normal again. "He's coming at six, and I don't know where we're going. He said it's a surprise."

June placed a hand over her chest. "That's so romantic."

"You have to let me do your hair," Bobbi said, swirling her hands in the air to mimic whatever elaborate style she'd envisioned. She shook her head and decided, "No, we won't put it up. Then he can't run his fingers through it. Let's go with a half-do. I'll pin up a few

strands around your face and leave the rest down—
maybe enhance your natural wave."

June nodded. "That'll look nice. And just a touch of
eye makeup."

"Keep it light," Bobbi agreed, tipping her head and
studying her subject. "And nothing on the lips except a
little gloss. Heavy lipstick's not kissable."

"As if *that* would stop him," June said with a laugh.

"True." Bobbi grinned at Leah. "We could send you
out in a potato sack and smear mud all over your face
and it wouldn't matter. He's over the moon for you."

*He won't be for much longer.*

"Has been for years," June added with a dreamy sigh.
"I'm glad you decided to give him a second chance."

*A second chance…*

The words settled at the bottom of Leah's conscience
and turned over and over, sparking a realization. Didn't
everyone deserve a clean slate after making a mistake?
Even herself? She'd forgiven Colt, so why wouldn't he
do the same for her? Maybe she shouldn't be so quick
to make assumptions. By automatically expecting Colt
to hate her, she was choosing to believe the worst about
him, and that wasn't fair.

"I am too," Leah said, resolving to think positively.
"Want to help me figure out what to wear? I'd rather not
go out in a potato sack."

—–∿∿–—

At six o'clock on the button, two hours after her friends
had left, the nearby rumble of a high-performance engine announced Colt's arrival. Leah grabbed her purse
and paused at the door for a quick prayer.

*Please give me strength to do what's right. And if it's not too much to ask, soften Colt's heart. Let him forgive me.*

The words left her with a feeling of peace that vanished as soon as she stepped outside and caught a glimpse of her date. Lord help her, Colt was more stunning than she'd ever seen him, and that was saying a lot.

He was impeccably dressed in a jet black tuxedo, the starched white shirt a perfect contrast against his dark skin. Creased trousers hugged his long, muscular legs and led to a pair of wingtips polished to a high gleam that reflected the setting sun. He'd smoothed back his hair into a low ponytail, ever-so-slightly tussled from the open air ride to her house. With a dazzling grin, he strode toward her and extended an extra motorcycle helmet.

"Honey," he drawled, "you look gorgeous."

Leah wiped both palms on her khaki pants before she took his helmet and gestured at her coordinated sweater set. "I think I should change."

"No, don't." He joined her on the top step and settled a hand on her lower back. Leaning down, he kissed her cheek in a teasing brush of lips that brought a flush to her skin. "I've got it all taken care of."

"You've got clothes for me?"

"Mmm-hmm."

He didn't elaborate, only offered a sly grin as he interlaced their fingers and led her down the steps to his Harley parked on the street. After helping her fasten the strap on her helmet, he donned his own and straddled the bike, then kick-started it to life. Leah slung her purse strap securely over one shoulder and climbed on behind Colt, settling close against his strong back and wrapping her arms around his waist. Instinctively, her feet found their resting spots, as if the memory of her rides with Colt had simply lain dormant for all these years. She rested her chin near his shoulder and closed her eyes to enjoy his warmth. With a twist of the throttle, they were off, cruising out of her small neighborhood and onto the county highway, where Colt opened it up and left her worries in the dust.

Leah's tummy fluttered with exhilaration. She'd missed this—the danger, the speed, trusting Colt not to let her fall. It felt natural, like taking flight after a decade inside a cage. The crisp wind chilled her bare hands, so she worked her arms beneath Colt's jacket and pressed her palms against the hard planes of his stomach. She wanted to keep going forever, to drive across Texas, then turn around and head for California.

"Where're we going?" she shouted over the engine's roar.

"My place," Colt hollered back.

The ride didn't last nearly long enough. He turned off the highway onto a country road, and after another mile, made a left onto a long private driveway that wound into the woods. The property suited him, rough and secluded, his house a simple ranch with cedar siding set against the backdrop of mature trees. Most of the foliage had fallen, but a few gold and orange leaves held firm in clusters of vibrancy against the pink sky. He'd made a beautiful home here.

He parked the Harley in front of a detached garage, cut the engine, and lowered the kickstand. Once they'd removed their helmets, he hung them on the handlebars and escorted her to the front door.

"Listen," he said. "I need you to do two things before we go inside."

Leah smoothed her hair and tried to fend off the butterflies that had resumed turning summersaults inside her. "What's that?"

"First, keep your eyes closed until I tell you it's safe to look."

"Okay." That seemed simple enough. "What else?"

"The second one's not so easy." His hand, cool from the ride over, cupped her face, and she leaned into it, drawing strength from his touch. His low voice shifted as his grin vanished. "I want you to live in the here and now. No problems, no worries. It's just you and me tonight. No one else exists." He caressed her cheek, his warm breath stirring the strands of hair on her forehead. "Can you do that? Give me all of you till midnight—no distractions?"

Leah hesitated. She wanted to say yes, but that would mean delaying her confession, and she'd driven herself half mad preparing for it.

"I don't want anything or anyone between us," he pressed. "Just for tonight. Then tomorrow we'll go back to normal."

His voice was so thick with promise and pleading that she couldn't say no. "All right. I promise." After everything she and Colt had been through, they deserved one perfect night together. She was tired of fighting him— she wanted to spend the evening in his arms, to enjoy as much time with Colt as she could get. She needed this. She could just as easily tell him about Noah tomorrow.

"I mean it," Colt said. "I'd better not see that far-off look on your face."

She laughed softly and raised one hand. "I solemnly swear to stay in the moment."

"That's my girl." He kissed the tip of her nose and shifted beside her, then she heard the door open. "You can come in. Close your eyes, and mind that first step."

Blindly, she held tight to Colt and let him lead her into the house. The scents of baking bread and grilled chicken greeted her, along with a slow country tune she'd never heard before. She stretched one arm into the space in front of her to make sure she didn't collide with the furniture.

"You're fine," Colt assured her. "Keep walking." They continued slowly for another twenty paces before he turned her through a doorway to the right. She heard the door click shut behind them. "Okay," he said. "You can open your eyes now."

The first thing she noticed was a king-sized bed draped in a simple gray comforter. From there, she took in a pine dresser and matching chest of drawers until her gaze settled on a long sapphire ball gown suspended from a hanger on the highest drawer pull. She recognized it instantly.

"Is that…" she began, doubting her own eyes.

"Your prom dress?" he finished. "Yep. It took a beating at the secondhand store, so I had it dry-cleaned."

He'd rescued her dress from the Goodwill and had it cleaned? She turned and searched his face for answers, and the pieces suddenly clicked into place. His tuxedo, her gown. "We're going to prom?" She felt silly saying it aloud.

"Yes and no." He pulled open his closet door and retrieved a shoebox, then handed it to her. "We're having our own private dance right here."

She lifted the lid and discovered a pair of nude, strappy stilettos in her size.

"Go ahead and change," he said, "but don't come out yet. I'll be in the living room. Knock when you're done, and I'll come get you." Without giving her a chance to ask if he was serious, he left and pulled the door shut behind him.

Apparently, he was serious.

She stared at the dress for a while, unsure of what to do. But then she remembered her promise to Colt—no distractions, no self-doubt—and she began unbuttoning her sweater. Once she'd undressed, she folded her clothes and placed them on top of the dresser, tucking her bra beneath the pile. She stepped into the gown and slid the spaghetti straps up the length of her arms, then zipped the back halfway, which was as high as she could reach on her own. After sitting on the bed to fasten her new sandals, she stood in front of Colt's mirror and finger combed her hair. Maybe the dress didn't look so ridiculous after all. She liked the way it flared out from the waist, and the shoes complimented it perfectly. Giving herself a small smile, she fluffed her skirts and straightened her bodice.

On slightly wobbly heels, she clicked across the hardwood floor to the bedroom entrance and knocked three times to let Colt know she'd finished changing.

When he appeared at the door, she noticed he'd smoothed his ponytail and pinned a single red rosebud to his lapel. A brilliant grin curved his lips while he studied her. He held up a corsage brimming with roses and baby's breath and motioned for her hand. "You still need one of these."

"I need help with my zipper too," she said, holding her wrist out to him.

He slipped on the corsage, but instead of circling behind her to fasten her dress, he closed the distance between them, embracing her while lifting the zipper one slow inch at a time. Once he'd completed the task, he brushed her hair aside and whispered, "This is exactly how I imagined you'd look. You're the prettiest girl in Texas."

The tickle of his breath in her ear made her shiver, and she unconsciously bared her neck to him. But instead of taking things farther, he placed her hand on his forearm like a true gentleman.

"Ready?" he asked.

She nodded, and he led her into the living room, where she stopped short at the threshold, her eyes widening in surprise. If discovering her prom dress in Colt's bedroom measured an eight on the Shock Scale, what he'd done in the living room rated a twenty.

A wide banner hanging across the foyer promised *A Night to Remember*, while crepe paper streamers crisscrossed the room and led to clusters of gray and white helium balloons in each of the room's four corners. A scattering of candles provided the only light, reflected in tinfoil stars Colt had affixed to the ceiling and walls, their twinkling glow a mirror image of the flickering flames below. He'd situated a small round table near the wall, draped in white linen and set with two covered dishes, champagne glasses, a basket of sliced French bread, and a small plate of olive oil for dipping. If that weren't impressive enough, he'd fashioned a photo station in the far corner, using a tripod with tall potted plants for the backdrop.

She couldn't believe it. He must have worked on this all day.

"Colt," she breathed in awe. "It's amazing."

He wasted no time ushering her across the room. "First things first," he said. "We need our picture taken."

"Absolutely." She slipped right into character, giddy with excitement. "Before we start dancing and get all hot and sweaty."

"That's right."

He pushed a button on the digital camera, and they rushed into the corner to assume the standard prom pose: Colt standing behind her with his hands resting lightly on her waist, her hands atop his. When the timer beeped, Leah lifted her chin and smiled more widely than she had in months. The camera flashed, and she blinked to restore her sight while Colt jogged around to check the LCD panel. He nodded in satisfaction and motioned for her to sit at the table.

After she took her seat, he helped scoot her chair forward, then filled their glasses with sparkling punch and joined her.

He raised his champagne flute and toasted, "Here's to getting it right the second time."

"I'll drink to that."

They clinked glasses and took a sip, and then Colt reached over and removed the silver trays covering both their meals. At once, savory steam wafted up from her plate of grilled chicken, scalloped potatoes, and green beans. Her mouth watered in response.

"I can't compete with you in the kitchen," he said, "but I did my best."

"CJ, this is too much." She gazed around the room

at the magical transformation. No one had ever put so much time and effort into a date with her. "I don't deserve all this."

When she faced him again, it was to find him watching her with amusement dancing behind his sea-blue eyes. The candlelight cast shadows beneath his strong cheekbones and full lips, sharpening the masculine angles of his face until she almost couldn't look at him. He was so handsome it hurt.

"You called me CJ," he said.

Heat flushed her cheeks, forcing her to glance down at her plate. "This means a lot to me."

"This is just as much for me as it is for you." He pointed his fork at her. "And don't forget our agreement. You better not go sad on me."

"Not a chance."

She cut into her chicken and began eating, Colt following suit. He'd underestimated his cooking skills, and she told him so with nearly every bite. They spent the next half hour dining and talking, laughing and remembering when. She couldn't recall the last time she'd had so much fun. After they finished their meal, Colt reached beneath the table and produced a small white bakery box. She already knew what was inside, and he confirmed it by lifting the lid. A single Richman's éclair rested atop a white paper doily.

"I was hoping we could share it," Colt said, watching intently for her reaction.

Leah faced her enemy, unafraid. "Fine. But I want the bigger half."

He quickly wiped his knife clean, probably afraid she'd change her mind, then cut the pastry in two and handed her an ever-so-slightly larger piece. Once again, he proposed a toast. "To living in the moment."

"*And* enjoying the sweetness in life," she added before tapping his half and sinking into hers. That first bite rocked her taste buds in a burst of chocolaty flavor and cool crème that had her toes curling inside her strappy sandals. She finished the rest in tiny nibbles, savoring each morsel while Colt gobbled his and licked his fingers clean. God bless, it was so good. She wanted another.

"Now that we've had dessert," Colt said, pulling two slips of paper and a pencil from his inside breast pocket, "it's time to vote for king and queen."

She laughed and motioned for the pencil. "I hope we win."

"Me too." He handed over a sheet. "Nobody here deserves it more than us."

They scribbled their votes and Colt read the results. "We win by a landslide!" He pumped his fist into the air while Leah clapped her hands and cheered. She played along with the ruse, but didn't expect him to leave the room and return with a two-tiered rhinestone tiara fit for an empress.

"Colt!" she chided. This *really* was too much.

Taking her hand, he led her to the "dance floor" in the middle of the living room and settled the crown atop her head. "Now, don't fuss at me. It was no big deal. I saw it in a Halloween clearance bin, and picked it up for next to nothing."

He was such a liar. A considerate, loveable liar.

"Then where's your crown?" she asked, automatically linking her fingers behind his neck for a dance.

He drew her close and took her waist between his

large palms. "Honey, no self-respecting lawman wears a crown."

"Is that so?"

"Common knowledge. Besides, I already feel like a king." He pressed a finger to her lips. "No more arguing. I've been waiting ten years for this dance, and I mean to enjoy it."

She didn't object—she'd waited a long time for this too. Instead, she rested her cheek on Colt's chest as they swayed to the slow, sensual rhythm of "I Wanna Make You Close Your Eyes" by Dierks Bentley. By the time the song ended, she'd eliminated any sliver of space between them in a compulsion to get closer.

Colt didn't release her. He held on tighter than before, continuing their lazy sway while he waited for the next song to play. When a man's voice crooned from the speakers, promising *there's no gettin' over me*, Leah couldn't help hearing her own story reflected in the lyrics. No matter how fast or far she'd run, she'd never escaped Colt's hold on her. She'd never gotten over him, and she doubted she ever would. This man was it for her—she loved him. A shiver of fear chilled her bones, reminding her she might lose him tomorrow, but she staved it off by burrowing her face deeper into his chest and pulling in his warm, woodsy scent.

Colt rested his cheek atop her head and caressed the exposed skin on her shoulders. In the gentle glow of starlight and flickering flames, they danced through song after song, clinging to each other with an urgency that charged the air. The prom night Colt had recreated easily trumped the one they'd missed. When Leah lifted her face to tell him so, he took her cheek in one hand and met her halfway with a soft kiss. It caught her off guard, but she didn't hesitate to open to him, encouraging his seeking tongue with the tip of her own.

Time got lost as they shared easy kisses, tentatively tasting and exploring, the music forgotten until they were no longer dancing but trying to complete one another. Her hips sought his and found him swelling with desire. A low groan rumbled from his throat while his hands slid down over her back and settled on her bottom. Matching his need, she ran her palms over the contours of his steely chest, eager to feel his burning skin against hers. Colt broke the kiss and moved to her neck, where he brushed his way to her ear. When he took her lobe between his teeth, she pushed lightly against his shoulder and asked him to stop.

Colt drew back, his breathing erratic. "What's wrong?"

Nothing was wrong. The night was flawless and she didn't want it to end. Leah knew with complete certainty what—and who—she needed. She cupped the smooth edge of his jaw and said, "I'm telling you right now, before you get me worked up and say I don't know my own mind, that I'm ready."

He swallowed hard, shifting his Adam's apple, the question clear in his eyes.

"I'm sure," she said. "I want you." When he didn't respond, she pointed between them. "We can dance all night, but it's never going to be close enough. I need to feel your skin against every part of me." She delivered a solemn look, an unspoken vow to love him as long as he'd let her. "I'm ready, CJ. Let me show you how much."

# Chapter 15

APPARENTLY, COLT DIDN'T NEED FURTHER CONVINCING. His lips moved against hers in a hot slide that sent her pulse rushing straight between her thighs. She barely had time to catch her breath before his thumbs pressed down on her jaw, opening her for his thrusting tongue. Now that she'd given him the green light, he consumed her with a pure passion that burned her all over. Once he'd had his fill, he swept her hair aside and made love to the sensitive spot at the top of her shoulder.

"Oh, Lord." Leah's head fell back, knees went slack. She whispered, "Take me to bed, Colt."

When he gazed down at her, his lips were swollen and slick, his eyelids half closed with lust. In a thick voice, he promised, "Don't worry, I will." He tugged his bowtie free and tossed it to the floor, then worked the top buttons on his collar. "But not yet. You don't have to be home till midnight, Angel. We're just gettin' started."

After shrugging out of his tuxedo jacket, he took her wrist and led her to the dinner table. He lowered to a chair and turned her around, then pulled her onto his lap so his burgeoning erection pressed against her backside. She gyrated against him, but he halted her movements and gathered her hair to one side. With teasing fingers, he pushed down each of her gown straps and unzipped her bodice so slowly she had to grip her knees to keep from finishing the job for him. He peeled apart the satiny panels and kissed a meandering trail from the middle of her back to her shoulder, where he scraped his teeth along the same spot he'd suckled moments earlier. Just when she began squirming with desire, he shoved the dress to her waist and pulled her back against his chest.

He cupped her breasts in his rough hands while she rested her head on his shoulder, letting her eyes flutter closed, arching her spine for a stronger touch.

"Has anyone ever made you come like this?" he asked, using his thumbs to brush her nipples. "Just from touching you here?"

She shook her head.

That seemed to please him. He nuzzled her ear and whispered, "*I will.*"

He removed one hand and reached across the table, and she opened her eyes in time to see him dip his index finger into the dish of olive oil. Balancing the bead of oil on his fingertip, he brought it to her breast and worked it lightly into one nipple, the warm, thick liquid dripping a trail down her skin. Then he did the same on the other side. With slippery fingers, he took hold and massaged her, softly at first, his grip tightening by degrees until he'd brought her nipples to stiff points. She sighed with pleasure, her breasts growing full beneath his skilled hands. The gliding pinch and pull felt exactly like the wet suction of his mouth. It was more erotic than she'd ever imagined.

She rocked her hips for friction, finding none. A heavy ache blossomed low in her belly with each firm tug of his fingers, and after a few short minutes, she couldn't take it anymore. She needed to feel something solid against her throbbing flesh. She brought her hand to the taffeta skirts bunched between her legs, but Colt snatched her arm before she made contact.

"Unh-uh," he murmured. "You can look, but you can't touch." When she objected, he tugged her wrists behind her back.

"Colt, please…"

He didn't relent. "Don't make me get my cuffs."

He released her, and she clutched two fistfuls of fabric to keep from touching herself as Colt resumed rolling her slick nipples harder and faster than before. He whispered all the wicked things he'd do to her next, swearing he'd make her come so many times she wouldn't remember how to walk by the end of the night. If that was his goal, he was off to a good start. Her breath came in shallow gasps, the growing pressure forcing her to squirm on his lap, her legs widening of their own volition. And then, just when she didn't think she could stand another second of torture, Colt twisted his wet fingers again, and the ache broke into ecstasy.

She sank her teeth into her bottom lip and felt her core pulsing in waves of release. She stiffened against him and rode the pleasure, unable to believe what he'd just done. Colt had brought her to orgasm without touching her below the waist. That had to be some kind of superpower.

While she fought for air, he pushed her dress down over her hips. Still too weak to stand, she shifted on his lap to shed her gown. Her tiara tumbled to the floor with it.

"Lose the panties," he ordered. "But keep the shoes."

She did as he asked and settled back against him, naked except for her stilettos. She expected him to let her recover and then lead her into the bedroom, but instead, he pushed aside his dinner plate and situated her right leg on the tabletop. He used his knee to spread her left leg open so she lay exposed on his lap.

"No, I can't," she said, closing her legs an inch. "Just give me a minute."

He tipped her head aside and kissed her neck while he slid one hand along her inner thigh, pausing when he reached her soft center. "Do you trust me?"

"Yes, but—"

"Then relax and let me touch you. I know what you need." To prove it, he dipped the pad of one finger inside and spread warm lubrication over her swollen flesh, sparking her to life and coaxing a moan from her lips. He was right. She wanted to feel him there. He stroked her long and slow until she arched back and pushed her knees farther apart in a silent plea for more. With a teasing whisper, he stilled his movements and asked, "You want me to stop?"

She didn't want him to stop and he knew it. But she'd submit to him if it meant more of the delicious pressure he was building within her. "No. Please don't stop."

At her assent, he took her stiff bud between two fingers and slid them up and down in a wet caress that had her gasping aloud. He shifted slightly to peer over her shoulder at his own talented fingers.

"I love seeing you like this," he breathed into her ear. "Wide open for me." With his middle finger, he slid barely inside and out again, then spread glistening moisture along her folds. "And so wet. God, honey, look how wet you are." She watched with him. Even in the dim glow of candlelight, she could see the dampness that matted her blond curls. "I love seeing how much you want me," he repeated.

"I do," she said, reaching behind her to lock her arms around his neck. "I want you right now."

"Soon." He brought his other hand between her thighs to work her in tandem. "You need to come for me again. When I take you to bed, you're gonna be slippery as sin."

She wanted to tell him she was already there, but he massaged her entrance with his middle finger while thumbing circles around her tender flesh, and she couldn't speak over the sound of her own moaning. He used shallow penetration to toy with her, pulling back when she strained her hips forward to take him deeper. No matter how often she begged, he refused to fill her.

"I can't wait to be inside you," he said, adding a second finger but lingering at the base of her femininity. "I'm gonna ease in real slow…" He gave her a precious inch before sliding out again. "Like this." He did it again, pumping her with nothing but his fingertips. "Then a little deeper…" He gave another inch, then pulled back. Groaning and incoherent with need, she clenched her fists and heaved against his hand. "And a little deeper." The erotic pressure was about to burst— she was so close. If he'd only go in farther… He ground his erection against her bottom, his rigid control clearly beginning to slip. "Until I'm all the way in."

With that, he pushed fully inside her as her inner walls clenched around him. She cried out and stiffened with pleasure, her muscles squeezing his pumping fingers so hard she feared it might split her in half. The sweet spasms went on and on until her legs trembled, and once the surge crested, she knew Colt was right. By the time this night was over, she wouldn't be able to walk a straight line.

She collapsed against him, still tingling with satisfaction and unable to lift her limbs. "CJ," she began weakly. "No more."

"Shh. Stay with me a little longer."

He gathered her limp body and carried her to his bedroom, then laid her down on the cool comforter and stepped back to undress. A sliver of moonlight escaped the window shade and cut across Colt's face as he stood at the foot of the bed, unbuttoning his cuffs and watching her with savage hunger. Ready or not, he would have her. But the anticipation of his solid weight, his smooth, burning skin covering every inch of hers, his thick length filling her to bursting, sent new moisture between her thighs. She already wanted him again. He really did have superpowers.

His gaze never left hers as he pulled off his shirt and unbuckled his belt. In the darkness, she admired the shadows of muscle flexing along his broad shoulders and beneath the russet skin of his forearms. He worked the button on his pants and shucked them to the floor along with his briefs, freeing his rigid shaft. While he kicked off his shoes, she admired his powerful body, the lean outline of his thighs and the hard curve of his backside, where he'd inked a tattoo in her honor. She lowered her gaze to his erection, eager to wrap her palm around his smooth, tight skin and take him inside her.

Once he'd stripped down, he joined her on the mattress and knelt between her parted thighs. He swept a lingering gaze over her body and shook his head in wonder. "I could look at you forever and never have my fill."

Out of habit, she covered the low scar on her belly. The motion drew his attention to the silvery line, and he pulled one of her hands free and pressed it to a stretch of marred flesh on his abdomen.

"I've got one there too." He released her, and she ran her fingers through his inky-black hair. "We match."

He lowered to kiss her scar, and once there, he continued downward and told her to spread wider for him. When she obeyed, he drew her into his mouth with a warm pull of suction that sent a shiver down the length of her legs and curled her toes. The sensation multiplied with each taunting suckle, but despite the exquisite pleasure, she wriggled free and tugged on his shoulder. She wanted to feel him close—as close as they could get.

"Come here," she whispered. "I need you."

He pinned her hips to the bed and kissed the insides of her thighs. "Not yet. I wanna make you come again."

She pushed to her elbows and used her heels to scoot toward the headboard, her cheeks growing hot. "No."

"What do you mean, no?"

She couldn't help snapping at him. "I don't want you to make me come—I want you to make love to me." If she didn't know better, she'd think an oversized check awaited Colt in the living room, the grand prize for giving her the most orgasms by midnight. "Do you know the difference?"

A flicker of pain widened his eyes. "Of course I do." He stretched out beside her and brushed the hair back from her face. "I've only made love to one woman in my life, and that's you."

"Then why won't you love me now?"

His lips parted in shock. "That's what I've been doing this whole time—trying to make you feel good. Trying to make you forget the—"

He cut off, but she suspected his next word would have been *doctor*. He'd mentioned Ari the last time they were intimate too, telling her to remember who made her feel this hot. It was like Colt had something to prove—that if he couldn't be the better man, at least he could surpass Ari as the better lover.

Leah gasped and turned to Colt. She couldn't believe she hadn't seen it before. He thought she cared for another man.

Guilt swam up inside her. No wonder he'd worked all day to create this magical experience—he was trying to win her back from an imaginary rival. "Colt, you don't need to make me forget anyone." She stroked his chest and repeated the words he'd told her when they were young, back when she'd struggled with her own insecurities. "There's only you."

His lips lifted in a grin, but his eyes were still cautious. "You mean that?"

"It's always been you." She wrapped one leg around his waist and rolled him on top of her. "I want to feel you inside me. Nothing else matters, and no one else exists. Just love me. Can you do that?"

———

Hell yeah, he could do that.

Loving Leah was second nature for Colt—giving himself to her came easier than breathing. Gazing down into her flushed face, brimming with emotion and lust, he shoved aside all thoughts of her bastard ex-fiancé and focused on what felt right. He let go and simply loved her.

Supporting himself on one elbow, he lowered onto her body until her curves molded to every inch of him.

When she sighed with contentment and pulled him closer, he gave her more of his weight and tipped their foreheads together. Her blue eyes mirrored the passion he felt, proof that she wanted him and no one else. This felt so good—all wrapped up in her soft skin and her scent. He never wanted it to end. Taking her face, he brushed their lips together and adored her with his mouth, using the tip of his tongue in a sensual invitation that she eagerly took.

While they kissed, he began rocking against her. Beads of arousal converged on his rounded tip and made him slick. She worked a hand between them to stroke his length, but he pulled her away, afraid of finishing too soon. It was a miracle he'd lasted until now. He laced their fingers together and pinned them above her head while using his free hand to caress the swollen bundle of nerves between her thighs until it grew engorged and throbbing.

"CJ," she gasped. "Now."

He couldn't wait a second longer. Nudging her wider apart, he settled himself at the base of her passage and eased inside an inch, pulled back, and slid a fraction deeper. Clenching his eyes shut and gritting his teeth, he continued playing at her entrance, ignoring the overwhelming urge to bury himself to the hilt with one thrust. She was so small, gripping him like a hot liquid fist, and he knew she'd need to stretch to take all of him. He worked inside her gradually, letting her set the pace with the slow undulation of her hips. Then she drew her knees higher and let them drop to the sides, opening her velvet walls enough for him to slide in to the base. She was a tight fit, but they locked together perfectly.

"Are you okay?" he asked.

She answered with a long groan, which he took as a yes.

He held there, giving her time to adjust to his thickness. Writhing with need, she panted against the curve of his neck and dug her nails into his shoulder. Instead of pulling back, he ground against her in a slow rotation, then another, stoking her pleasure and making her impossibly wetter. When he opened his eyes, it was to find her biting her lip and staring back in unchecked ecstasy. It was then that they joined on every level— hands, gazes, bodies. He'd never felt more connected to her or more exposed. He had to know if she felt the same.

"Tell me you love me," he whispered against her lips. "Say my name and tell me you love me."

She nodded against the pillow and squeezed their linked fingers. "I love you, Colt."

He closed his eyes to savor the words and began moving inside her in a fluid glide. "Say it again."

"I love you."

His body trembled with the mingled pleasure of taking Leah's body along with her heart. Nothing had ever felt sweeter, the joy so powerful he could burst from it. He set a gentle tempo, sliding in and out while searching her face, savoring the pleasure reflected in her eyes, each quiet sigh and whimper urging him deeper. They shared the same heaving breaths, too overcome with pleasure to manage a kiss but unwilling to put an inch between them. With her free hand, Leah unfastened his hair and let if fall around her, then danced her fingertips along his cheek. She couldn't seem to get close enough to him, her legs wrapping tighter around his hips, the spikes of her high heels digging into his thighs.

He gave her more, thrust harder, the tension coiling in the pit of his stomach with each slippery stroke. Her silken warmth tensed around him, and he whispered, "Come with me" right before she arched her neck off the pillow and cried out. Her inner muscles contracted in viselike spasms that milked a climax from him he felt all the way to his toes. With a grunt, he bucked against her, then pulled back once and plunged as deep as he could go and tensed there, spilling inside her in scalding release. God, he'd never come so hard in his life.

They trembled together for a while, the only sound the harsh pull of air into their lungs. Even after they'd floated back down, Colt didn't want to leave the haven of her body. He remained buried within her as he rotated them to the side and wrapped her in his arms. For the next several minutes, they loved each other in silence — stroking hair, brushing skin, sharing warmth — until their lips met and their kisses stoked another fire within them.

When they made love again, he rolled Leah atop him and watched as she rode his hips, her back bowed with rapture, her long golden waves falling in a wild tangle over her breasts, her mouth agape as she touched herself and rose and sank onto his drenched erection. She was pale against his dark skin. Their contrast was somehow a testament to their perfection, proof that they belonged together. When she came, gliding over him hard and fast and sobbing his name, the sight of her abandon brought about his own explosive climax. She fell against his chest, weak with bliss, and he held her like that until it was time to take her home.

Helping her dress and driving her home almost proved more than he could bear, and after he walked her to the door and left her with one final kiss, she disappeared inside the house, taking his heart with her. He stood on her front stoop, staring at the door, his feet unwilling to move, his arms aching to hold her again. A couple of his other parts missed her too.

When he returned home to his empty bed, his pillow mocked him with Leah's lingering scent. He hugged it close and vowed not to spend another day without her by his side. There was only one cure for what ailed him, and the idea set a smile in motion across his lips. Tomorrow he'd ask her to be his wife.

"Leah Nicole Bea," he said to himself. Her name tasted mighty good on his tongue.

# Chapter 16

"LEAH MCMAHON, HUH?"

"Yeah," Colt said, handing his old friend a mug of coffee. It was the least he could do, considering Greg had driven all the way out here at the ass-crack of dawn. "She's the one. I knew it back in high school."

"Congrats, buddy." Greg sipped his coffee and set the mug on the end table. "You called the right man. I'm gonna hook you up." He opened the travel case balanced on his lap and lifted a gold ring from inside. "This one's a popular style with the ladies because it sits low on the hand. It won't snag on fabrics or hair. Good for a nurse—she's a nurse, right?"

"Uh-huh."

Colt took the ring and held it to the light, where a tiny diamond caught the sun and sprayed rainbows on the sofa. It seemed wrong buying an engagement ring from a pawnbroker, but the nearest jeweler was two hours away, and Colt didn't want to wait that long to ask for Leah's hand. Being apart from her for the last ten hours had him more jittery than the addicts he'd busted stealing copper from the air conditioners on Main Street last week.

He passed the ring back to Greg. "Got anything bigger?"

"How big you want it?"

Colt spread his palms wide. "The biggest you've got." Despite Leah's promise that she wasn't interested in Dr. Douchebag, he still wanted to outdo the asshole. Colt's grandma had passed down a ring for his future wife to wear, but the modest garnet wouldn't catch anyone's eye. He'd give Leah a diamond so friggin' huge it'd make her forget whatever sparkler had rested on her finger before.

"Okay." Greg nodded appreciatively and plucked another ring from his case. "This one's a two-carat round brilliant solitaire set in platinum. It's an I-1 but you can't tell because of the way it's set."

"An aye-what?" Colt asked.

"I-1. That means it's got flaws visible to the naked eye. This one's got a pretty hefty carbon spot." Greg scooted closer on the sofa and pointed to the edge of a marble-sized diamond that appeared crystal clear. "The jeweler who set the stone was smart enough to cover it with a prong." He turned it upside down. "But if you look at it from this angle, you can see a dot of carbon near the girdle. See what I mean?"

Colt took the ring and squinted at the tiny black spot, then flipped it over and scrutinized the diamond from the top. Greg was right. A shiny platinum prong completely concealed the imperfection. When Leah wore this enormous rock on her hand, the only thing her admirers would see was a blinding sparkle that said *Back off, motherfuckers! This girl's taken!*

"It's perfect," Colt said. "How much?"

"For you? Ten strong."

Ten thousand dollars? That was a lot more than the two paychecks DeBeers suggested he spend when he visited their website last night. He didn't have that kind of cash on him. He didn't have it in savings either. He could take out a loan or cash in some retirement, but that didn't seem like a good way to start a marriage.

Colt slipped the tiny band on his pinky and watched the stone refract the morning sunbeams over his hand in an array of dazzling prisms. He'd never given a shit about jewelry, but even *he* was impressed. There was no way Leah would say no to this ring. He imagined the way her baby blues would widen in shock when he knelt at her feet and pulled it from his pocket. He simply had to give it to her. Maybe he lacked the greenbacks, but he did have something Greg had been drooling over for years.

"I don't have ten grand," Colt said, then nodded toward the garage. "But I've got a fully restored 1978 Harley-Davidson XLCR Café Racer with upgraded transmission and suspension. Custom paint job too."

Greg froze. He'd been after that bike since high school, when Colt had bought it out from under him at the junkyard. "You'd better not be shitting me."

Colt held up one hand. "Zero shit. I'll even throw in the helmets."

They sealed the deal in less than sixty seconds, and Greg hauled ass out of there with the title in his fist, probably afraid Colt would come to his senses and give back the ring. With a promise to return for his truck later, Greg left it parked on the driveway and elected to ride the Harley back into town. Then he revved up the hog and rode out of sight.

It stung to lose the old girl, but Leah was worth it. Besides, they'd adopt a couple of kids, and Colt would be a family man. What did he need with a motorcycle?

—◆◆◆—

"I'm going to tell him today," Leah said to Rachel's image on the iPad. "For real this time."

"Whatever you say." To her surprise, Rachel didn't lecture her like Daddy had done. "I know how hard this must be for you. Just try not to put it off too much longer, because it won't magically get easier tomorrow."

"Oh, there's no chance of backing out," Leah said. "Colt called and I told him we need to talk, so he's on his way over. I sent Daddy to the grocery so we'd have some privacy, and he has my permission to tell Colt the truth if I chicken out." Which wouldn't happen. She loved Colt too much to let him learn about his son that way.

Rachel nodded and blew a kiss into the screen. "I'm still sending all my good mojo in your direction. But this time, don't use it to get laid."

"Shh!" Leah cringed and glanced over both shoulders before she remembered she was alone. "I hate that term. We didn't get laid. We made love."

Rachel rolled her eyes and pretended to gag herself. "I'm gonna make *vomit* if you don't shut up."

Leah stuck out her tongue. "One day you'll understand."

"Sex is sex, no matter what you call it. Some guys are better than others, but it's still just bumping uglies."

Bumping uglies? That sounded so…ugly. Definitely not a fair description of what she and Colt had shared last night.

The doorbell rang, sending a chill skittering down Leah's spine. She darted a glance out the living room window and noticed Colt's cruiser in the driveway. Oh, God bless, he was here.

The panic must have shown on her face, because
Rachel used a firm voice to bolster her confidence.
"Listen to me, Tink. You're the strongest, most selfless
person I know. You can do this. Go face him and then
call me. I'll have my cell in my pocket all day."

Leah nodded and licked her lips. She could do this.
She had to. Numbly, she said good-bye and powered
off her iPad, then stood from the sofa, wiped her palms
against her jeans, and answered the front door.

Colt greeted her with a fistful of daisies. "I know tu-
lips are your favorite," he said, "but they're hard to come
by this time of year." He smiled and drew a shaky breath
while blotting his forehead with his sweater sleeve. He
looked even more nervous than she felt.

"Thanks, they're beautiful." She took the bouquet
and brought it to her nose, even though daisies didn't
have much of a scent. "Come on in."

He followed her inside, where she rested her flowers on the coffee table and took a seat on the sofa. Colt
lowered beside her and quickly captured her cheeks between his palms for a kiss. She didn't resist him. A small
voice at the back of her mind warned this might be the
last time her lips moved in perfect synch with Colt's, so
she linked her wrists behind his broad neck and let him
capture her mouth for a few blissful minutes.

When they parted, Colt told her, "I missed you."

Leah's heart warmed. She'd missed him too, but she
knew she was in danger of losing her nerve if she spent
another moment in his arms. She scooted back to give
herself some space. "Thanks for coming. There's something important we need to talk about."

Colt's expression flattened, his gaze flickering to the

newly vacated spot beside him. His already dewy forehead paled a few shades, and suddenly she understood
the reason behind his jitters. He probably thought she'd
called him over here to break up with him.

"It's not about last night," she clarified, taking his
hand in both of hers. "I'm not sorry for what happened."

"You're sure?"

"It was perfect. I want us to share a thousand more
nights just like it." Steeling her resolve, she drew a deep
cleansing breath and blew it out slowly. "That's why
I asked you over." *You can do this. Stay strong.* She
dropped her gaze into her lap and then peeked up at him.
"I've been keeping something from you. There's a reason
I left Texas and stayed away so long, and I can't let things
go any farther between us until I tell you the truth."

He squeezed her hand and laughed dryly. "You're not
married, are you?"

She only wished it were that simple. "No."

"Then whatever it is, it can't be so bad."

Oh, Lord, yes it could. "I did something really awful,
Colt. I made a choice a long time ago that affected us
both, but I didn't give you any say in the decision. Now
I have to ask you to forgive me."

He lowered his brows in confusion. "You're starting
to make me worry. Are you hurt or someth—"

"I was pregnant," she blurted, the words amplified in
the small space. Softer, she added, "When I left home
at the end of senior year, I was two months pregnant."

His grip tightened around her fingers before going
slack. It took a few beats for him to find his voice.
"Was?" He swallowed hard. "Did you miscarry? Or
have an…an abortion?"

"No," she answered, "I had the baby. I hemorrhaged afterward, and they had to do an emergency hysterectomy. That's why I can't have children."

He worked free from her grasp and raked a hand through his loose hair. His gaze traveled absently around the room before settling on her again. "You're serious?"

"I wouldn't joke about something like this." She reached for her iPad and pulled up a photo of herself at seventeen, her eyes hollow with grief, her belly swollen with Colt's child. "That was taken two weeks before I delivered."

He stared at the photo in silence.

To maintain some distance, she anchored the tablet on the sofa between them, then swiped through the albums in chronological order. Next came a waterlogged Noah swaddled in his hospital bassinet, a tiny blue cap covering his cone-shaped newborn head. Other pictures followed: Noah sitting up on his own, drooling beneath a gummy smile; Noah standing for the first time, arms stretched toward the camera; Noah perched on Santa's lap, face frozen in a hysterical wail.

"You had a baby," Colt muttered, more to himself than to her.

"*We* had a baby." She continued swiping through the digital account of their son's life, stopping when she reached his third grade portrait. "His name's Noah. He looks just like you."

"We had a baby," Colt repeated, "and you never told me."

"No, I didn't."

His eyes were glassy, his voice vacant. "I have a son."

This was the hardest part—ripping the rug out from

beneath him—telling Colt that even though he had a son, he couldn't be a parent. "Yes and no."

"What's that supposed to mean?"

"I put him up for adoption when he was born."

For several long moments, he stared at her blankly, but Colt's gaze shifted and darkened as he processed her confession. Then his eyes narrowed in clear resentment. His anger left her with an odd sense of relief. Finally he was seeing her for who she was—a flawed, dishonest human being instead of an angel.

"It's an open adoption," she explained. "That means I get to see him about once a month and talk to him on the phone when he feels like calling. They usually give me visitation around the holidays too. Noah understands that I gave birth to him, but he doesn't call me Mom. He's not my son—not legally. I'm not allowed to sign his school permission slips or talk to his doctor when he's sick. So he's our child biologically, but not in any other way."

"And you didn't tell me," Colt repeated, but this time his tone sharpened, taking on a dangerous edge.

Leah's throat grew thick and her eyes prickled, but she refused to let herself cry. After what she'd done, she didn't deserve to cry. "I was young and scared, Colt. I didn't know what to do. We'd just broken up and—"

"Is that why you did it?" he asked. "To get back at me for sleeping with you and telling Tommy after?"

"No!" She couldn't let him think she'd made this decision out of spite. "I was trying to do the best thing for our baby." Memories of that time trickled into her consciousness, causing tears to well up and blur her vision. "It almost killed me to give him up. I cried myself to sleep every night for the first six months, and each morning when I woke up, I wanted to die." She knew better than to try and take Colt's hand, so she wrung hers together and pleaded for understanding. "There's no pain in the world like carrying a child for nine months and watching another woman take him home, especially knowing I can't get pregnant again."

"Stop trying to sound like a martyr," he said. "You did this to yourself."

"But I was only thinking of Noah." How could she make him understand? "I loved him more than I loved myself—or you."

"Bullshit." He glared at her like she was something he'd scraped off the bottom of his shoe. "If that were true, you would've kept him."

Leah gasped at the malice behind those words. If he was trying to hurt her, he'd done a thorough job. "You're wrong. It would've been easier for me to keep Noah, but it wasn't the right thing to do. His happiness was more important than mine. I couldn't take care of him—not like he deserved."

Colt shook his head, unmoved. "I would've helped."

"You were in jail."

"For a few days," he argued, raising his voice. "Once I found out about the baby, I would've gotten my act together. I would've married you and worked my ass off to support us."

"You and me, married at seventeen?" She remembered how wild and arrogant he'd been, even if time had made him forget. "It would've been a train wreck. Neither of us was ready."

"Our parents could've helped out while—"

"I didn't want that for Noah."

"*You* didn't want that? What about me?" Colt pointed to the iPad, where Noah smiled at them beneath a mop of black hair. "That boy's half mine. Who were you to decide all this without asking how I felt? You took my child and gave him to strangers and then you kept it a secret for—" Fire flashed behind his gaze, his voice cutting sharper than a razor blade. "That's why you stayed gone so long. So I couldn't get my boy back from his so-called *parents*." Colt stood and demanded, "What're their names?"

"They're not bad people—"

"Their names!" he shouted.

Leah cringed beneath the weight of Colt's fury and tried to soften him. "Jim and Diane Ackerman. They're good parents, I swear. I'll introduce you and explain everything. I'm sure they'll let you meet Noah."

Colt's countenance transformed into an eerie calm that made the hair on her arms stand on end. "Oh, will they?" he asked, smooth as cream. "How generous of them to let me see my own son, especially after they adopted him illegally."

"It's not like that," she insisted. "I lied to them too. I told them I didn't know who the father was."

"Did they run a notice in all the newspapers here?" Colt asked, his voice deceptively placid. "Did they at least try to find me, or did they hurry up and hire some shyster to push the adoption through?"

She could see where this was headed, and she had to stop him from disrupting Noah's life. "They're Noah's parents and he loves them."

"We're his parents."

"Listen, please." She wanted to run to her bedroom and hide under the covers, but she stood and faced Colt, squaring her shoulders even though she felt naked and two feet tall. "What I did was wrong, and I'm sorry. Sorrier than you'll ever know. But don't punish Noah because you're mad at me. You can't do anything to—"

"Don't you dare," he said, colder and harder than winter steel, "tell me what I can't do." He reached into his back pocket and retrieved his wallet, then began fishing through it, pulling out credit cards and scraps of paper. "You took my child and gave him away when he could've lived with family. I never got to hold him or hear his first words." Colt used his wallet to point to Noah's image on the iPad. "Or watch him get on the bus for the first day of kindergarten, or teach him how to throw a football. You got to see all of it, but I missed everything, and I can't ever get it back. It's like you stole a whole other life from me." For a moment, his anger faded and he pinned her in place with a wounded look. "I didn't think you were capable of anything so heartless. All these years I loved you because you were the finest person I knew." He shook his head sadly. "I didn't know you at all."

"I kept telling you I'm no angel." The words sounded flippant, and she regretted them the instant they left her lips.

"Well, you sure showed me, didn't you?"

"I'm sorry—I didn't mean it like that."

"Whatever. It doesn't matter." He found what he'd been searching for in his wallet and tossed it onto the coffee table beside her bouquet of daisies. It was her driver's license, the one he'd confiscated all those weeks ago. "I'm not sure what I'm gonna do about this, but either way, my decision won't involve you. Since you didn't bother involving me, it only seems fitting. So feel free to go back to Minnesota whenever you damn well please." He stalked to the front door and left her with two words before walking out of her life. "Good riddance."

# Chapter 17

COLT AWOKE THE NEXT MORNING WITH A MOUTHFUL OF rancid cotton and a jackhammer battering away at his temples. He squinted against the sunlight streaming through his window shade, cringing when his skull throbbed in tandem with his stomach. Every little sound rattled his brain, the whoosh of forced air through the ceiling vents louder than an ocean's roar. He pressed the heels of his hands over his scratchy eyes in an effort to block out the stimuli. God damn, he couldn't drink like he used to. When had he turned into such a lightweight?

Once he adjusted to the harsh light, he turned his head on the pillow and glanced at his nightstand, where a half-empty bottle of Jack Daniels distorted the alarm clock's red glow. He shoved the bottle aside and struck an object with a faint *clink*. Propping on one elbow, Colt peered closer to investigate and immediately wished he hadn't. Because for a few fleeting seconds, he'd managed to forget the reason he'd taken a bottle to bed in the first place. Mocking him from atop the snooze button was Leah's ring, the one he'd never given her. The one he'd traded his Harley for. The one hiding a big, ugly black spot beneath a facade of gleaming platinum.

How fucking appropriate.

He still couldn't believe it. The girl he'd called his angel for the last decade—whose deceptively innocent face had haunted him night and day—was a liar and a thief. What she'd done trumped the crimes committed by every slimy bastard currently taking up residence in the county lockup, because she'd stolen something that couldn't be returned. Unlike a car or a box of tools or a flat screen television, she couldn't give back the years he'd missed with his son.

Christ. He had a son.

He couldn't believe that either. The kid looked just like him—the living spit of himself at that age, his blue-green eyes twinkling with a hint of mischief, his black hair scraggly and a few inches too long, a gap between his two front teeth wide enough to hold a Tic Tac. If he'd passed that kid on the street, he would've assumed a rogue scientist had cloned him. No wonder Leah had moved to Minnesota. It was the last place Colt would visit and spot the boy, though he should probably remedy that soon. A quick scan of the database last night had turned up the Ackermans' street address. He could drop in on the happy little family whenever he pleased, but at the same time, he didn't want to scare the boy by showing up on his doorstep. Colt had tried calling Granddaddy for advice, but couldn't reach him in Oklahoma. He wondered if he should lawyer up now, just in case Leah had already called her co-conspirators to warn them. Or was that overreacting?

Hell, he didn't know what to do.

But since he was already late for work, he dragged his aching ass out of bed and shuffled to the bathroom, figuring a warm shower would clear his head. But while the steam soothed the throbbing between his temples, it did nothing to alleviate his confusion or to expel thoughts of Leah. He couldn't stop replaying their

night together, especially the sound of his name spilling
from her parted lips and the clench of her tight silky
walls around him. By the time he shut off the water and
grabbed his towel, his johnson was hotter and harder
than asphalt in July. Damn it, he still wanted her, even
after the awful shit she'd done. He hated himself for his
weakness. Hated her too.

Reminders of her lingered throughout the house—the
deflated balloons drooping in every corner of the living room, the crumpled prom banner he'd torn from the
ceiling, the wooden chair where he'd pulled her into his
lap and made her come twice with only his fingers. Colt
found himself rushing though his morning routine in an
effort to escape Leah's ghost.

During his drive to work, he cranked up George Strait
on the radio and sang "All My Ex's Live in Texas" at
the top of his lungs. Just when he'd gone five minutes
without thinking about Leah, Colt strode into the station lobby and noticed an angel atop the old artificial
Christmas tree, her hands pressed together in prayer,
blue eyes turned toward the heavens, waves of blond
hair rippling to her waist.

A bubble of rage burst inside his chest, and he locked
eyes with the nearest deputy, who happened to be
Horace. Colt barked, "Have one of the boys take that
thing down!"

The old guy cocked a brow. "What? The tree?"

"No, damn it!" Colt pointed at the topper. "The angel.
I told y'all about keeping it secular in here!"

Horace tipped back his hat, clearly confused. "I
thought you changed your mind."

"Well, I'm changin' it back."

Without another glance at the cursed tree, Colt turned and stalked down the hall toward his office. Darla met him halfway there, her eyes brightening when she saw him.

"Congratulations!" She threw her arms around his neck and pressed her giant tits against his chest in a tight hug.

He pushed free, in no mood for another of her advances. "What the hell for?"

She smiled and bounced in place, making the buttons on her sweater beg for mercy. "I saw Greg Cowan at the gas station filling up your old Harley, and he told me the news!"

Colt froze while his stomach dropped. "What news?"

"That you and Leah are getting married, silly."

Oh, shit. It hadn't occurred to him that Greg might spill the beans. By now, half the town was probably abuzz with news of the impending nuptials. And he knew firsthand that shutting down a rumor took a hell of a lot more work than starting one. He'd be fielding questions about his broken engagement until *next* Christmas.

"I wasn't gonna say anything," Darla continued, "but I noticed how happy you've been since Leah came back to town." She winked. "You know what they say about the preacher's daughter…"

"We're not engaged," he told her. "So you can keep—"

"Oh!" She clapped a hand over her cherry-red lips. "You haven't popped the question yet. Don't worry, boss. I won't spoil the surprise." Then she patted him on the shoulder and sashayed to the reception desk.

Son of a bitch. It was only nine o'clock, and already this day couldn't get any worse.

Colt hid inside his office for the next couple of hours and let his calls go to voice mail while he Googled adoption laws in Minnesota and Texas. He stumbled across a ruling that overturned an adoption in favor of the biological father, but the child in that case was only fourteen months old. Colt didn't know his son's birthday, but the boy had to be nine, maybe ten. The best Colt could hope for at this point was visitation rights. He'd have to file a motion, and for that, he was definitely going to need a lawyer.

Three quick knocks sounded from his door before Bobbi Lewis poked her red head inside and said, "I just heard the news! Ohmygod, I'm so excited for you!"

Colt hung his head and groaned. He couldn't take much more of this. "Who told you?"

"I heard it from June, who heard it from Luke, who heard it from—"

"Never mind," Colt interrupted. "It doesn't matter. Just come in and shut the door behind you."

Bobbi's smile fell. "What's wrong? Trouble in paradise already?"

More like trouble in hell. "Just shut the door. I don't want this getting around."

She stepped inside and slung her laptop bag over the back of his guest chair, then took a seat on the edge of his desk. "Talk to me."

So he did. He told her everything, starting with the proposal that never happened and ending with the news that he had a son who belonged to strangers. Bobbi listened passively the whole time, never betraying any emotion. Loyal as she was to him, he expected her to rage against Leah or at least call her a few choice names, but she didn't.

"Well, they're not strangers," she finally said when he'd finished unloading. "Not to that little boy. They're his mom and dad, and you're the stranger. I know that hurts, but it's the truth, and you need to remember it before you go off half-cocked and do something stupid."

Colt drew back, offended. He'd just learned that his flesh and blood had been snatched out from under him, and Bobbi made *him* sound like the villain. "I have the right to know my own son."

"Of course you do," Bobbi said. "But there's a right way to get to know him, and threatening the stability of his family isn't it."

"*I'm* his family." Why couldn't she see that?

Bobbi shook her head. "Family's about more than DNA. I know firsthand." She dropped her gaze to the tips of her ankle boots, warning him the conversation was about to get heavy. "My mom abandoned Luke and took me with her when she left, but she did a shit job of raising me. It wasn't until she OD'd and two *strangers* adopted me that I knew what a real family was. Now I can't imagine my life without my dads in it. I'm not saying you would've done a shitty job too—"

"Good," he interjected. "Because I would've manned up, but Leah never gave me the chance."

Bobbi offered him a sympathetic grin. "I know. I'm just trying to say that what's done is done. You have to think about what's best for the child."

*What's best for the child.* Colt was really friggin' sick of hearing that. Why did everyone else get to decide what was best for his son? He was the father. Why didn't he get a say?

"For what it's worth," Bobbi said, "I wouldn't judge Leah too harshly."

"It's not worth shit, so save it."

She flashed a palm. "Fine. But I want you to see something real quick, then I'll leave you alone."

Bobbi unzipped her bag and pulled out her laptop, then situated it on the desk in front of him. Leaning over his shoulder, she clicked and tapped through several files until she found some old footage of him from the *Sex in the Sticks* project. When she hit the play button, he recognized the scene instantly. It was from Trey Lewis's farewell party at the church fellowship hall, right before he shipped out to Dubai. It was also the night Barbara Lee had run Colt down in the church parking lot.

"*Got something to say to the camera*," Bobbi said from the computer speakers. Her hair was shorter then, but otherwise she looked exactly the same. "*You're the last one*."

Even though the footage was only two years old, Colt seemed so much younger in his short-sleeved deputy shirt, leaning back in his chair with both arms folded behind his head. He still had that cocky, easygoing look in his eyes, the one he'd lost after the accident. He smirked and told Bobbi, "*I've got somethin' to say to both of you*."

"*Both of who?*"

"*You and Lewis*."

Bobbi turned away from the camera and gazed off into the distance, probably at Trey. She was clearly sprung for the guy. Colt had seen it from day one.

"*Yeah*," Colt said, "*you got it bad*."

Bobbi shrugged. "*I'll live*."

"*No, you won't*." Colt leaned forward and rested his forearms on his knees, his expression hardening.

"*You'll survive, but you won't live. Trust me, there's a difference.*"

"Look." Bobbi paused the footage and pointed at Colt's image: his eyes unfocused as he stared at the floor, his mouth pressed into a line. "I remember how miserable you were back then."

Not much had changed. He was miserable now.

"I'm not saying what Leah did was right, because it wasn't." Bobbi closed the file and his image disappeared from the screen. "She should've told you about the baby as soon as she found out she was pregnant. But she was just a kid, Colt. I'm sure you did a few things at that age you regret."

"Nothing like that." His drinking and whoring and stealing had never hurt anyone. Not long-term, anyway. "I was stupid, but I wasn't cruel."

"You still love her." It wasn't a question, and he didn't deny it. Bobbi rested her hand near the top of his shoulder and gave a light squeeze. "I want to see you happy. Why not try and forgive her?"

Why not? Because that would defeat the purpose. The reason he'd fallen in love with Leah in the first place was because she had the purest heart on earth. She was good, all the way down to her soul. Or so he thought. Now she was no different from any other woman in town.

Another rap of knuckles sounded from the door, this time soft and timid—a knock with an apology behind it. Colt knew who was on the other side of that oak barrier, and his chest constricted in a mingling of dread and anticipation.

Just as he expected, Leah stepped inside, wearing her Vikings sweatshirt over jeans, hair pulled back in a sloppy ponytail. Her puffy, red-rimmed eyes widened when she spotted Bobbi sitting on his desk with her hand resting on his shoulder. Colt realized how it must look, but he didn't care. Let her think the worst. Let her cry some more. Why should he be the only one to feel like his heart was about to explode?

Leah lowered her gaze to the tile. "I've been trying to call you all morning, but I keep getting your voice mail."

"Mmm-hmm," he replied flatly, making no effort to move Bobbi's hand. "There's a reason for that."

Bobbi scooted off the desk and stuffed her laptop inside her bag. "I'm gonna head out and let you two talk." She told Colt, "Remember what I said," and then gave Leah a consoling hug on her way out.

Traitor.

"Is she the only one who knows?" Leah asked after the door shut.

"For now." But that wouldn't last long. "Why? Worried about your reputation?"

She ignored his question and sank into the chair opposite him, keeping her gaze fixed on her folded hands. "On my way over here, three people stopped and congratulated me on our engagement." She peeked up. "I don't get what that's all about, but I thought you should know."

"Duly noted," he said and nodded at the door. "You can go now."

Pain flashed across her ivory features, and he felt it like a mule kick to the gut.

"That's not what I came here to tell you." Her voice was so damned pitiful that he had to hold back from offering her a glass of water. Shit, what was wrong with him? "I talked to the Ackermans last night."

"I figured you would."

"I asked them to bring Noah for a visit so you two can meet."

Colt raised a brow. "What'd they say?"

"They said yes. They're flying down next week." She bit her lip and flicked a glance at him. "There's just one thing…"

He didn't like the sound of that.

"…I told Jim and Diane that if they'd come to Sultry Springs, the four of us would sit down and resolve all this without lawyers."

"Ah, Jesus." This was un-friggin'-believable. Colt slapped his desk and shot to his feet. "There you go again, making decisions for me! You had no right to tell them that." He still hadn't figured out what course of action to take, but he lied and said, "I've already got a lawyer."

"Just listen. Please." She begged with her eyes, and he couldn't bring himself to toss her into the hall. He really was going soft. "We all love Noah," she said. "It's in our best interest to work together and balance his needs with our own. Let's try it and see what happens, and if we can't come to an agreement, then bring in your attorney. I'm surprised he hasn't already advised you to try this before taking it to the next level."

Colt dodged that last bit by grumbling something about not having time for a formal consultation yet. Then he lowered to his chair and tried to think over the rush of anger dulling his brain. Leah was probably right, even though she went behind his back—again—to facilitate the meeting. It made sense to try and work out a deal with the Ackermans before involving the courts.

"Fine," he decided. "But don't ever speak for me again. You're not my go-between, and you don't have a say in what I do. Stay the hell out of my business. Are we clear?"

"Perfectly clear." She stood from her chair but made no move to leave. Instead, she clasped both hands behind her back and chewed her bottom lip, just like the first day she'd returned to town. And the first time he'd kissed her. "I just want to say again how sorry I am. I know what I did was wrong, but I had good intentions. I swear I didn't do it to hurt you."

Colt couldn't look at her. He grabbed his clipboard and flipped through the citizens' complaints, hoping she'd take the hint and go.

"I know you're angry," she went on. "And hurt. But I hope you can forgive me someday. Is there anything at all I can do to make this right?"

Unless Leah had discovered a way to time-travel, that wasn't going to happen. But there was one thing she could do to make his life a little easier. The reminders of her were bad enough inside his empty home. He couldn't survive bumping into her at the Sack-n-Pay and the coffee shop for the rest of his existence.

"I want you to go home to Minnesota," Colt said. "When your daddy's back on his feet." He chanced a split-second glance at her—it was all he could bear. "If you stay, it's gonna be difficult for both of us to move on."

She fell silent for several beats while Colt stared at his reports, seeing nothing. He didn't want to think about her moving on with another man, but it would eventually happen.

"I'll…um…" A soft sob choked off her words, but

he refused to make eye contact. If he saw her cry, he'd never get the image out of his head. "I'll think about it."

"Thanks. I'd appreciate that."

She sniffled and hiccupped in an effort to hold back her tears—awful noises that tore through his guts like shrapnel. Then she bolted from the room, leaving the door open so he heard the quick, light tap of her shoes retreating down the hall.

Colt tossed aside his clipboard and tipped back his head. His insides felt raw, as if he'd injected acid into his veins and the burning solution was working its way into each and every muscle fiber beneath his skin. He hadn't ached this badly since the day he'd woken up in the hospital wearing a full-body cast. If there was a pill for this, he'd pop it in an instant, no matter what the cost. This was probably how addicts felt. Now he understood what drove them to steal for a fix. He'd give anything to make the pain stop.

But a warning voice at the back of his mind told him there was no escape…and this was just the beginning.

# Chapter 18

"*WHAT?*" A DOLLOP OF CHILI SLIPPED FROM RACHEL'S spoon, splattering against the diner's Formica tabletop. Rachel licked the spoon clean and used it to point at Leah. "Don't you dare let him run you out of town! I need you, Tink. This is where you belong, and if Sheriff McSensitive can't handle seeing you around, then let *him* leave."

Leah sipped her iced tea and glanced around the room. Was it her imagination, or was everybody staring at her? "It's not just Colt, it's hard for me too. I ran into him at the drug store yesterday, and again this morning when I passed his cruiser on the way to the farmer's market. I get butterflies every time I see him, and then I remember we're not together anymore and it hurts so bad I want to throw up." She slumped over and rested her chin in her hand. "It's awful."

Rachel used a napkin to clean up her mess. "I get that, but the way I see it, you're gonna hurt for a while. You can either hurt all alone in Minnesota, or here with friends and family who can help lift you up. If you stay, we can start over together—maybe get our own place." She smiled and crumbled a cracker over her chili. "Think of all the trouble we could get into if we were roommates."

Yeah, but *trouble* made Leah think of getting arrested, which made her think of Colt, which made her ache all over. She stared into her tea and used her straw to poke at the ice cubes. No matter what she did, her life was in shambles.

"Excuse me, Miss McMahon."

Leah glanced up at the waitress, a timid sixteen-year-old with a sweet smile on her lips and an enormous slice of cherry pie in her hand.

"The owner said to tell you this is on the house." The girl set the plate on the table with two forks and some extra napkins. "And congrats on the wedding." She leaned down and whispered, "I think he wants to cater the reception, just so you know." Before Leah had a chance to set her straight, the girl waved and strode away.

Leah stared at her fruity offering. As if passing Colt twice a day wasn't painful enough, she couldn't take two steps in any given direction without someone congratulating her on an engagement that'd never happened. And never would. Maybe she *should* move back to Minnesota. At least there, nobody wanted to take her dress shopping or discuss color schemes.

"Well, that was weird," Rachel said with a shrug. "But at least it came with a side of pie."

The tart scent of wild cherries turned Leah's stomach, and she pushed the plate away. "Go ahead and dig in. I don't want any."

"Aw, come on, Tink. You haven't touched a bite all day, and it's not like you've got extra padding to—" She paused, her gaze shifting to someone behind Leah. "Hey there, hon."

Leah turned and spotted June approaching their table, her complexion a bit more peaked than it was a few days ago. Something in June's gait seemed off, maybe more sluggish than usual, so Leah scooted over and patted the spot beside her on the booth.

"Sit down before you pass out," she told June, who nodded and lowered to the vinyl cushion. "I thought you were staying off your feet."

"I am, mostly." June started eyeing the cherry pie. "But I can't sit around the house all day. I mean, I'm pregnant, not dead. Besides, I had a craving for something, but I couldn't figure out what." She spoke directly to the pie crust now. "That looks pretty good."

Leah handed her a fork. "You and Rachel can share it. I can't eat a thing."

"Oh, yeah." June tore her gaze away from the pie long enough to offer a pitying look and squeeze Leah's hand under the table. "Bobbi told me what happened, but we haven't said a word to Luke or Trey. We figured you'd wanna keep it private as long as you can."

"Thanks." She wondered how long before the news leaked. Probably a few days at the most.

June grabbed a fork and divided the pie in half, then tore right in. They spent the next several minutes in contented silence until June brought the last bite to her lips. She paused and pressed one hand over her chest, her face contorting in discomfort.

"You okay?" Rachel asked from the other side of the table.

"Wicked heartburn," June explained.

"Oh, yeah." Leah remembered that well. Even water had given her heartburn during the third trimester. "One of the many joys of pregnancy."

"My stomach hurts too." June sat back and brought a hand to her belly. Leah took the liberty of touching her friend's tummy to feel for the tightening of contractions, but the muscles beneath her fingers were relaxed and springy. Nothing out of the ordinary. "Probably just something I ate," June said.

Leah didn't like this. June hadn't seemed like herself when she'd joined them, and now a fine sweat had broken out on her cheeks. "You don't have a headache, do you?"

She opened her mouth to respond and everything happened in a flash.

June's body lurched and she started to gag. Rachel dashed for the nearest trash can, returning just in time for June to vomit into it. When June's shoulders and legs began twitching uncontrollably, Leah knew what was wrong.

"Where's your car parked?" she asked Rachel.

"Back at the store." Rachel pulled back June's hair and patted her back. "Why?"

Leah jammed her hand inside her pocket and retrieved her keys. "We'll have to take mine." Bruiser wasn't as fast as Rachel's Subaru, but they didn't have a minute to spare. "We need to get her to the ER right now."

"Should we call an ambulance?"

Leah shook her head. "They won't get here and back to the hospital in time."

June moaned and wiped her mouth with a handful of napkins. "In time for what?"

"Hey," Leah called to the busboy. "Can you help us get her outside?"

The kid eagerly complied, and the three of them managed to get June settled in Bruiser's front seat with a small wastebasket wedged between her legs. Leah pressed a twenty into the boy's palm to cover their bill and dashed to the driver's side door while Rachel sat in the back. After cranking the ignition, Leah checked over her shoulder for traffic and then peeled down Main Street, leaving clouds of rubber in her wake.

"In time for wh—" June began before heaving into the trash can.

Leah was ninety-nine percent sure June needed an emergency C-section, but she didn't want to worry her, especially considering the baby wasn't full-term. She told Rachel, "Call the ER and hand me the phone when they're on the line," then pushed the pedal to the floor and prayed to God that the engine wouldn't explode and kill them all. They tore down the highway as fast as Bruiser could haul them, which turned out to be sixty-eight and a half miles per hour.

"Here," Rachel said, handing over the phone.

With June coughing and retching so violently from the passenger seat, it was impossible to hear the staffer on the other end of the line, so Leah said loudly, "I'm on my way to the ER with a friend. She's…" Dang it, how far along was June? She couldn't remember. "She's in her mid-third trimester, and I'm almost positive she's got HELLP syndrome." Just to be safe, she repeated, "That's H-E-L-L-P. She was complaining of chest and abdominal pains, then she started vomiting and having seizures. She might have internal bleeding. The baby's not full-term yet, so have your neonatal staff ready."

Did Sultry Memorial even have a neonatal department? For June's sake, she hoped so, because this baby would have to make her entrance into the world in the next few minutes—ready or not.

"What do you mean, neonatal staff?" June croaked.

So much for trying not to scare her. Leah handed the phone into the back seat and glared at the road as if to propel them faster to their destination.

"They can't…take the baby," she said between dry heaves. "It's too soon."

When they pulled up to the Sultry Memorial emergency entrance, Leah honked the horn like a lunatic and jumped the curb. She burst out of the car to meet the staff, who'd already come running with a stretcher.

Leah opened the passenger door and said, "Her name's—"

"June Gallagher," finished one of the nurses. "I know. She's a regular customer here. We see so much of June, we should give her a Fast Pass."

Before Leah could supply the team with any more information, they wheeled June inside and she disappeared behind twin sliding doors.

Poor June. Growing up, she always *had* seemed a little unlucky. Leah hoped she'd gotten here in time. She decided to park the car and head inside to the chapel. Maybe God had stopped hearing her prayers, but it couldn't hurt to try.

———

Colt slouched against his granddaddy's leather sofa and idly toyed with a fuzzy fishing lure he'd plucked from the wall. His low position put him eye-level with the desk in front of him, where stacks of bench warrants and rulings awaited the judge's signature. As deputy and eventually sheriff, Colt had been to court so many times it felt like a second home—a really dysfunctional home where you had to pass through a metal detector to get inside. The last thing he wanted was to spend the next year of his life duking it out in court and racking up a mountain of debt.

"Well, slap my ass and call me Sally," Granddaddy said with a shake of his half-bald head. "I never would'a guessed it. Didn't I warn ya Leah wasn't the same girl you remembered?"

Nice. Leave it to Granddaddy to bust out *I told you so* at a time like this.

"Well, guess what," Colt retorted. "The Lord didn't call her home to Sultry Springs like you thought. She and her daddy were in cahoots the whole time—bet you didn't see that coming." Pastor Mac was such a hypocrite, always asking, *What would Jesus do?* You know what Jesus wouldn't do? Steal people's kids, that's what. "But you were right about Leah. Does that make you feel better?"

White bushy brows furrowed above rheumy eyes. "Course not, son." He sat back and pulled his pipe from the middle desk drawer. "I hate seein' you upset, and what she did to you was mighty low. But let's focus on what we can control. It's good that you're meetin' with the boy's parents. Just don't sign anything till I have a look at it." He tossed a sack of tobacco onto the desk. "Speakin' of which, what're you gonna ask for?"

Colt shrugged. He hadn't given it much thought. "Ideally, I'd like joint custody, but I'll settle for visitation. It'd be great if we could divide the school year and alternate summers so Noah splits his time between Minnesota and Texas."

Granddaddy huffed a dry laugh. "Well, that ain't

what you're gonna get—not even if you'd raised the boy from birth."

"Why not?" He'd heard joint custody was standard practice now. In fact, half the deputies on the payroll needed flex schedules because they never knew which days of the week they'd have their kids.

"First off, that boy doesn't know you from Adam," Granddaddy said, stuffing tobacco shreds inside his pipe. "And second, kids need more stability than that. It's not good to bounce 'em from school to school every year. Don't you want what's best for him?"

Colt's whole body flashed hot. How many times would he have to hear that? He shouted, "No, damn it!" before realizing what he'd just admitted. His face heated, but not from anger this time.

The worst part was that Granddaddy didn't look all that surprised. He struck a match and lit his dried tobacco, then sucked a few leisurely puffs. "Well, that's what the court wants, so best prepare yourself and lower your expectations."

"I didn't mean it that way." Colt wasn't being selfish, was he? All he wanted was to form a relationship with his son—something that went deeper than a few phone calls now and then. There was nothing wrong with that. "Of course I care about what's best for Noah."

The phone rang, interrupting their strategy session. Granddaddy answered the call and spent the next few minutes uttering *Uh-huhs* and *Mmm-hmms*, and *Well, I'll be*. Then he slammed down the receiver and abandoned his pipe.

"C'mon, boy." Smiling, Granddaddy pushed to standing and grabbed his Stetson. "We're goin' to the hospital to meet my new step-grandbaby!"

Step-grandbaby? But June wasn't due until January. "Everything all right?"

The old guy scooted around his desk with a spring in his step. "There was some ruckus, but mama and baby are both doin' fine."

"Only one baby, huh?" Colt would've bet his left nut there were twins inside that Kong-sized belly. "It must be built like a linebacker."

"Five pounds 'n change," Granddaddy said. "Not bad for a preemie. Now get the lead out so I can go see the little peanut."

As Colt hustled alongside his granddaddy to the cruiser, he couldn't help feeling a twinge of envy for June and Luke. They weren't family—not really—but Granddaddy would be there to gush over their newborn and take a dozen pictures, which would probably go on display beside Emma's portrait on his desk. Just add that to the list of experiences Colt had been denied. Aside from the giddy old coot beside him, none of Colt's family knew he had a child, and he didn't have a single photo to share.

During the drive to the hospital, Colt tuned out his granddaddy's yammering and tried to narrow down his list of requests for the meeting in a few days. He didn't want to come across as a pushover, but in order to avoid a drawn-out court battle, he had to keep his demands reasonable. It was a fine line, and he didn't know where to draw it.

The possibilities tumbled in his head, and by the time Colt pulled into the parking lot, he was no closer to reaching a decision than before he'd left. He stood from the cruiser and heaved a sigh. Might as well give his brain a rest, especially considering they'd arrived at the hospital. He'd never told anyone, but every time he returned to Sultry Memorial, his flesh practically crawled off his bones. There was no use trying to think straight while he was here.

He ambled across the foyer and took the stairs while Granddaddy waited for the elevator. Colt was in a lousy disposition by default, but his mood darkened when he reached the fifth floor nursery and spotted a familiar blond ponytail at the other end of the corridor.

Leah didn't see him. She was too busy gazing into the nursery with her fingertips pressed against the glass. The longing on her face made his chest heavy and his arms twitch to wrap around her. *There's no pain in the world like carrying a child for nine months and watching another woman take him home*, she'd told him. *Especially knowing I can't get pregnant again*. Colt clenched his fists. He didn't want to remember her words, and he sure as hell didn't want to feel sorry for her.

He was about to duck back into the stairwell when a man wearing a white lab coat joined Leah at the observation window and handed her a Styrofoam coffee cup. Colt leaned forward and squinted at the guy's smooth cheeks and the stringy blond hair brushing his shirt collar. It was Dr. Benton, that Doogie Howser wannabe. He said something that made Leah smile, then cupped her lower back and steered her toward a door marked *Staff Only*.

A surge of red hot jealousy scalded the inside of Colt's throat. Benton, that baby-faced bastard, was touching Leah, and he made no move to drop his hand even after she pushed open the door. Colt wanted to drop-kick Benton into next week, but he missed his chance. The two of them vanished inside the room—for something that looked an awful lot like a coffee date—and the door whispered shut.

"Hey," someone said from nearby. "Thanks for coming."

It was Luke Gallagher, who'd already begun towing Colt by the shirtsleeve toward the nursery while Granddaddy followed. Colt gritted his teeth and tried not to imagine what Leah and the doctor were doing inside that private room—whether Benton was making her laugh or complimenting her beauty or asking her out for dinner. Her personal life was none of his business anymore, and if she wanted to date another doctor, then so be it. Benton was a better match for her anyway. What had she and Colt ever had in common?

"There she is," Luke said, pointing at the glass. "Third one from the left."

Colt peered at a squirming bundle of blankets encased in a plastic bassinet, but he couldn't stop seeing Benton's pale hand at the base of Leah's spine.

"How's our Calamity June?" Granddaddy asked. "Feelin' rough, I expect."

"She's a little beat up, but she'll be fine—thanks to Leah."

Colt snapped to attention and turned to face Luke. "McMahon?"

"Yeah, she didn't tell you?" Luke dragged one hand over his face and shook his head in reverence. "She's the one who figured out something was wrong with June and drove her to the ER. Just in time too. Doc Benton said in another ten minutes her liver would've ruptured." He clapped Colt on the arm and said, "Congrats, man. You've got a real keeper. I think Doc Benton's trying to recruit her for intensive care."

Benton was trying to recruit her, all right, and not just for the nursing staff. Colt shouldn't give a damn, but he did.

While Luke and Granddaddy made kissy noises at the windowpane, Colt tried to ignore the acid burning a hole in his gut. Leah had done him wrong, and yet *he* was the one taking karma's size twelve boot up the ass. What had he done to deserve this?

# Chapter 19

LEAH SAT IN THE EMPTY PARKING LOT OF ELLA-MAE'S Waffle Shack, otherwise known as The Awful Waffle, and drummed her nails on the steering wheel. With its limited menu of doughy hotcakes, watery syrup, bitter coffee, and rubbery eggs, the Shack's nickname was well-deserved. Nobody ate here—it was a miracle the place stayed in business. But if you wanted a quiet breakfast free from prying eyes, The Awful Waffle marked the spot.

That's why she was here: to introduce Colt to the Ackerman family in a neutral place where neither side would feel threatened.

Now to survive the waiting…

Nervous tingles danced across her chest. Colt wasn't her biggest fan these days, and he could be a real wild card when angry. For the last nine years, she'd walked a meticulous line with Noah's parents, careful not to rock the boat and lose the privileges they granted her. She'd damaged that relationship by lying, and she prayed Colt wouldn't fly off the handle and make it worse.

Speak of the devil, the good sheriff pulled up in his cruiser and rolled to a stop. He could've parked beside her, but instead he put four wide spaces between them in a silent message that he still wanted nothing to do with her. He turned off the ignition and stared out his front windshield, refusing to acknowledge her with even a glance.

His rejection stung. Each cold-shouldered snub pricked her heart like thistle, and he'd given her no reprieve in the week since she'd told him the truth. Her hopes of forgiveness were fading fast. It was probably time to admit that Colt's anger was stronger than his love.

But even if it was too late for them, she could try to salvage her friendship with the Ackermans, and to do that, she'd have to talk to Colt and make him see reason. Taking a fortifying breath, she stepped out of her car and charged toward his cruiser.

The brisk morning air condensed into fog when she exhaled, and she pulled her sweater lapels tight over her breasts to hold in the warmth. When she reached Colt's passenger door, she bent at the waist and knocked politely on his window.

He gave her nothing. With one arm slung over the steering wheel, the immature jerk sipped his coffee and continued ignoring her.

This was ridiculous. Leah tried opening the door but found it locked. Temper flaring, she pounded on his window. "I can do this all day!"

He still didn't look at her, but he rolled his eyes and hit the automatic unlock button. She took a second to calm down and climbed in before he had a chance to change his mind.

The inside of Colt's cruiser was warm and thick with the scent of his aftershave, a smell that conjured bittersweet memories of their single night together. It was hard to believe that just days ago, they'd fused their skin and twined their limbs in a compulsion to get as close as possible, to join their bodies and souls. Now Colt couldn't get far enough away.

A pang of loss shot through Leah, so acute she struggled to catch her breath. It seemed there was no limit to how much she could suffer. Every interaction with this man, no matter how trifling, cut to the core. It was then that she knew what she had to do. She would give him what he wanted—she'd leave town. The sooner the better. Maybe she could return to Sultry Springs someday, but for now the pain was too fresh. She needed time to heal her bruised spirit, and she couldn't do that with Colt in her life.

"Well?" The low timbre of his voice sent another ripple of agony through her. "What's so important that you had to beat down my door?"

Even though it hurt, she forced herself to face him, blindingly handsome in his starched uniform. "I thought it'd be a good idea to talk before the Ackermans get here. We should make sure we're on the same page."

He took a long, slow sip of coffee, forcing her to wait on needles for a response. Several seconds ticked by, and then he took another sip. Finally, he said, "We're not on the same page. You made sure of that ten years ago."

Leah leaned back against the leather seat and huffed a sigh. Clearly, Colt wasn't going to make this easy. "Look, I know you're mad, and you have every right to be. But I need you to pretend for one minute that you don't hate me. Can you do that?"

He made eye contact now—in the form of an icy blue-green glare.

"We need to talk before we go in there," she continued. "Or we're going to make the situation worse than it already is."

"Fine." He faced front and raised his mug to his lips. "Then talk."

Leah glanced out the back window for Jim and Diane's rental car. They should be here any minute. "The Ackermans have always let me see Noah, but we don't have a legal agreement. There's nothing in writing. They could cut me off anytime, and I wouldn't have a leg to stand on in court. They don't have to let you see Noah either, so keep that in mind before you start making demands."

"What do you think I'm gonna do?" He spoke into his coffee, sounding offended. "Go in there and order an omelet, then draw my Glock and kidnap him?"

"Don't rock the boat. That's all I'm trying to say. You've got a temper, CJ, and—"

"Hey," he objected. "I don't have a temper!"

"Oh, please." She cocked her head to the side. "Need I remind you of The Great Condom Incident, where you pulverized Tommy's liver right there at the Sack-n-Pay checkout line?"

"It was his kidney, not his liver. And besides, that doesn't count." Colt waved her off. "Tommy needed someone to take him down a peg. Anyone but *you* would understand, Saint Leah the Passive."

She made a frustrated noise from the back of her throat. "You're infuriating, you know that?"

"Now who has the temper?"

Leah's head came dangerously close to exploding, but fortunately, a silver Ford Taurus pulled up beside the cruiser and forced an end to their argument.

"Noah's a sweet boy," she said with an artificial smile and a wave out the window. "So you be sweet too."

Colt nestled his coffee mug inside the dashboard holder. Before opening his door, he left her with a sarcastic jab. "Got it. Thanks for having so much faith in me, as usual."

His words stunned her and she sat for a silent beat with her fingers frozen around the door handle. Colt had thrown the barb at her in spite, but a tug of guilt from the pit of her stomach told her there was a kernel of truth behind it. She hadn't had faith in his ability to parent their baby all those years ago, so she'd arranged the adoption behind his back. Had she made the same mistake by expecting him to cause trouble today? Colt got under her skin like a deer tick, but he was probably right. She still lacked faith in him. By the time she geared up to apologize, he'd already stepped out onto the sidewalk.

She joined Colt near the Waffle Shack entrance and linked arms with him to present a united front. He stiffened the set of his elbow but didn't pull away. Leaning in, she whispered, "I'm sorry. I do have faith in you."

He didn't answer, just pulled off his Stetson and alternated nervous glances between his boots and the son he'd never met. She decided to help him along. It was the least she could do.

She waved Noah over with an enthusiastic grin. "Hey, Bud! Come here—I missed you!"

A toothy smile split her boy's face, and she felt it like sunshine warming her from scalp to toes. He looked so handsome in his tan corduroys and the dinosaur sweater she'd given him last Christmas. As he ran toward her, she lowered and reached out her arms to him.

He gave her a tight squeeze, surrounding her in his signature little boy scent of outdoor air and grape shampoo. She hugged him back and closed her eyes to soak him up until he got fidgety. Noah hugs never lasted long enough.

When she stood, she nodded at Colt. "I want you to meet my good friend, Colton Bea." Then she widened her eyes and said in a super-serious voice, "He's the sheriff of the *whole* county."

"Whoa." Noah turned an equally wide-eyed gaze at Colt. After taking in every gadget, badge, and patch along Colt's uniform, he surprised her by matter-of-factly stating, "You're my birth dad."

She and Colt shared a quick glance. "That's right," Leah said. "Did your mom and dad talk to you about that?"

"Uh-huh, they told me yesterday." Noah motioned to Jim and Diane, who held back a few feet to give them some space. "Mom said a man named Colton Bea put me in your tummy a long time ago, but he couldn't take care of me 'cause he was still in school, just like you were."

Leah felt her cheeks flushing. She didn't know how much Diane had explained about the birds and the bees, so she didn't elaborate. "That's right. Colt is your birth father like I'm your birth mother. And he loves you just as much as I do, even though you two have never met. Isn't that cool?"

Noah thought about it a moment before deciding, "Yeah. He's got a cowboy hat and a pistol and everything." Colt chuckled at that, and Noah asked him, "Do you get to arrest a lot of bad guys?"

"I sure do. We've got a whole jail full of 'em. And I brought something for you." Colt reached into his breast pocket and pulled out a silver star. He bent at the knees until he was eye-level with Noah and leaned in as if to share a secret. "Now, don't tell anyone, but these are the badges we give *real* deputies. We don't hand these out to just anybody."

Noah's black brows shot up his forehead.

"I was thinkin' you could be my deputy in training," Colt told him. "I can't give you a cruiser since you're not driving age, but we could probably wrangle up a hat in your size. What do you think?"

Noah whirled around and asked Diane, "Can I, Mom?" She nodded and Noah didn't wait another moment to accept his gift. Colt pinned it to his sweater, careful not to pierce the dinosaur's head, while Noah beamed like a sixty-watt bulb. "Thanks," he said, admiring his star.

"You're welcome." Colt extended a hand. "Nice to meet you." When Noah gave it a vigorous shake, Colt nodded appreciatively and said, "Nice grip."

Leah figured it was time to introduce the Ackermans. She waved at them and touched Colt's shoulder. "Jim and Diane, this is Sheriff Colton Bea."

The three of them leaned in to exchange greetings and handshakes, their postures stiff and their smiles tight. Diane, whose wardrobe typically consisted of yoga pants and long-sleeved T-shirts, had dressed in a pantsuit paired with pearls. She fidgeted with her designer purse strap and clung to Jim, who looked more like a math professor than a graphic designer in his tweed sport jacket. It seemed everyone had something to prove today, including Colt, who could've worn street clothes but obviously felt more powerful in his uniform.

What they all needed was to relax and bond over a greasy second-rate breakfast. Leah wrapped an arm around Noah and led him toward the front door. She called over her shoulder, "Everyone ready? The food's great here. I hope you're hungry!"

—〰—

"That's not a T-rex." Noah tapped his finger against the green dinosaur embroidered on his sweater. "It's an allosaurus."

The boy said it with so much authority that Colt believed him, but he still asked, "How do you know?"

"T-rex was bigger." Noah shrugged as if the answer should be obvious, then sipped his herbal tea like a little scholar. "He weighed three times as much."

Colt mirrored his son and took a swig of the pond sludge that passed for coffee in this joint. Why Leah had insisted on meeting here was beyond him. "You know an awful lot about dinosaurs."

Noah darted a glance at Diane. "My mom takes me to Dino Camp at the museum every Saturday."

Private school, museum memberships, science camps—Colt couldn't deny the Ackermans had given his boy the kinds of things he couldn't have provided at seventeen. Judging by the couple's fancy clothes and trendy haircuts, they had plenty of cash to drop on Noah, but that didn't make Colt feel all warm and fuzzy about the adoption. Money and education weren't everything. He could've taught his son how to throw a perfect spiral and how to catch a catfish using nothing more than a night crawler and a few yards of fishing line. And if you asked him, that kind of knowledge was more practical than how to tell dinosaurs apart.

"You play any sports?" Colt asked.

Leah answered from the other end of the long table, "He sure does. Noah's soccer team is going to regionals again this year, aren't you, Bud?"

"Uh-huh."

Soccer? A deep-in-the-heart-of-Texas Bea man playing *soccer*? "That's great," Colt ground out while clapping his boy on the back. "But a big, strapping guy like you? I took you for a football player."

"Nah," Noah said. "I don't like football."

Colt almost choked on his coffee. This kid needed an intervention. "Well, you can't judge the sport by the Vikings. Next time you're in town, I'll take you to a Texans game so you can see what *real* football's all about."

"Hey," Leah objected. "The Vikings have a good team this year."

Colt rolled his eyes and whispered to Noah, "Girls."

Noah gave a conspiratorial giggle. "Yeah, girls."

The waitress returned with their orders and began dealing out plates like poker cards. Colt scowled at his lumpy grits, runny eggs, and a buttermilk biscuit hard enough to qualify as a lethal weapon. He glanced beside him at Noah's bowl of diced fruit.

"That's all you're gonna eat?" Colt asked him.

Diane spoke up from the opposite side of the table. Until now, she and her husband had done a good job of keeping to themselves so Colt and Noah could get to know each other.

"I brought a packet of gluten-free oatmeal," she said. "He's got a slight allergy to wheat. Nothing serious, but it gives him a tummy ache." Then she pulled a pouch from her purse and used the boiling water from her teapot to mix up a bowl of oats.

Gluten? Colt didn't even know what that was. And how was it related to wheat?

"Can I have something in it?" Noah asked, pointing to the maple syrup and an assortment of jelly packets.

Diane dug inside her purse and produced a tiny plastic bottle. "Here, I packed some organic honey." She handed it to Noah, and he drizzled it over his oatmeal without a single complaint, even though the stuff looked like gruel.

Gluten-free oats, organic honey, diced fruit, and herbal tea? Was this the kind of breakfast Noah ate every day? Colt thought back to all the times he'd let Emma nosh on Pop Tarts and glazed doughnuts, giving her a jug of Sunny D to wash it all down. His sister had always yelled at him about sugar and preservatives, but the way he'd figured it, the cherry filling counted as a serving of fruit. Besides, his parents had let him eat junk once in a while, and he'd survived.

Colt brought a forkful of eggs to his mouth and froze when he noticed Noah lay a napkin across his lap. He hurried to do the same before the boy assumed his "birth father" was a redneck cretin. Not only was Noah smart and well-nourished, but he had impeccable manners too. Colt felt a flash of shame, but he snuffed it out. Maybe he would've fed Noah too much sugar and let him rest his elbows on the table. Maybe he'd have allowed the boy to slack off in school now and then, but that never killed anyone. He would've been a good father in other ways if Leah had given him the chance.

While Colt was busy brooding to himself, a family of four settled loudly in a nearby booth. He didn't pay them much mind, but Noah kept turning around to watch the two kids sitting opposite their parents. The boy and girl kept needling each other—just your standard sibling rivalry—until their dad hollered at them to shut up. They mouthed off in a way that would've earned most kids an ass whoopin' in these parts, but then they pulled out a pair of handheld video games and sweet silence ensued.

Noah asked his mom, "How come *they* get to play their DSs at the table and I can't?"

Diane leaned to the side and glanced at the kids in question, then simply stated, "Because I'm not their mother."

Noah turned to Leah, but she cut him off before he got a single word out. "You know better than to ask me."

Then Noah bit his lip and blinked up at Colt. Personally, Colt didn't see the harm in kids playing video games in public. It kept them quiet and let the adults talk. But the glare Leah was firing from the other end of the table told him to shut Noah down fast, so he shook his head and tried to remember the trick his sister was always talking about—redirecting.

He turned Noah's attention away from video games by asking, "What kind of stuff do you like doing back home?"

Noah lit up and started talking about Japanese animation. Colt was pretty sure the boy was speaking English, but he had his doubts. Names like Pikachu, Polywag, Weedle, and Magnemite flew at him at a thousand words per minute, forcing Colt to nod thoughtfully and pretend he had a clue what Noah was saying. But he listened patiently, entertained by his son's passion for battle arenas, whatever those were.

The next topic was more Colt's speed. Jim mentioned that Noah had taken the remote control apart and put it back together at age five, and then Noah filled him in on his favorite hobby—building motorized racing boats with his dad. The two would spend all year tweaking the engine performance before traveling to an annual showdown to race the competition. They'd never won, but Colt could tell from the admiration in Jim's eyes that victory wasn't the point. It was all about father-son bonding, like the fishing and hunting trips Colt had taken with his own dad.

Colt felt a stirring of envy and gratitude for Jim. It rubbed him the wrong way to hear his son refer to the man as "Dad," but as time passed, he began to see all the ways Jim had made Noah the center of his universe. Would Colt have done the same? Would he have put his child first? At seventeen, his whole world was football. Even Leah had come in second place behind the team. He wanted to believe he would've manned up, but the truth was he wasn't much of a man back then.

"Do you build stuff too?" Noah asked, drawing Colt away from thoughts he didn't want to explore.

"Sure, always have," he said. "I started rebuilding a motorcycle when I was in high school. Got it running better than new."

"Is it fast?"

"Faster than a greased bullet."

That spurred a discussion about pistons and gear shafts. It made Colt proud to know his son had inherited an aptitude for mechanics from him. At least he'd been able to contribute something to the life of this remarkable boy.

Colt never imagined it could happen so quickly, but he fell in love with Noah over the course of that long meal. Leah was right when she'd called Noah sweet. That wasn't typically a word Colt used to describe boys, but it fit. Noah had a gentle spirit. He spoke respectfully to his mama, he said *please* and *thank you*, and he didn't whine. He wasn't perfect. Like all kids, he tried to push the line when he didn't get his way, but compared to Colt at that age, Noah was an angel.

*Just like his mother.*

Colt didn't want it to be true, but he couldn't deny that Leah and the Ackermans had shaped Noah into a fine young man. That didn't mean he was happy about missing his son's first decade, but he began to understand what was best for Noah, and it wasn't uprooting him from his parents for half the school year.

"Look at Miss Leah." Noah tugged on Colt's shirt-sleeve and stared at the other end of the table. "Why's she so sad all the time?"

Colt turned to find her staring out the window with her chin in her hand while Jim and Diane carried on a side conversation. With her blond waves catching the morning sun, she looked beautiful but broken, so heart-sick that his breath caught. He said, "She's probably just tired," but that was a lie. He'd been flogging her all week, stomping her down until he'd smothered the happiness she'd found here.

"I wanna make her feel better." Noah stood and pulled a small plastic ball from his pocket. "I traded my friend for a new Pokemon. It's a powerball—it beats almost everything. I'll battle her, but I'll let her use this and she'll win. I always feel better when I win."

"That's real nice of you," Colt said. "You should hug her too. Girls like that kind of thing."

Noah made a *yuck!* face. "The girls at my school like kisses too, but that's gross."

Colt chuckled, remembering a time when he'd felt

the same way. He watched Noah present his toy to Leah and sling his arms around her neck. Her ivory face brightened, brimming with love for their boy. The sight made Colt's heart swell. Add *compassion* to the list of Noah's virtues, something Colt couldn't have taught him at seventeen because he'd been a selfish bastard in boots. Hell, sometimes he still was. He probably would've ruined that sweet boy.

"I have an idea," Leah said to everyone. "Why don't I take Noah to meet his granddad—uh, I mean Pastor Mac—while you guys chat?"

Colt shared a glance with Jim and Diane. He'd been dreading this part of the meeting, but they did need to iron out a plan for the future.

"That sounds fine," Jim said. "Why don't you bring him back here in..." he tipped his head at Colt, "what? An hour?"

"An hour sounds good," Colt agreed. He waved at Noah. "Maybe when you come back, I can take you on a tour of the station." He realized too late that he should have cleared that with his parents first. "I mean, if it's okay with your mom and dad."

Jim grinned, but the sentiment didn't reach his eyes. "Let's see how our schedule looks."

In other words: *Let's see if we're friends or enemies*.

Colt couldn't blame him for being protective. Any good father would do the same.

Leah took Noah by the hand and led him into the parking lot. Before she disappeared from view, she gave Colt an encouraging smile as if to repeat, *I do have faith in you*. It left him with a sense of warmth he didn't want to feel for her.

An awkward silence hung in the air for a few seconds. Diane was the first to break it by clearing her throat and nervously folding and unfolding her hands on the tabletop.

"Before we begin," she said, "I want you to know that we never would've pursued the adoption if we'd known you wanted to parent Noah. We had no idea."

"I know," he said. "Leah already told me."

Diane pressed a hand to her chest. "Still, I feel responsible on some level. She was so skittish back then—completely terrified. Those first few weeks, she barely spoke a word. I should've known something was wrong."

Colt remembered the picture Leah had shown him last week. He hadn't told her so, but the most striking part of the image wasn't her round pregnant belly. It was her eyes—haunted and vacant.

It hadn't occurred to him until right now, but he'd put that look in her eyes. As a teen, he'd selfishly set out to seduce her without a care for using protection. Yes, she'd hurt him by hiding Noah, but hadn't he done the same by putting her in that position to begin with?

"We figured her parents were abusive," Jim added, bringing Colt back to the present.

Colt picked up his Stetson and turned it over in his hands. "Look, I'm grateful for everything you've given Noah. You've done a fine job with him—much better than I could've done."

"He's a special boy," Diane said. "He makes it easy."

Colt smiled in agreement. "But that doesn't change the fact that Leah placed him with you without my consent." He flashed a palm and quickly added, "Don't get the wrong idea. I'm not interested in disrupting Noah's life. But I want to be a part of it."

"We understand that," she said.

"I'd like to see him on a regular basis, like Leah does." Even though he and Noah had gotten off to a great start, Colt said, "It's probably a good idea to begin with supervised visitation until he gets to know me. But after that, I'd like it if he and I could spend one weekend together every other month. Then maybe when he's a teenager, a couple of weeks over the summer here in Texas."

Jim and Diane shared an agreeing glance. "I think we can make that work," Jim said.

"But I'd like it in writing." Colt recalled what Leah had said earlier, how she feared losing her visits with Noah. He didn't want that threat hanging over his head. "Not that I don't trust you, but I'd feel better if we made it official."

For the next few minutes, they hashed out a few minor details, then came to an agreement over a handshake. Colt insisted on settling the bill. These people had given his son a loving home, so the least he could do was buy their god-awful breakfast.

While he left the tip, Diane said, "I don't know how much Leah told you about us…"

"Not much." He counted out thirty percent, figuring it wasn't the waitress's fault the food was so horrible. "Just that you're good people."

"When Leah contacted us ten years ago," her voice thickened, and she paused. "I'd just had my fifth miscarriage and we decided to quit trying."

Colt gave her his full attention, but it wasn't easy.

Her eyes had started to well up, and he hated to see anyone cry.

"Leah gave us a tremendous gift," she went on. "And that's one of the reasons we agreed to keep the adoption open. I know it came at a great cost to the both of you."

He agreed with her, but he didn't know what to say to that. *You're welcome* didn't seem to fit.

"Noah saved me." She turned her watery gaze to her husband, who pulled her against his chest and kissed her forehead. "I know that sounds dramatic, but it's true."

Colt had to look away, and not just because he hated to see a woman cry. He'd never been a churchgoing man and he didn't believe in fate, but her words resonated with him straight to the pit of his stomach. Noah belonged with these people. He felt that truth deep inside.

He hated to admit it, but Leah had done the right thing. If she'd come to him ten years ago and asked for his consent, he would have asked his parents to keep the baby until he got his shit together. And God only knows how long that would've taken.

She'd done the right thing, and he'd punished her for it.

This past week, he'd grieved the loss of his angel, the flawless woman he'd loved half his life, but what right did he have to hold her to that impossible standard? Nobody walked on water, least of all himself. Just look at the way he'd behaved since Leah returned to town—vowing to win her back by any means necessary, stooping to lies and manipulation to get her naked. But when she made a mistake, he tried running her out of town. Why was her perfection so important to him? Was he trying to make himself good by association, like he'd done in high school?

Colt didn't know, but he began to understand why karma was kicking his ass lately. Leah still had the purest heart on earth…and he'd broken it.

# Chapter 20

LEAH SAT ON HER SUITCASE AND BOUNCED IN PLACE A few times until she flattened the clothes inside. She zipped the top shut and hauled it to the bedroom door, where it sat looking more like a time bomb than a Samsonite. Since she hadn't brought much with her, it didn't take long to pack. All she needed now was to gather her toiletries and she'd be ready to hit the road.

"You're insane," Rachel said from the other side of the bed. "You know that, right?"

And say good-bye to the people she loved. She had to do that too.

Rachel pushed off the bed and stood in the doorway. She used her foot to knock over the suitcase. "I should hogtie you and stuff you in the closet until you come to your senses." She raised her chin and promised, "I'm bigger than you. I could do it."

Leah sniffed a laugh. Rachel always had a way of making her feel better, and she'd needed her best friend's support after saying good-bye to Noah half an hour ago. Her visits with him left her fragile, which was why she had to get out of Sultry Springs. If she bumped into Colt again, she'd shatter completely.

"Enough with the wounded bird routine," Rachel demanded. "Say something."

Leah stopped what she was doing and locked eyes with her best friend. "I'm going to miss you."

In typical Rachel fashion, she held up both palms to block the emotions from touching her too deeply. "Don't do that—don't go all sappy on me, Tink. Just stay." She tilted her head and pleaded, "C'mon, stay. Please?"

Rachel wasn't making this easy, and she wasn't the only one. Even though Daddy's heart was beating stronger than ever, he'd called Doctor Benton, hoping her new acquaintance would coerce her into overseeing Daddy's cardiac rehabilitation therapy. The doctor wouldn't take Daddy's side, but only because he had his own agenda—Benton wanted her working with *him* in the intensive care unit. He said the hospital had offered her a nursing position contingent on the renewal of her license. She'd tried telling him no, but much like Rachel, he didn't want to hear it. He'd insisted the offer would remain open, and he encouraged her to reconsider.

"At least tell me this isn't about Colton," Rachel said. "Because really, Tink. He's just a man. They're a dime a dozen, and we grow 'em big here in Texas. We'll find you another one—a sexy cowboy who's packin' some serious heat, and I don't mean a pistol!"

Leah smiled at the joke but shook her head. A heart's true match wasn't easily replaced, and she hoped one day Rachel would meet a man who proved that to her. "This isn't forever," Leah said, dodging the question. "I just need some time to heal."

"Are you coming back for Christmas?"

Leah opened her mouth to say *yes* but closed it just as quickly. The Ackermans would take Noah to Paris, so she wouldn't be able to spend Christmas Eve with him. There was no reason she couldn't return to Sultry Springs for the holidays. No reason besides seeing Colt and reopening the wound she was so desperately trying to close. She offered a weak grin and said, "Maybe."

The skeptical twist of Rachel's lips said she didn't buy it. "You're not gonna stay with me, are you?"

"No."

"And there's nothing I can do to stop you, is there?"

"No."

"Then let's get this over with." Rachel held out her arms reluctantly, like the hug might carry rabies. "I don't want to be here when you drive away."

Leah agreed it was easier like this. Watching Daddy's house in her rear-view mirror would be hard enough without Rachel's reflection fading into the distance alongside it. She embraced her friend tightly, careful not to allow the stinging tears behind her eyes to overflow. If she started crying now, she wouldn't stop until she hit Iowa.

Rachel seemed to struggle too. But just when she started to break down, Rachel abruptly pulled back, turned on her heel, and fled down the hall. Leah called after her, but she wouldn't stop. A glance out her bedroom window showed her friend jogging across the front lawn to her car and then speeding away.

This wasn't the farewell she'd imagined.

Leah tipped her face toward the ceiling fan and blinked her eyes dry. The tears wouldn't hold back for much longer. A pressure was building inside her chest, sobs trying to work their way free. She had to hurry and get out of here.

After throwing her cosmetics into an oversized Ziploc bag, she wheeled her suitcase outside and stowed it in the trunk of Benny's Escalade. The thought of driving the massive luxury SUV didn't appeal to her. All that extra space inside made her feel lonely, not pampered. During the past month, she'd grown accustomed to the cradle of a cracked vinyl seat and duct-taped arm rests. She cast a wistful glance at Bruiser, parked at the curb. She'd miss him too. Despite his hideous facade, he'd been good to her. Besides, he was her first real car—and a girl never forgot her first.

Daddy made his way outside to join her, dragging his feet, both hands wedged in his pockets. The crisp autumn air brought a healthy flush to his cheeks that she hadn't seen since the surgery. He still had work to do, but he looked better than she'd seen him in years, and she told him so.

"That's the power of good old-fashioned TLC," he told her softly. "I don't think you understand how much I miss you when you're gone, Pumpkin."

Oh, she understood perfectly. She felt the same way between visits with her own child. She hated to leave Daddy, but she had to put herself first for once, take care of her needs before she could give any more of herself to others.

"I'll be back to visit before too long," she said. "And I want to see you back in those size thirty-fours you used to wear." She didn't tell Daddy, but she'd asked old Ms. Bicknocker to come around and make sure he was eating real food. "No more frozen dinners, and no more drive-thru meals. I don't want you undoing all my hard work. Promise?"

He tried to say, "Promise," but it came out in a wet whisper that almost tore out her heart. She had to go now, or she'd come undone. She threw her arms around his neck and pulled in the smell of minty antacids and Aqua Velva. The smell of her daddy. She held that breath a while to make it last.

Once Leah had scaled the Escalade and fastened her seat belt, she turned on the navigation system and waved to Daddy one last time. Then she pulled onto the street and didn't look back.

—∿∿—

Darla leaned over the reception desk and pointed one red fingernail at Noah. "Don't tell the other guys I said this, but you're the cutest deputy in here."

Noah tipped back his miniature Stetson. The cowboy hat looked strange paired with his preppy tan pants and the toothy dinosaur on his sweater, like Indiana Jones meets Wyatt Earp. The boy smiled at her and said, "I know."

Everyone laughed at that, and then Colt noticed Jim checking his watch again. Colt knew the Ackermans had a plane to catch, and they'd been more than generous with their time, so he steered them through the lobby and out the front doors to the parking lot. After a round of handshakes and good-byes, he told Noah he'd see him next month and watched to make sure the family made it safely down Main Street before he headed inside.

"I still can't believe you're a daddy," Darla told him. "He looks just like you."

Colt felt himself beaming. He glanced down at his phone, where he'd captured Noah's image—blue eyes bright beneath the brim of his hat, mouth curved in a gap-toothed smile. Now he could see his boy whenever he pleased, and in a few weeks, they'd be together in

Minnesota. He should probably apply for one of those frequent flyer credit cards, because he'd rack up some serious miles before long.

"I see a little of Leah in him too," Darla said, pointing to her own face. "Around the eyes, don't you think?"

*Leah*. At the mention of her name, a dull ache spread though his chest. "Yeah," he mumbled. "Around the eyes."

What was he going to do about her? He'd screwed up again, big time. They needed to talk and set things right, but she'd already forgiven him once, and that had taken a month of solid effort on his part. Even if she gave him a third chance, he didn't know what he wanted from her. When he'd sold her engagement ring last week, he'd felt certain there was no shot of a future for them.

"Is Noah gonna be your ring bearer?" Darla asked. "Or your best man? 'Cause I think he'd look so handsome standing up there beside you in a little-bitty tux."

Colt scratched his forehead and repeated, "Little-bitty tux" while he absently strode down the hall to his office. A sense of urgency warned him to repair the damage now, before it was too late. But what should he say to her? What about their relationship—could they salvage it? Hell, he didn't know. He needed to shut his office door and think.

He didn't expect to see Rachel Landry sitting in his chair with those damn dirty garden clogs kicked up on his desk. God bless, why did women insist on wearing those things? Maybe Rachel used them as man-repellent.

"How'd you get in here?" he asked. "I know Darla didn't let you in this time."

She shot him the bird, not even bothering to flash her usual sarcastic grin. "I came here to tell you I changed my mind. I *do* hate your face, Colton Bea."

"Good to know things are getting back to normal."
He hitched a thumb over his shoulder. "Now I can tell
you to take a hike."

Her nostrils flared and she started eyeing his letter
opener. He didn't think she'd shank him, but just to be
safe, he grabbed it and tossed it onto the filing cabinet.

Rachel stood from his chair and folded her arms.
"Well, you did it. You rode her out of town on a rail.
You happy now, asshole? Or you wanna tar and feather
her too?"

Colt's stomach sank as he processed her psychotic
rant. "Leah left already?" But he'd just seen her a couple
of hours ago at the Waffle Shack when she'd dropped
off Noah.

"Yep. Gone. She's probably in Hallover County by
now." She touched her forehead with two fingers in a
mock salute. "I just lost my best friend—for the second
time—thanks to you. I'd like to kick you in the nuts so
hard your granddaddy feels it."

A cold sweat broke out across Colt's brow. Every
fiber of uncertainty vanished, leaving behind an ironclad
truth that he felt in the pit of his soul: he still wanted
Leah. He'd barely survived losing her the first time, and
he simply could not lose her again. His first instinct was
to hop in his cruiser and speed after her, but that was a
bad idea. He had no clue which route she'd taken—if
she'd stuck to the highway or ventured down back roads
to reach the interstate.

"Is she driving the Cadillac," he asked, "or that old
purple beater?"

"The Caddy. Why do you care?"

"Move." He nudged Rachel aside and pulled open

his top desk drawer. He tore through receipts, messages, and Post-it notes for the slip of paper he'd used to write down Leah's license plate number when she'd come to town last month. Once he found it, he left Rachel without another word and dashed to the dispatch room.

He shoved the wad of paper at the deputy manning the dispatch station. "Tell the Hallover boys I need a quick favor."

---

Leah fiddled with the satellite radio controls until she found a peppy station. She cranked up the volume and sang along to "Shiny Happy People" as loud as she could, but her vocal cords refused to cooperate. She kept choking off at the end of each line, so the shiny happy people were holding "hah" instead of hands. Since there was no use trying to trick herself, she changed strategies and drowned her sorrows in some old George Jones. "He Stopped Loving Her Today" was a more appropriate song anyhow.

Through a thin veil of tears, she admired the rolling hills and hayfields as they blurred past at sixty miles per hour. Fall had dulled the colors of the typically green landscape, but at least it wasn't covered in two feet of Minnesota snow. She'd just passed an abandoned barn when red and blue flashing lights caught her eye in the rear-view mirror. A brown sheriff's cruiser blasted his siren in two short wails, and Leah's gaze flew to the speedometer. She was going five miles under the speed limit, thank goodness. She took her foot off the gas and looked for a good spot to pull over. Twenty yards ahead, she spotted a gravel path running between two soybean fields, so she turned onto it and came to a stop, then cut the engine.

She watched the officer pull in behind her and waited to see what he'd do. When he stepped outside and approached her door, she rolled down her window.

"Afternoon, ma'am." He touched the brim of his hat in a firm greeting. "You headed out of town?"

"Yes, sir." She noticed her reflection in his mirrored sunglasses. With her puffy eyes and reddened nose, he probably thought she'd been drinking. "Is something wrong?"

He took a moment to study her, his poker face revealing no emotion. "Just stay in the car, please." Then he walked back to his cruiser and climbed inside.

That was weird. She wondered what he wanted. Benny knew she was on her way back to Minnesota, so he wouldn't have reported the Escalade as stolen. She sat patiently, watching him in her rear-view while she waited for him to return.

Five minutes passed. Then ten. And fifteen. Twenty minutes later, a Sultry County cruiser joined them on the path, kicking up dirt and gravel as he pulled to a stop in front of her. After that, the Hallover deputy backed onto the main road and drove away.

Leah didn't like this. She peered out her front windshield to catch a glimpse of the other officer, but the air was too clouded with dust to identify him. She gripped the leather steering wheel while his door swung open, all the while praying to herself, *Please don't be Colt. Please don't be Colt. Please don't be Colt.*

One brown Laredo hit the gravel, then the other. A large tawny hand gripped the door frame, and the man hoisted himself to standing. At once, she recognized the loose black hair brushing his broad shoulders. Of course it was Colt. Because she hadn't suffered enough today.

He closed his door and ambled toward her, the brim of his Stetson concealing his face in shadows. When he reached her, he knocked twice on the window, and she reluctantly rolled it down.

"License and registration," he said, keeping his head tipped down to inspect her tires.

If she and Colt had parted on friendly terms, she'd assume this was a joke. But there was no humor in his smooth, deep voice. She didn't know what he was up to, but she didn't want any part of it. She couldn't take another one of his cold shots.

"Leave me be," she said weakly. "You don't even have jurisdiction here."

He held out his hand, palm up, and repeated, "License and registration."

She made a frustrated noise and reached for her purse. "Fine." Maybe if she gave him what he wanted, he'd go away. She dug Benny's paper out of the glove box, then thrust it out the window along with her license.

He took the documents from her and made a show of appraising them, even though he'd seen them before. "Here," he said, handing back Benny's registration. "You can have this." But instead of returning her license, he tucked it in his back pocket.

She pointed to the vicinity of his backside. "I need that."

He ignored her and ordered, "Step out of the car."

"Why?" she asked. "There are only so many ways I can say I'm sorry. I tried to—"

"Because you're not goin' anywhere." He tipped

back his hat, revealing sea blue eyes alight with fire. "Not till I have my say."

She stayed put, trying to hold herself together while her chin trembled.

"Damn it, Leah." Colt pointed to the ground. "Get out here so I can apologize."

She slid a glance at him and lowered one brow, figuring he couldn't mean that. "Is this a trick?"

He answered by opening her door and offering a hand to help her down. When she unbuckled her seatbelt and swung her legs around, he surprised her by wrapping his palms around her waist and carefully lowering her to the gravel. Once there, he was slow to release her, standing so close she felt the heat rolling off his chest.

"It's not a trick," he murmured into her hair. "I wanna tell you I'm sorry." He tipped her chin until their faces met, his gaze full of contrition when he whispered, "I'm sorry."

She believed him, and yet her feet took a step back in a warning to keep her shields up. She was too raw inside, too vulnerable to risk her heart again if *sorry* was all he had to say.

He noted the distance between them but didn't object. Instead, he shut her car door and respected her space. Humbly, he pulled off his hat and told her, "I'm not trying to excuse the way I behaved, but it was a shock—learning about Noah that way. I was hurt and angry, and I think I wanted you to feel some of that pain."

She leaned back against the Escalade and folded her arms protectively.

"If we're being honest," he said, "I'm still hurt. I have a son, but I don't know his favorite flavor of ice cream or if he still sleeps with a stuffed animal."

Unable to hold his gaze, she stared at the ground. "Cotton candy is his favorite, and he sleeps with a little blue bear, but he doesn't want anyone to know because he's afraid his friends will make fun of him. I feel awful for shutting you out, Colt. I hope you believe me. If I could go back and do it again, I'd—"

"I wouldn't want you to change a thing," he insisted. She glanced at him in disbelief and found him raking a hand through his hair. "That's the hard part—that's the rub. I hate that I missed Noah's first nine years, but I know I couldn't have been a decent father to him back then. Hell, I even wonder if I'd make a decent dad now. And if you'd asked me, I never would've agreed to give him up. You sacrificed your happiness for our boy, and that's the truest kind of love." He shook his head as if he didn't understand his own words. "You did the right thing, even though it was terrible and wrong. Does that make sense?"

Leah caught her bottom lip between her teeth and nodded. It made perfect sense.

"Staying mad at you is a lot of work, and I'm tired. I don't want to let all that bitterness and regret eat me up." He reached for her hand, a silent message that the next move was hers. "I love you too much for that."

Her heart jumped. He still loved her? A cautious smile pressed her lips as she took his hand.

"I know you're not perfect—I don't expect that of you." He eliminated the space between them and lifted her chin again. "But you'll always be my angel."

The tears she'd suppressed all day leaked down her cheeks. Colt used a thumb to brush them away. He whispered against her lips, "Tell me you still love me."

It took a few moments to find her voice, but when she did, she promised, "There's only you."

He dropped a soft kiss on her mouth, just a taste of his sweetness, then lowered to one knee. "I've never loved anybody but you, and if you'll let me, I swear I'll love you and no one else until I die."

He pulled a gold ring from his shirt pocket and studied it for a moment. A faceted burgundy stone glowed warm and shimmered in the light until it resembled a beating heart. "I know it's not a diamond," Colt said, "but my grandmamma gave me this before she passed. She used to say garnets symbolize pure sacrifice, and I can't think of anything more fitting for you to wear on your finger."

Leah wanted to tell him it was the most beautiful thing she'd ever seen, but emotion had thickened her throat until she could barely breathe.

Colt presented the ring to her and squeezed her hand. "I never felt like I deserved you, and today's no different. But I promise no man will love you harder and no man will give more of himself than I will. I swear I'll never let you down. Please say you'll marry me. It hurts too much when we're not together."

Leah pressed her free hand over her mouth to stifle a sob of joy. Colt's stunning face, so filled with adoration, blurred through her tears, and she blotted her eyes to bring him back into focus. "Yes." It was more a husky whisper than anything, but she didn't care. "Yes, I'll marry you."

With a smile bright enough to shame the sun, he slid the ring on her finger and stood to take her face between his palms. "Thank you," he said.

"Oh, no." She remembered something. "What about Benny's car? I still have to drive it to Minnesota."

"It can wait a few weeks." He pressed her body against the side of the Escalade. "I just got you back, and we've got some catching up to do." To prove it, he brushed his mouth against hers and ran the tip of his tongue along her bottom lip. The kiss deepened, growing hotter and wetter until she felt him hardening against her belly. He moved his lips to her ear and whispered, "You really wanna take a road trip right now?"

"No," she breathed, tipping her head aside to welcome the slide of his mouth on her neck. She wasn't going anywhere today, except to the moon. "I wouldn't mind climbing into the back seat, though."

"Why, Leah McMahon!" Colt drew back and tried to sound scandalized, but a wicked grin betrayed him. "Are you leading me into temptation?"

She beamed up at him—her future husband—so exquisite that she wanted to cry again. There was too much happiness inside her. She couldn't make room for all of it. "You bet I am. And what I have in mind is illegal in some states."

He opened the door and tossed his Stetson inside. "In that case, I'm all in, honey. They don't call me Crazy Colt for nothing."

No, they sure didn't. Colt was the devil in cowboy boots, and Leah was no angel. But together, she knew they'd make their own brand of heaven on earth.

~~~

After their back-seat adventure, they sped home to Sultry County, where they spent the rest of the afternoon making up for lost time in Colt's king-sized bed. Even when they weren't making love, Leah clung to him, locking her arms around his broad neck in a compulsion to get closer, afraid the dream would evaporate like mist if she loosened her embrace. He must have felt the same way, because he left her side only once—to make a phone call to her daddy—before returning to bed and loving her again, stronger than before.

Finally at suppertime, Colt insisted they venture out to the Main Street Diner, and Leah's grumbling stomach agreed. But instead of driving toward town, he made a left onto the old country road, continued another mile, and pulled into the church parking lot.

"Are we turning around?" she asked.

"Nope," was all he said as he cut the ignition.

Leah glanced at the church and the adjoining fellowship hall, both equally dark and showing no signs of life. She remembered his earlier phone call with Daddy and wondered if he'd staged an impromptu wedding. "We can't get married without a license, you know."

"I know." He stepped out of the cruiser and jogged around the front end to open her door, then extended a hand to help her to standing. "Besides, when I marry you, it won't be in the dark. I'm gonna throw you the biggest wedding this town's ever seen."

Leah smiled at his enthusiasm, figuring she'd rein in his plans later. She didn't need a flashy extravaganza— just her family, her friends, and Colt. It was the marriage that mattered, not the wedding.

"Then what're we doing here?" she asked him.

He didn't answer, only linked their fingers and towed her toward the fellowship hall. When they reached the door, he knocked twice and let himself in, then ushered her into the darkness.

Leah had just opened her mouth to object when the lights flashed on and a chorus of whoops and hollers broke out, followed closely by thunderous applause.

She drew back, hand flying over her heart, as half the church congregation stood in front of their folding chairs, clapping wildly for her. At once, her eyes focused on the church's well-used "Welcome Home" banner that hung from the ceiling—the same one she'd seen at the Lewis homecoming. But below the faded lettering, someone had added the word *FOREVER* in bright-red paint. From there, she noticed a few old photos of herself affixed to the walls, and in the center of the room, platters of cold cuts and appetizers were arranged near the punch bowl on a long, cloth-draped table. Through the clamor, someone whistled loudly, and Leah glanced to her right to find Rachel, who bounced on her toes and waved beside Daddy.

It took a moment for Leah to absorb what was happening. She turned to Colt with an unspoken question in her gaze. *Is all this for me?*

"Pru and your daddy put this together," Colt said. "They couldn't use all the fancy decorations on such short notice, but I figured you wouldn't mind."

"Mind?" Leah's vision flooded with tears while she warmed all over with gratitude. This was what she'd wanted since coming back to town—a true welcome. Who cared if a few streamers were missing? "It's amazing."

Everyone she loved was here, even June and Luke, who sat in a quiet corner with their new baby. With a little nudge from Colt, Leah stepped inside and let the congregation embrace her, one set of arms at a time. When she'd finished circulating through the hall, her cheeks ached from smiling but she'd never felt more cherished.

She was finally home.

# Epilogue

THE CALL CAME TWO YEARS LATER WHEN LEAH WAS fast asleep, wrapped in Colt's arms. She awoke with a start and glanced at the bedside alarm clock, instantly worried, because the only news that traveled at three in the morning was the devastating kind. She shot out an arm to answer the phone. But instead of bad news, Leah heard the two most glorious words in the English language.

"It's time."

A surge of adrenalin shot through her, more energizing than ten pots of coffee. She giggled loudly and shook Colt's shoulder. "It's time!"

He yawned and stretched, blinking at her in confusion until understanding dawned in his eyes. "*Time* time?" She nodded and he bolted upright in bed with an instant smile, his teeth bright in the darkness.

They jumped out of bed and scurried around their bedroom, clumsily hopping into pant legs and yanking shirts over their heads. Five minutes later, they dashed down the front walk to Colt's cruiser, looking disheveled and mismatched, but giddy as kids on Christmas Eve. Colt flipped on the siren, and they barreled to the hospital, linking their fingers and holding tight to one another.

Once they arrived, Colt parked at an awkward angle, taking up two spaces, but he didn't seem to care. They jumped out of the car and jogged to the afterhours entrance.

Leah flashed her employee badge to the security officer stationed at the front desk, and he waved her through. When they reached the elevator, the excitement that had propelled her into a frenzy began to morph into the sick weight of anxiety. Colt noticed at once, which didn't surprise her. He knew her better than anyone.

"You okay?" he asked, punching the *up* button.

She took a deep breath and let it out slowly. "What if she changes her mind?"

Leah had refused to allow a single baby item inside their home for that reason. Not one pacifier. She'd even made Rachel promise not to throw her a baby shower. If the adoption fell through, she didn't want to come home to a painted nursery or heaps of presents to remind her of their loss.

The elevator doors parted, and Colt wrapped an arm around her shoulders, leading her inside. He pushed the button to take them to the fifth floor, then cupped her face. "If she changes her mind, we'll try again. As many times as it takes." He pulled her into a tight hug that promised he'd never falter. When they parted, he made sure to add, "And whatever happens, you've always got me."

She warmed all over with loving him. "We've got each other."

The doors opened, and they walked hand-in-hand to the labor and delivery waiting room. Shannon, their adoption facilitator, was already expecting them. With a wave, she stood from her chair, and Leah immediately scanned her face for signs of trouble, finding none.

"Congratulations," Shannon said with a sleepy smile. "It's a girl."

Salty tears rushed Leah's vision, forcing her to blot her eyes with her shirt sleeve. "And Rosaria?" she asked. "Is she okay?"

Leah knew firsthand the agony the young woman was facing. They'd never met the birth mother in person, because Rosaria had insisted on a closed adoption with no contact whatsoever. But they knew she was a young second-generation citizen without much family support, and the baby's father had been deported to Ecuador. Leah's heart broke for the girl, and she finally understood how Diane had felt all those years ago—overjoyed to add a child to her family, but bereaved for the woman making the sacrifice.

Shannon nodded, but dropped eye contact. "I keep offering to have the baby brought to her room, but she insists she doesn't want to see her. It's easier that way for some women."

Leah couldn't hold back the tears any longer. At first they leaked silently down her cheeks, but then memories of Noah's birth resurfaced, and a series of wet sobs wracked her chest. Colt snatched a tissue from the nearby coffee table and handed it to her before surrounding her in his embrace. She clung to him and cried violently for what seemed like forever—first for herself and then for the woman who'd given her a second chance at motherhood. When the pain finally dulled, she apologized to Shannon.

"You have nothing to feel sorry about," Shannon said. "This is an emotional process for everyone involved." Then she said the only thing that could possibly make Leah smile. "Are you ready to hold your daughter?"

She and Colt shared a bittersweet glance, sorrow

from their past mingling with hope for the future. "Absolutely," Leah said.

They followed Shannon to an empty recovery room and washed their hands, then sat beside each other on the bed while Shannon called for the baby. Minutes later, a nurse wheeled in a plastic bassinet with a pink tag affixed to the top, labeled *Girl, Sanchez, 6.2 oz. 19 in.*

Leah's pulse quickened, and she couldn't sit still any longer. She stood and peered down at the baby girl, barely visible beneath white swaddling blankets and a pink-striped newborn cap. Leah had already been invited to do so, but she felt like she needed permission to touch the child. She gave the nurse a questioning glance.

"Go ahead," the woman prompted with a smile.

With careful fingers, Leah worked one hand beneath the baby's delicate neck and the other beneath her diapered bottom. Supporting her head, she lifted the tiny sleeping bundle from her bassinet and cradled her against her chest. She was so light, and yet she pulled at Leah's heartstrings with ten tons of force. With her puffy eyes, smooshed nose, and light bruising along her forehead, she was the most beautiful baby Leah had ever seen. Tufts of jet black hair peeked out from beneath her cap, just like her daddy's, even though they weren't genetically linked.

Leah took a step back and rejoined Colt on the edge of the bed so they could share this moment. He scooted closer and wrapped an arm around Leah's waist, admiring their baby in silence for a while. With one light fingertip, he stroked the baby's cheek and said, "Hello, Grace. We've waited a long time to meet you."

"Grace," Leah repeated. Until now she'd barely

allowed herself to speak the name for fear of jinxing herself. But she wasn't afraid anymore. "We love you, Grace Rosaria Bea."

Leah lifted Grace high enough to take in her sweet newborn scent. She bonded to her baby at once, her body recognizing this child as her own and overwhelming her with a maternal urge she'd only felt once before—when the timing wasn't right.

Gazing into her baby girl's cherubic face, Leah wondered how she'd ever believed God had forsaken her. How shortsighted she'd been. He hadn't left her side for a moment—instead, He'd guided her to the perfect family for Noah, and when she was ready, He reconnected her with the only man she'd ever truly loved. Now He'd blessed them with a child of their own.

A warm feeling of peace stirred inside Leah's breast, faith that she'd found her purpose on this earth, and realization that she deserved the gift of happiness.

Leah rested her head on Colt's solid chest, and they cherished their baby girl together. As a family.

# About the Author

Macy Beckett is an unrepentant escapist who left teaching to write hot and humorous romances. No offense to her former students, but her new career is way more fun! She lives just outside Cincinnati in the appropriately named town of Loveland, Ohio, with her husband and three children. In addition to romance, she publishes young adult science fiction under the name Melissa Landers. Visit her on the web at macybeckett.com.